Essie's Way

PAMELA COOK

hachette
AUSTRALIA

Published in Australia and New Zealand in 2013
by Hachette Australia
(an imprint of Hachette Australia Pty Limited)
Level 17, 207 Kent Street, Sydney NSW 2000
www.hachette.com.au

10 9 8 7 6 5 4 3 2 1

National Library of Australia
Cataloguing-in-Publication data

Cook, Pamela, author.

Essie's way / Pamela Cook.

978 0 7336 3208 2 (pbk.)

A823.4

Cover design by Christabella Designs
Cover photographs courtesy Corbis
Text design by Bookhouse, Sydney
Typeset in 12/17.5 pt Sabon LT Pro by Bookhouse, Sydney
Printed and bound in Australia by Griffin Press, Adelaide, an Accredited ISO AS/NZS
14001:2009 Environmental Management System printer

MIX
Paper from
responsible sources
FSC
www.fsc.org
FSC® C009448

The paper this book is printed on is certified against the
Forest Stewardship Council® Standards. Griffin Press holds
FSC chain of custody certification SGS-COC-005088. FSC
promotes environmentally responsible, socially beneficial
and economically viable management of the world's forests.

For my mother, Gwen.
With all my love.

Prologue

*T*he wind howled – a long low mournful sound that spiralled around the edges of the house. She peered through the window and wondered what he was doing down there in the stable. When she closed her eyes she could smell the earthy sweat of his skin, feel his muscles ripple beneath her fingertips as she ran her hands across his shoulders and down his spine. He was out there in that tiny room that passed for his home, surrounded by the scent of hay and horses. She pictured him reading by lamplight, dark curls framing his face as he bent his head over the books she had bought for him, learning all he could, educating himself so they could one day be together.

One day.

In the distance the sky and sea merged into an opaque sheet of black, the only light shed by a sliver of moon. A crack of lightning split the darkness, illuminating the cauldron that was the ocean for just a few moments. She tilted her chin up *and stretched forward, straining to see. Something was out there. Rubbing at the glass, clearing the mist her breath had made, she stared harder. Another flash. There it was. A boat. Waves pouring over the bow, and in the half-second that she managed to focus, a tiny figure clinging on for dear life.*

She heard herself gasp as her body froze in recognition at the familiar scene. This had happened before: a boat tossed against the rocks in a raging storm, the passengers' screams devoured by the wind as they struggled against the rising swell, clinging to broken remnants of timber and steel. But she was the only person listening, the only one who could hear their cries for help, because they were trapped in her dream. Over and over the same dream, night after night, until she knew their terror, the sharpness of the icy cold water leaving her winded as it pricked her skin, clawed at her, pulling her down into the depths with them until they were completely submerged and their cries could be heard no more.

But this was not a dream. This was real and it was happening now, before her eyes, not behind them. What should she do? Her father was away in Sydney on business. It was just her and her mother here in the house. And him out there in the stables.

There was only one thing to be done. She pulled her jacket from the hook behind her door, struggled into it and dived out into the night.

Part One

Sydney

Miranda stared at the woman in the wedding gown. She watched as she ran her fingers over the scalloped edge of the neckline, tracing the pattern on the lace: small sprays of roses joined by delicate vines that curled around one bunch and looped to the next. The silk lining swished deliciously beneath the ivory satin waistband as the woman turned one way and then the other in front of the full-length mirror. She reached up and unpinned her hair from its bun, letting it fall loosely across her shoulders. A faint smile skimmed her lips and then vanished. Her gaze flickered briefly to the floor, as if she was uncertain of something, but then, squaring her shoulders, she lifted her chin and peered straight into the eyes of her reflection.

'Beautiful, so beautiful.' The dressmaker hovered, hands clasped across her chest. 'Let me see from the front,' she said, making a circling motion with her hands.

Miranda spun around as instructed.

'So tall and slim, so lucky,' the dressmaker clucked, patting her own portly stomach. She was small and round with a thick accent and a permanent grin that reminded Miranda of one of those Russian dolls that fit snugly inside each other. 'You like?'

'Yes, Hilde, it's perfect.'

You could sound a little more convincing, that annoying voice in Miranda's head suggested.

'You don't seem so sure.'

'No, I love it. Really.' She turned back to the mirror. The dress was everything she'd dreamt of and more. Not genuine antique lace but as close as she was going to get. She waited for the anticipated euphoria to kick in but instead a wave of nausea rippled through her stomach. Probably just nerves, seeing herself for the first time in her wedding dress. She swallowed and forced a smile.

'I think we need to take in a little bit here, yes?' The seamstress pinched a fold of material on either side of Miranda's hips.

'Yes, I think so. It doesn't make my bum look too big, though, does it?'

'Your bottom.' Hilde peered over the top of her rectangular glasses and frowned. 'No, absolutely not. Gives you more shape. Stand still now.'

Miranda nodded and glanced towards the door. It would've been nice to have a second opinion, but despite her mother's promise to join her for the fitting, she hadn't shown. As if she'd read her mind, the woman removed a pin from between her pursed lips and asked, 'Your mama not coming with you today?'

'No, she couldn't make it.' Just like she couldn't make the last two fittings, or the visits to the reception lounge or the meeting with the priest. A flush of heat flooded Miranda's cheeks.

'Such a shame. I'm sure she'll be here next time.'

I don't think so!

That damned voice, butting in again. Something must have happened to hold her mother up – she'd probably arrive any minute now. She might not have been completely reliable in the past, but surely she'd want to be part of the wedding preparations for her only daughter?

Don't bet on it.

Miranda blinked away the tears that were lurking. What did it matter? As long as her mother was there at the actual wedding, that was the main thing.

'There. All done.' The dressmaker beamed, clearly pleased with her handiwork. 'You will make such a beautiful bride.'

'Thank you, it's perfect,' Miranda sighed, sliding her hands down the sides of the dress. 'Ouch!' A pin pricked the tip of her finger and a drop of blood oozed onto the lace, creeping across a rose petal. 'Shit.'

The dressmaker leapt into action, licking the corner of a white handkerchief she'd pulled from her pocket, and dabbed at the stain.

Miranda drew in her stomach as far as she could while Hilde rubbed away. 'Isn't it a bad omen to get blood on a wedding dress?' She didn't know where she'd heard it and she usually wasn't so irrational but the idea of it made her chest tighten.

Hilde wobbled her head. 'No, no, just silly superstition.' She unbuttoned the back of the dress while Miranda sucked her injured finger. 'You can take it off now, please. And watch out for the pins.' She tapped Miranda's arm and disappeared behind a set of gold brocade curtains.

In the change room Miranda peeled the dress from her shoulders and slipped out of it, being careful not to do any more damage. She held the dress up to the light feeling the weight of it between her hands. There was no sign of the bloodstain – Hilde's quick thinking had thankfully worked. Snatches of conversation between two other customers filtered in from the shop and Miranda once again felt her mother's absence. She pulled her phone from her bag, scrolled through her contacts and pressed 'Mum'.

You know she's not going to answer.

One ring, two, three . . . but no answer. She pulled on her blouse and slid into her skirt. When had that voice in her head started to get so bossy anyway? She'd never been one to give in to self-doubt. Until recently. Until the voice had started murmuring. Zipping up her skirt and shrugging her arms into her jacket she gave herself a good talking-to. There was no use dwelling on the negatives. Everything was falling into place – engagement to a wonderful man, a potential partnership at work, financial security. All those boxes had been ticked. Even things with her mother had seemed to be getting better – until now. But hopefully that was only a hiccup. Life was working out just as she'd hoped it would, so now was definitely not the time to be questioning herself. She brushed on a fresh coat of lipstick, fastened her hair back into place and dabbed away the eyeliner that had smudged beneath her lashes. Laying the dress over the velvet chaise longue outside the change room, she said goodbye to Hilde, now busy with other clients, and stepped out into the bright lights of the Queen Victoria Building.

Should she try calling her mother again? Where could she be? Her heartbeat quickened. It had been a long time now since she'd gone off the rails. There was sure to be a logical explanation. Rummaging in her bag, she found her phone again and dialled the number. Apart from a group of Japanese tourists browsing the opals in the window next door, the whole top floor was deserted. The shops on this level were designer boutiques, way out of the price range of the average person. Just as Miranda was about to hang up, she heard a faint voice on the other end of the line.

'Hello?'

'Hi Mum, it's me, where are you?'

'I missed the train.'

'So where are you now?'

'I'm waiting for you downstairs, in the middle.'

Miranda held back a sigh. 'Okay, well stay put and I'll come and find you.' She hung up and drummed her fingers on the timber balustrade. Had her mother really missed the train or was that yet another excuse? She was here now, that was the main thing. Better not to make a fuss.

Her heels sank into the caramel swirls of the carpet as she made her way to the centre of the building. Keeping her eyes peeled she rushed down the stone stairs straight into the path of a gaggle of lunchtime shoppers. As she stood back to let them pass she saw her mother sitting on a bench seat beneath the white scrolled archways, surrounded by that same old air of sadness that Miranda had known since childhood.

She stepped forward, painting on her most animated expression. 'Hi, Mum.'

Her mother stood and hitched her handbag over her shoulder. 'Hello, darling, sorry I missed the fitting. I must have got the train times mixed up.'

Miranda bent down and kissed her mother on the cheek, conscious of Kathleen's slight drawing away. 'That's okay. You're here now – how about some lunch? What do you feel like?'

'Whatever you want,' her mother replied, not quite looking at her.

Determined to make the most of what was left of her lunch hour, Miranda took her mother's arm and led her towards the café area. The Queen Victoria was one of her favourite buildings – the high arches, the way the light diffused through the purple and green glass of the dome, the geometric patterns of the heritage tiles, the wrought iron and timber hand rails. There was something so old-fashioned and romantic about it all. It was the sort of style she dreamt of one day having in a home of her own – on a much smaller scale of course.

Not much chance of that if you marry James.

'Oh, shut up,' she mumbled.

'I beg your pardon?' Her mother stopped walking and looked up at Miranda.

'Not you. Sorry, Mum.'

'Well, I don't see anyone else here.'

Shit. I must be losing it.

She grabbed her mother's elbow and started walking again. 'I was just thinking about something at work – a discussion I was having this morning with this dickhead who thinks he knows everything. Must have spoken out loud without realising it.'

'There's no need to use that language, Miranda. And anyway, you worry too much about work. You need to slow down a little.'

'You're probably right.' She'd learnt over the years it was better to agree than to argue. The smell of freshly cooked bacon and brewed coffee caught her attention. 'How about here?'

'Looks good.'

Miranda chose a table and the two of them settled in to peruse the menu among the thrum of passers-by, the tinkling of ice in glasses, a girl giggling at the table beside them. She knew her mother would choose whatever she did, but asked her anyway, then ordered two caesar salads, some sparkling water and coffees for after.

Sensing her mother's unease, she decided to get the elephant out of the room first. 'The dress fitting went well.'

'That's good. Have you booked your honeymoon?'

So that's all she's got to say about it?

At least she's here, I suppose, and she's making an effort at conversation.

'No, we're still deciding. James wants to do some river rafting thing in Vietnam but I want to go somewhere more romantic, Paris maybe, or Rome.'

'Perhaps you can do a little of both.'

'It's a bit hard, Mum – they're not exactly in the same vicinity.'

'Marriage is all about compromise, Miranda,' her mother said. 'You should know that, you two have lived together for long enough now.'

Good old Mum, never letting the chance go by to remind her daughter that she was 'living in sin'. At least once they were married she wouldn't be able to dig the knife in about that.

'True,' Miranda conceded.

Why are you letting her off the hook so easily?

Miranda pondered the question while she sipped her mineral water. From past experience she knew there was no point making a big deal of it when her mother let her down. She'd always rationalised any strange behaviour as part of her 'condition', but Miranda's yearning to have a normal mother was starting to get the better of her after all these years.

'I pricked my finger on a pin during the fitting,' she said. 'It drew blood and stained the lace. Hilde, the dressmaker, was so good about it.' She resisted sharing her fears about the omen. The memory of the crimson spot stealing along the vines sent a tremor up the back of her neck.

'Well, it's her job, I suppose.'

The waiter arrived with their salads and that was all her mother said on the subject. While they ate, Miranda watched the world bustling around her – women in smart black suits similar to her own carrying laptops and briefcases, men in ties grabbing a bite to eat between meetings, a few frocked-up shoppers laden with bags from Guess, Country Road and an assortment of up-market boutiques. Everyone on the treadmill – work, eat, sleep, then get up and do it all

over again. Lately she'd been thinking there had to be more
to life than just getting ahead, but she didn't know what.

Her mother interrupted her musings. 'Are you going to
have something old, something new, something borrowed
and something blue at the wedding?'

This is impressive – she's showing some interest.

Miranda finished her mouthful of lettuce and nodded. 'Yes,
I am. We're using James' father's Bentley, so that's something
borrowed. And I've bought new underwear.' Probably more
information than her mother was looking for. 'Not sure about
the blue or old part, though.'

'Usually they do a blue garter.'

'Hmm, not sure about that. It's a bit demeaning, having
the groom rip it off your leg while all the men have a good
old perv.'

'Well, it was good enough in my day. And I'm sure the
men wouldn't be perving, as you call it.' Her mother sounded
slightly offended and Miranda decided it was time to tread
more carefully.

'I'd like a piece of antique jewellery for something old – I'm
just not sure what.' But as she stirred the froth on the top
of the skinny capp the waiter had just delivered, an image
floated on the fringes of her mind, something she remembered
from childhood. 'Didn't you have a pearl necklace, an old
one, with some sort of stones – amethysts, I think? That
would match the irises perfectly. And Belle's dress is purple.
Do you still have it?'

The colour drained completely from her mother's face as
she set down her knife and fork and pressed a napkin to
her lips. When she replied her voice was barely more than

a whisper. 'No, I don't recall anything like that – you must have imagined it.'

Ignoring the warning signs, Miranda blundered on, the memory stronger now. 'Yes, I'm sure you did. I found it that time I was snooping around in your bedroom, trying on all your jewellery. You came in and yelled at me and told me to take it off. Don't you remember?'

Her mother lurched to her feet, sending her chair toppling backwards, surprising a waiter who was clearing an adjacent table. A couple of glasses on his tray teetered before falling to the floor and shattering into pieces. Everything and everyone around them stopped. Everyone except her mother. 'I told you I don't remember,' she shouted. 'Why are you badgering me about it? Why can't you just take no for an answer?'

Miranda gripped the edge of the table, her heart galloping beneath her ribs. She knew she should take a breath but it wouldn't come. Not until a man, presumably the manager, appeared and broke the silence that had fallen over the entire café. 'Is everything all right?' he asked, pointedly.

'I'm so sorry, yes, everything's fine,' Miranda said, 'just a small misunderstanding. We'll pay for any damage.' She took a few seconds to calm herself as he moved away to help the waiter clean up the mess. Her mother picked up her bag and made her way through the carnage to stand well away from the café, staring into a shop window.

Wishing that she could somehow shrink to the size of an ant and crawl away, Miranda stood and headed to the counter to pay the bill, avoiding the questioning looks from the other tables. She left a ridiculously generous tip as compensation and apologised again before she summoned up the courage to approach her mother.

'Mum, are you okay?'

Her mother turned, a crumpled tissue in her hand, and nodded. 'I think I'd better be getting home.' Dark circles rimmed her eyes, which were focused on the floor again, anywhere but at her daughter.

'Are you sure you don't want to stay for a bit, do some shopping?' Maybe there was a chance of salvaging some of the day.

'No, I'll get going. Your father's home at four.'

'I'm sorry for upsetting you, Mum.' She tried to hug her but her mother pulled away.

'I'm fine. Bye.' And with that she turned and merged with the crowd, her neat blonde bob hardly moving as she walked briskly away. Miranda felt the air leak completely out of her as she watched her mother disappear. What had she said that had made her so distraught? Was it the reminder Kathleen had yelled at her or the mention of the necklace itself? Had it even been a real memory or one that she'd only imagined?

As she wandered past the shops on her way to the office she cast her mind back. How old would she have been when she'd snuck into her mother's room? Six? Maybe seven? Her mother had been watching some show on TV where the women always wore too much make-up and the men gazed into their blue-lidded eyes. Miranda knew she wasn't supposed to touch the jewellery, so she made sure she was extra quiet. Her heart was thumping like a rabbit's foot inside her chest as she opened the drawer. At the front were the everyday beads her mother wore – mainly in shades of brown and beige, which 'went with everything'. Miranda rifled through them to see what else she could find. When she spied the black velvet case tucked away at the back she knew it would be something special. She ran her fingers across the lid of the box and clicked it open, her eyes widening when she saw what was inside – strands of tiny pearls with purple stones set on either side of a small horseshoe. She lifted it from the box and undid the clasp. It was too hard to do up so she held it around her neck and ran the fingers of her other hand over the horseshoe as she looked at herself in the mirror, twisting slightly from one side to the other to see how the stones caught the light. 'It's beautiful,' she whispered to herself.

'What do you think you're doing?' Her mother looked back at her from the mirror, with a face the colour of beetroot, hands planted on her hips. Before she could answer her mother was screaming. 'Haven't I told you not to go through my things? Wait until your father gets home and hears about this. You'll be lucky if you don't get the wooden spoon. Now put that down and get out.'

Throwing the necklace down on the glass top of the dresser Miranda ran as fast as she could to the back door and out into the yard, to the tree house, where she knew her mother wouldn't follow. She climbed the ladder and sat sobbing on the floor. So what if she'd touched a dumb necklace – she hadn't broken anything, so what did it matter? Still, it was probably a good idea to lie low for a while until her mother got over it. It was almost dark when her father came out and found her there, half-asleep and shivering, arms wrapped around her bent-up knees, stale tears dry on her cheeks. He coaxed her out and put his arm around her shoulder as they walked back inside.

That same wave of shame and confusion she'd felt as a child when her mother caught her in the act washed over Miranda again now. Strange how vivid the memory was even though she'd never thought of it in all the intervening years. And even stranger that her mother would still have the same hysterical reaction. Perhaps the necklace held a clue to the past that her mother flatly refused to speak of? Perhaps if Miranda could find out more about it she could understand why her mother had always been so distant and, frankly, so unhinged. Perhaps it would bring them closer?

Ever the optimist.

She shrugged away the cynicism of the voice, put the last few hours out of her mind and made a beeline for the office.

Pelican Point

The old woman stood on the verandah, her hair tossed by the sea breeze that had blown in with the setting sun. She tucked the violin beneath her chin and closed her eyes. The strings were taut beneath her fingers and as she caressed them with the bow her body relaxed into the sad, sweet sound they made. Notes drifted into the air, mingling with the whisper of the ocean and the gentle snoring of the black dog who lay at her feet, before they lilted across the sand and out over the waves into the dusk. As the music dipped and soared she swayed in time to its song, the wrinkles on her cheeks and around her eyes softening as she sank into the dream she was weaving. A gust of wind grabbed at the screen door behind her, opening it and then banging it shut. The dog jerked and lifted his head before flopping back down to the wooden floor, but the woman played on, lost in the music, oblivious to everything.

Sydney

- Grocery shopping
- Dress fitting
- Call travel agent

Miranda ticked off the last item on her weekly to-do list and checked the time on her phone. James had texted to suggest they have a quick drink before heading home. After the day she'd had, she hadn't needed to think twice. Which was why she'd darted out of the office earlier than usual and was already sipping on a glass of red. It was one of their favourite places, tucked away in a side street down towards the Quay – small and quaint, with a quirky menu and a range of boutique beers that James adored. As she waited for him to arrive she wondered how much she should share about the day. His parents were so conventional and stable, and while her dad was Mr Dependable, her mum was . . . well, her mum.

'You look like you're off with the pixies.' James kissed her forehead and slid into the seat opposite her, beer already in hand. There was a rosy glow to his cheeks that told her he'd been hurrying to get here, and his hair, always meticulously groomed, had drooped a little. But as usual, he looked mighty fine in a suit. He loosened his tie and ran his finger around the inside of his collar. 'Looks like you've had a tough day.'

Miranda shook her head and groaned. 'That's an understatement.'

'Did something go wrong with the fitting?'

'Not the fitting itself, just . . .'

'Let me guess, your mother.'

Miranda nodded and gulped at her wine, her resolve not to discuss the incident at the café crumbling. She told James the whole story, including her memory of the necklace. 'Why do you think she would have reacted that way?'

He studied the neck of his beer bottle and shrugged. 'No idea. But it is Kathleen we're talking about.'

'She's not that bad.' Despite everything, Miranda always felt defensive when anyone criticised her mother.

'Maybe you were asking her too many questions. You can be like a dog with a bone sometimes, Mindy.'

'Dog with a bone? Thank you very much. And I wasn't asking too many questions. I just happened to remember something from when I was a kid and asked my mother about it. Is that a crime?'

James held up his hands in defence. 'Don't go getting all hysterical, I just meant maybe you should have backed off a little when you saw she was going to lose it.'

Miranda huffed and sat back against the wall of the booth. He was right, there had been warning signs and she'd chosen to ignore them – chosen to listen to the voice instead – and look what had happened. But it was more than just her mother's explosion that had her worried. Her own lack of enthusiasm about the dress was playing on her mind. She'd put on a good show for Hilde but inside had felt ill rather than elated. Was that normal?

'So, how about we get some takeaway on the way home and later on I'll give you a nice long back rub to take your mind off your mother?' He gave her a boyish grin as he chugged back the last of his ale.

Although James' suggestion didn't exactly answer her questions, maybe it would be a good distraction. Lately her libido had seemed to be on the wane, another thing she'd put down to wedding stress, but she really should make more effort. 'Sounds good.'

But that look in her mother's eyes in the mirror as she stood behind her all those years ago, the same tortured look she'd seen again today, stayed in her thoughts all the way home.

⁓

It was Friday night, James had gone on a boys' weekend away, and despite the pressure from a few of her colleagues to join them for drinks, Miranda had opted for a quiet night in. All they ever seemed to talk about was work, and at the moment that meant the main topic of conversation was who was most likely to be offered the junior partnership – herself or Damien Blount. They'd tried to maintain a friendly rivalry about the whole thing, but in reality both of them would kill for the recognition. It was one more game she just didn't feel like playing tonight.

She scrolled through the songs on her iPod, selected one and set it up on the Bose dock she'd given James for Christmas. Probably the one useful thing she had ever bought him – or at least the one thing he used that she'd ever bought. Apart from the three thousand dollar bicycle he'd taken away with him – but he'd chosen that himself, all she'd done was hand over her credit card. She turned up the volume and felt her shoulders loosen as the bewitching voice of Florence Welch drifted through the speaker.

In the kitchen she poured herself a glass of wine – a sauv blanc tonight to go with the leftover Thai. She didn't normally drink alone, but after the strain of the last couple of days she needed it. Hard to believe it was already mid March – only eight weeks until the wedding. They'd opted for a May date so the trees in the gardens of the church grounds would be working their magic. Miranda had always loved autumn, the cooler mornings after the heat of summer, the bright, clear days that were just the right temperature and the crisp nights that meant you could put the doona back on the bed and snuggle in. And she loved the vibrant colours of the leaves. As a kid she'd spent hours collecting the unblemished ones from the maple tree in her front yard, organising them in her scrapbook, pressing them between layers of waxed paper under piles of the heaviest books she could find. I wonder what ever happened to those leaves, she thought. The question reminded her once again of the one she'd asked her mother just yesterday. She'd considered calling and probing some more but she knew that idea was a dead end. Maybe her dad would know – but he was a man and, like James, would probably have zero interest in jewellery, family or otherwise. As far as Miranda could remember, her mother had never ever worn the necklace – why was that? – so he probably wouldn't have a clue what she was talking about.

There's only one thing to do – go and find it, said the voice.

Miranda frowned. 'I'm not breaking in to my parents' house to steal something that might no longer even be there.'

Suit yourself. But it wouldn't be breaking in – you have a key.

She sat up and glanced around the room just to make sure she was completely on her own and it was in fact the voice she was having this conversation with. Maybe her mother wasn't the only one in the family with mental health issues.

So?

So what? Snooping around would be totally deceitful, Miranda thought. If my mother doesn't want to talk about the necklace then there must be a very good reason and I have to respect that. End of discussion.

She picked up the TV remote, pressing play on the DVD. With James away it was the perfect opportunity to watch one of her old black-and-white movies. She loved the ambience of them, and the romance, the way the camera closed in on the characters' tormented faces, the desperate sighs and declarations of undying love. Tonight's selection was *Casablanca*. She curled up on the lounge and snuggled between the cushions to spend a little time with Rick and Ilsa.

She woke the next morning feeling less than healthy, wishing she hadn't polished off the whole bottle of wine, and decided to give the gym a miss. Her mind had been racing all night, and as much as she hated to admit it, the voice was right. There was only one way to find out if the necklace actually existed, and that was to go looking for it. And this weekend was perfect timing. Her parents had gone away up to the Hydro Majestic in the Blue Mountains for their fortieth wedding anniversary, leaving the house empty. Who was it going to hurt if she went for a peek around the place?

After a quick shower, a bowl of muesli and a couple of panadol she was in the car contending with the weekend traffic. It was about forty minutes from Erskineville where she and James lived to her parents' place in the leafy suburb of Oatley in the south of Sydney. It was a sunshiny Saturday morning and Miranda pressed the button and folded back the roof on her cream-coloured VW convertible. She'd wanted a true vintage one but James had convinced her they weren't safe, so she'd opted for the more modern version. Not as impressive as his glossy black BMW, but it did have its perks: the retractable roof, the front and rear air conditioning, and the pièce de résistance – a sound system that had to be heard to be believed. She turned up the volume on the radio and sang along to Missy Higgins' new single. Such good lyrics, all about following your heart and listening to your inner voice. Nice in theory, but unfortunately her inner voice had way too much to say these days. She suspected it was the same voice that had told her to take up the dare to run naked through the street at Laura Simpson's eighteenth, which had ended in tears when the police turned up and she'd been driven home wrapped in nothing more than a blanket. It was probably the same voice that had coerced her into trying on that necklace in the first place, turning her mother into the wicked witch of the west. But at least on this occasion she hadn't just acted as soon as it had spoken. She'd slept on it, considered its wisdom, and although what she was about to do did seem slightly underhanded, it was the only way to quash the nagging feeling she had that the necklace was in some way connected to her mother's past.

She pulled into the driveway and a smile sprang to her lips. Her parents still lived in the same place she and her brother Simon had grown up in, a beautiful old Californian bungalow complete with stained-glass windows and hedges in the garden. As much as she loved living so close to the city, she missed the space and the green leafiness of the suburbs. Everything about this house said home: the neatly mowed lawns and manicured edges, the path lined with blossoming Iceberg roses, the black-and-white cat sunning itself on the front porch. A stark contrast to the renovated warehouse apartment she shared with James, which was all white surfaces and minimalism. As Miranda walked up the steps, Pepper jumped down from the chair and curled around her shins.

'Hello there, sweet one – all by yourself this weekend?' The cat purred loudly and dived through the plastic flap beside the door that allowed her to slip in and out whenever she felt like it.

Miranda slid the key into the door, looking over her shoulder as she heard it click. She couldn't escape the feeling that she was being watched, but that was ridiculous – it was just her guilty conscience playing tricks. She gave herself a shake and stepped inside. A faint scent of lavender hung in the hallway, a remnant no doubt of one of the many candles her mother burnt – much to her father's disgust. 'You'll set the bloody place on fire one day,' he was fond of saying, usually from behind the paper or a book. But so far the place was still standing.

In the dining room Miranda dumped her bag on the table, and before she could think better of it headed straight to her parents' room. It hadn't changed much over the years, apart from a few coats of paint. Matching timber side tables beside the flower-quilted bed, sheer white curtains drawn across the holland blinds on the windows and a collection of her mother's favourite perfumes decorating the mirrored dressing table.

The dressing table containing the jewellery drawer.

Heart racing, she stood in front of it and hesitated.

What are you worried about? You're only taking a look. It's not as if anyone is going to know.

'You're right,' she said out loud, since there was no one around to hear her craziness. She grabbed the handle of the top drawer, pulling it out as far as it would come. Sifting carefully through the contents so as not to disturb anything, she searched beneath the strands of beads for the box. Nothing. The drawer was long and narrow. She leant down and peered into it, sliding her hand right to the back. From the corner of her eye a sudden movement forced her upright.

'Argh!'

The cat jumped up onto the dresser. 'For god's sake, Pepper, did you have to do that?'

Miranda rubbed her knuckle where she'd banged it on the edge of the drawer and returned to her errand. But it was useless. There was no black velvet box, no necklace. What the hell was she doing anyway? Her mother might have sold it or given it away years ago. But even as the thought crossed her mind, she remembered her mother's reaction at lunch and knew she was wrong.

She rearranged the beads and earrings back in place as best she could and closed the drawer. Okay. So if it wasn't in the drawer, where else would it be? She slumped onto the bed and looked around the room. Her mother wasn't into clutter. Everything had its place, from the three perfume bottles on the top shelf of the dresser underneath the mirror to the three family photos arranged in perfect symmetry on the shelf below. One was of her and Simon when they were around twelve and fifteen, the next was one of those family shots her mother had received a discount voucher for at a local studio, and the third was her parents on their wedding day. You look so happy, Miranda thought as she picked up the photo and stared at the two joyful faces, feeling a sinking sensation as she thought about her own impending nuptials. She didn't really like being the centre of attention, and soon it would be her and James smiling for the camera. Just silly nerves again.

Letting out a long, loud sigh she stood, turning her attention back to the task at hand. Feeling like even more of an intruder than before, she opened each of the other drawers in the dressing table one by one and rummaged through the contents. Scarves, socks, underwear – but nothing else. The only place left was the built-in wardrobe. At one end were her father's shirts and pants, all perfectly pressed and arranged in colour blocks, and at the other her mother's clothes, similarly organised, with shoes stored on a rack beneath. Miranda lifted her eyes to the shelf at the top, leaning back to see what was stored up there: a few boxes, hats and bags. Something small could easily be tucked away. She grabbed the chair – upholstered to match the floral quilt – from beside the bed and stepped up, moving things aside to get a closer view of the back of the cupboard. Nothing. It was hard to see right into the corner where the shelf extended behind the wall, so she stretched her hand around to see if there was anything hidden there. Just as her fingers spidered along to the furthest point they could reach, they landed on a soft, slightly furry object a couple of centimetres high. It could definitely be the box but she couldn't get a grip on it.

Damn, I need something higher to stand on!

She jumped down and raced out to the pantry, found the folding set of steps stored behind the door and hurried back to the bedroom. As she climbed up she felt a surprising rush of adrenaline at the thought that she might have found what she was looking for. Maybe it was the thrill of doing something illicit, but her instincts told her it was more than that: whatever was inside that box had upset her mother to a shocking degree and she was determined to find out why.

Wriggling her fingers back to the same spot she managed to place her whole hand over the object and drag it out. For a few seconds she froze on the top step as she looked down at the case, about the size of a large wallet, before climbing down and sitting on the bed. Hardly daring to breathe, she flipped the box open and there it was: the necklace. A perfectly shaped horseshoe set between two rectangular amethysts on a double strand of large creamy pearls. The horseshoe itself was beaded with smaller pearls and a teardrop-shaped diamond dangled from its centre. Miranda ran the tips of her fingers across the pearls. They were smooth and cool to touch. Very carefully she lifted the piece from its box and held it up towards the window. The pendant sparkled – it was definitely the real deal. She walked to the dresser, undid the white gold clasp and fastened it around her neck. Her mouth curved into a smile as she looked into the mirror. The horseshoe rested right in the middle of her chest. It was light to wear and she imagined it with the milky lace of her wedding dress. Perfect. She'd never seen anything more beautiful in her life – well, only when she was a kid doing the same wicked, deceitful thing, feeling the same sick swirling in her stomach. A flush of red stained her cheeks at the thought and she glanced around. But this time she was the only one here.

She picked up the box and looked underneath. On the inside of the lid, printed in gold lettering on the satin lining, were the words *Taylors Jewellers*. Miranda jammed a fingernail down the side of the box and prised up the soft padding of the case. Her eyes watered as she stared at what lay concealed inside. As she pulled out the folded piece of newspaper, something fell against her leg and onto the floor. Shaking, she picked up the small photograph and held it in front of her. It was a studio photograph of a woman in a lace wedding dress, in sepia and tinted by hand. Miranda bent her head to the photo, astounded. The pattern on the lace was almost exactly the same as on her own gown. There was no more than a hint of a smile on the woman's lips as she gazed into the camera. Her long hair fell softly around her face and was pulled loosely to one side in a braid. There was a kindness in her eyes that Miranda warmed to immediately.

'Who are you?' she asked out loud. Did this woman own the necklace? Miranda squinted but it was impossible to tell if she was wearing anything around her neck.

She placed the photo on the bed beside her and unfolded the piece of paper. It was faded and brown with age but the headline and print were still legible.

Courageous Young Woman Rescues Storm Survivor on Horseback

Local beauty Esther Wilson is the talk of the town after rescuing the lone survivor of a boat sunk in the wild storm just off the coast near Pelican Point.

The nineteen-year-old Miss Wilson saw the flare of the sinking boat as she gazed out the window of her bedroom at approximately 10 pm Tuesday evening. Realising someone was in dire trouble, she ran to the stable and roused the station hand, who assisted her in saddling her horse, and the pair made their way through the howling wind and lashing rain down the slopes of the farm to the beach.

With no moonlight to guide her, Miss Wilson pushed her horse forward into the raging waters and swam with it out to where the boat was now almost completely submerged. Clinging to the wreckage of the stricken vessel was Sydney merchant Leonard Clarke, returning from a business trip to Eden, who climbed onto the horse's back behind Miss Wilson and made it safely back to shore. Sadly, Mr Clarke's business partner had already been lost at sea. God rest his soul.

Clarke was rescued just in the nick of time according to a doctor who was called to examine him after he had been helped back to the house. He is now recuperating at the home of Arthur and Elizabeth Wilson, who are both extremely proud of the valour shown by their daughter.

Police Constable Eric Moore said he will be recommending Miss Wilson for a bravery medal, which we are sure the local community will support.

Beneath the story was a photograph of a young woman wearing a fitted button-down dress. She was tall and slim with an ethereal beauty that defied the faded newspaper. Miranda picked up the wedding photograph, placed it on the bed next to the clipping to compare the two images – it was definitely the same person. She rubbed a finger across her bottom lip. Sitting in front of her were three pieces of a puzzle relating to a woman named Esther Wilson. But what were they doing here and why had her mother hidden them?

'Could this be my grandmother?' she wondered. The only grandparents she'd ever known had been her father's parents – her mother's had both died before Miranda and Simon had been born. She'd asked about them a few times but backed away when she realised it was too painful for her mother to discuss, and as she grew older she had just accepted that was the way it was. But Clarke was her mother's maiden name, so this Leonard could have been her father.

Which was exactly where Miranda would start her next search. She had a name – two in fact – Esther Wilson and Leonard Clarke – and a place – Pelican Point. Her earlier apprehension about searching through her mother's things was replaced now by excitement at the thought of discovering more about her mother's past. She'd always been such a closed book, but now maybe, just maybe, Miranda would be able to turn a few pages and find some answers.

She leapt from the bed, folded the page back up and placed the photo inside the case along with the necklace. She was just about to pop it in her handbag when she stopped. What if her mother went looking for the case and it was gone? Would she put two and two together and realise Miranda had been nosing around? Possibly. It was better to put it back where she found it. But she needed some sort of proof that it existed – not only for herself, but to show her mother, if she ever mustered the courage to question her about it and she tried to deny it. Delving into her bag she pulled out her phone, then took all three of the pieces back out, laid them on the bed and photographed them one by one, checking each picture to make sure it was clear. The writing in the newspaper article was too small to read, so she dug around in her bag for a notebook, copied it down word for word and, feeling immensely satisfied with her private detective skills, climbed up the steps and put the box back exactly where she had found it. She felt a twinge of regret at having to leave it there, now that she had finally discovered it, but it was better to be safe than sorry.

As she was deadlocking the door on her way out, congratulating herself on her cleverness, a voice behind her on the porch made her jump.

'Hello, Miranda – your mother didn't say you'd be around this weekend.'

'Oh, hi, no, she wouldn't have, I mean I just had to pick something up that I'd left last time I was over.'

Mrs Edwards, the next-door neighbour, nodded and grinned. 'Very good, I'm feeding the cat for your parents while they're away, so I just wanted to make sure everything was all right. Not long until the big day now, is it?'

'No, it's not. Lots to do.' Miranda jangled her keys in her hand. 'So I'd better be off. Bye.'

She felt Mrs Edwards' eyes on her as she hotfooted it to the car and turned on the ignition. Waving sweetly, she drove off up the street wondering what the hell she was going to tell her mother about why she had been there, now that she was sure to find out.

Pelican Point

Her eyes were closed. She felt the movement of the bow on the strings, the way it caught the edges and slid across, like light rippling on the surface of the sea. The music was her and she was the music. The notes rose into the air, floated and dissolved, like a lingering kiss, like a part-remembered dream. She was somewhere else. With him. She could feel the curve of his lip against her cheek, hear the smile in his voice. She was young again, at the beginning of something. The dog lay quietly at her feet, looking out across the wide expanse of grass to the ocean beyond, a half-chewed ball next to him, waiting for the walk that always came when the music stopped and she was returned to herself.

Sydney

The apartment was blissfully quiet, apart from the Café Classics CD Miranda had playing in the background. She laid the puzzle pieces on the table beside her laptop and studied each one in turn. The photos of the necklace and the woman weren't going to be much help in an internet search, although the name of the jeweller just might. More useful were the notes she'd copied down: the name of the boat, the place, the man who was rescued and of course the heroine.

Her fingers skipped across the keys – *Esther Wilson*. It was obviously a long time ago and there wasn't much likelihood that her Esther Wilson was going to be at the top of the Google search results. But when the list came up, a zing of excitement bounced around her insides. Right at the top was an Esther Wilson, a nursing sister in the army in World War I, who was born in 1864 and died in 1952. Maybe this was her? Miranda clicked on the link and skimmed through the information. This Esther had lived in Queensland and Adelaide as well as serving in both the world wars, but there was no mention of Pelican Point. She married late in life and had no children. Not the Esther she wanted.

She hit the back button and scrolled down the rest of the results for a few more pages, clicking on each one and finding out what she could about them – a singer, an American socialite, an actress, a real estate agent and a few images of gorgeous-looking girls on Facebook who were clearly not the Esther Wilson she was seeking.

Next she searched for Leonard Clarke, wading through pages of information, but found no one who fitted the bill.

Then she tried the newspaper article. After typing in the headline word for word, she pressed enter and waited, eyes glued to the screen, willing something useful to appear. But no luck. There was a story about Grace Bussell, a woman who had saved shipwreck survivors in the late 1800s in Western Australia – also on horseback – but the rest of the page referred to asylum seekers and stories about resilience in the war.

She gave a heavy sigh. The article must have come from a small local paper, so there would be no records of the story in any government archives. Not sure what other leads to follow, she typed in the name of the place mentioned in the article. Bingo! Pelican Point – a small rural community about four and a half hours south of Sydney. According to the snippet she found, it was the site of quite a few boating incidents, going right back to the 1800s, when a ship was wrecked just off the coast. The two survivors managed to get themselves to shore and stagger through the bush, but the other passengers went down with the ship. There wasn't much more information about the place. Further googling revealed only that it was now a haven for summer holiday-makers but had a permanent population of under a thousand people. And that was about it. The jeweller's name was a similar dead end. So all she'd found in over – what was it, two hours and thirty-nine minutes of research – was that a place called Pelican Point existed. Great! That was an afternoon well spent.

She switched off the computer, slouched in her chair and pondered her lack of progress. It was almost three o'clock and she'd promised to meet Belle for a coffee this afternoon. Maybe her friend would have some ideas on how to go about uncovering more information? She scooped up her finds and slipped them inside a plastic sleeve before putting them in her bag and heading out for a good strong dose of caffeine.

Miranda tapped her fingers on the table and checked her watch – five minutes after the last time she looked and Belle was now twenty-two minutes late. Well, technically she was only seventeen minutes late, since Miranda had arrived five minutes early, as usual. At least the sun was shining and there was plenty of people-watching to be done. The café was a bustle of twenty- and thirty-somethings, wearing an eclectic assortment of ripped jeans, faded T-shirts and trendy streetwear, the typical Newtown crowd.

Just as Miranda beckoned to the waiter – she really couldn't wait any longer for that coffee – there was a brush of a cheek against hers and the heady smell of a vanilla musk perfume as Belle made her appearance. And an appearance it was. Belle was one of those people who turned heads – not only because of her beautiful features but because of her unique sense of style. Today it was as obvious as ever – mid-calf Docs, black tights, a figure-hugging dress in a burnt-orange floral fabric that looked like it belonged on an armchair and a collection of beads that jingled as she sat opposite Miranda and greeted her breathlessly.

'So sorry I'm late, my lovely, you know how it is. Have you ordered yet?'

'Just about to.' Miranda did know how it was with Belle, and any irritation she'd felt at her lateness vanished as her friend gave a bewitching smile.

'So, tell me all your news. How's your week been? How's work? How's *Jamie*?'

'Work's the same old same old, too much of it and too little time. Still no news on the partnership.' Miranda ignored the sarcastic reference to her fiancé and launched straight into an account of the strange day with her mother and this morning's detective work, finishing her story just as the waiter delivered their skinny capps.

Belle licked the froth from the back of her spoon. 'So your mother denied knowing anything about the necklace?'

'Yes. Point-blank. She said I must have imagined the whole thing.'

'But the necklace you remembered was the one you found this morning?'

'Absolutely. Exactly the same.' Miranda picked up her phone from the table, found the pictures she'd taken at her parents' earlier that day and showed them to Belle. Then she filled her in on the contents of the article.

'Wow. Why would she lie about something like that? Do you think she stole it? Or it belonged to someone on the boat that went down? Whatever, she obviously doesn't want you to wear it to your wedding.' Belle gave her coffee another stir and dropped the spoon into the saucer. 'So what are you going to do?'

Miranda sighed. 'I don't know. I mean, it's not that big a deal, I guess, but I just have this feeling that the woman in the photo is . . . well, I think she could be my grandmother.'

'Your mum's mother?'

Miranda nodded. 'Mum's always been so secretive about her parents and childhood – it sort of makes sense.'

'Well, just bloody well ask her – show her the photo and ask her.'

'I can't, Belle. I don't want to upset her again.' Miranda quaked at the memory of the scene at the restaurant. Even though she was well and truly an adult now, it made her feel like the frightened child who had hidden away in her bedroom whenever one of her mother's stormy moods was brewing.

'It's the only way you're going to find out anything.'

'You think she's going to just come out and tell me? Not after the way she reacted the other day. I need to find out more information about the woman and the man mentioned in the newspaper clipping first. Try and work out if it actually is my grandmother and then maybe go and talk to Mum about it, when I have proof. My grandmother died when Mum was young and it's always been one of those no-go zones. Whenever I brought it up when I was younger she'd go all quiet and just change the subject. I figured it was too painful for her to talk about it so I never went there. Now I really want to know more. I've just got a feeling that it could explain a lot of things about my mother I've never understood.' Miranda swallowed back the lump in her throat.

'And besides, you really must wear that necklace at the wedding. It's divine!' Belle laughed. 'You should investigate through the Births, Deaths and Marriages registry.'

Miranda brightened up. 'That's a great idea.'

'But you're going to have to talk to your mother about it at some stage.'

'Hmmm.' The thought of bringing it up again made Miranda cringe but at least she had a plan A to get working on.

'So you didn't answer my other question,' Belle said.

'About?'

'Your lovely husband to be. I'm sure there must be something riveting you can tell me about him.'

Belle was determined to bait Miranda whenever it came to James, but she wasn't going to bite. 'He's good. I think. Away on a boys' cycling weekend.'

Her friend smirked. 'Oohh, that sounds like so much fun!'

'Lay off, Belle. I know you think he's boring, but there's a lot more to him than you realise.'

'Hmm. Well, he must keep it well hidden. You've been with him for the last five years and I haven't seen it yet.'

'He's quiet, that's all. Anyway, there's no point discussing it any more, we're never going to agree.'

Belle shook her head. 'I just want you to be happy, Mirry. I know he makes good money and comes from a good family, blah blah blah, but there are other things that are more important. I just don't think he's the man for you. I hope you prove me wrong, I really do.'

Miranda changed the subject, asking Belle about her love-life, which she was always happy to provide details on. After more chatting about work, the books they'd been reading and life in general, Belle reached over and rubbed Miranda's arm. 'Keep me posted on the necklace mystery. I have to run. We have a rehearsal this afternoon – there's only a week until opening night.'

They stood and hugged. Miranda clung on for a little longer than usual, stifling the urge to cry. Belle was the only person in the world who Miranda felt completely safe with, the only person in the world she could confide in when things went wrong. But for some reason she just couldn't bring herself to mention the anxiety she'd felt as she looked at herself in the wedding dress.

What are you so afraid of?

There's nothing wrong with wanting life to be calm and easy, she told the voice.

She watched Belle hail a bus and waved as it disappeared down King Street. There probably weren't two people in the world who were more different than she and Belle. Although they'd gone to school together, they hadn't been friends until they found themselves on the same train to Sydney Uni most mornings, and often in the same lectures. Both had enrolled in an arts degree but Miranda took a tangent into law while Belle left to see the world. It was the fact that they were so different that had drawn them together. Miranda had always played by the rules: performed well at school, waited for the 'right' one to have sex (although he subsequently turned out to be very much the wrong one), excelled academically and done a law degree just because she could. From what Belle had told Miranda about her past, she'd done almost exactly the opposite: hated school apart from drama, lost her virginity at age fifteen in the back of a Torana and had a series of low-paying but interesting jobs ranging from nannying to selling flowers to designing clothes. Anything that supported her true passion – acting. She'd spent every last cent to put herself through drama school as a mature age student. You had to admire it. Even if she was absolutely skint, she was happy.

Miranda unhooked her bag from the back of the chair. Something about the conversation with Belle had unsettled her. It wasn't her implied criticism of James, Miranda was used to that – he just wasn't out there enough for Belle. She tried to put her finger on it as she stopped and looked in the window of a chic little boutique at a wraparound dress in a shade of peacock blue. A blurred image of herself looked back, not a hair out of place, her clothes straight from the pages of the latest fashion magazine, and in an instant she knew what it was that was making her uneasy. Belle was content – with her life and with herself. She didn't want more of anything and she wasn't waiting for something spectacular to happen; she didn't care what people thought and she wasn't afraid to be herself.

You need to loosen up and live a little.

The voice again, right on cue.

She dipped her head to avoid any further confrontation with her reflection and took a closer look at the dress. A bit of retail therapy might perk her up. Heading into the shop, she put all thoughts of James and Belle and her mother right out of her mind, convinced that a new addition to her wardrobe was all she needed to make herself feel better.

Pelican Point

As the boat motored towards the shore she lifted her hand and gave a wave. The young man raised his in return as he cut the engine and drifted a little closer before climbing over the side, rope in hand, dragging the boat in behind him. It was good of him to be helping her out like this, delivering her shopping. Since the road had been blocked off there was no transport into town other than on foot or by boat. And two miles was a long way to lug your shopping bags along a dirt track.

'Not a bad day for it,' he called as he approached.

'Not bad,' she agreed.

The dog waddled up to the man as he tied the rope to an outcrop of rock, then followed him through the gently breaking surf back to the boat. She followed too, reaching in to grab a bag in each hand and carry them higher up the beach out of the water's reach.

'Doing any fishing?' she asked.

'Not today. Too much work on. You?'

'Threw a line in this morning but came out with diddly squat. Might give it another shot this evening.'

'Fair enough. Do you want a hand up with these?' He motioned to the bags sitting on the sand.

'Nope. Buster and I can manage. Thanks all the same.' The dog gave a small whine at the mention of his name, looking up at his mistress, eyes shining.

The man felt around in his pocket. He handed her some coins along with a small pile of envelopes. 'Not much change from fifty, I'm afraid.'

'Doesn't surprise me,' she huffed. 'Thanks for your trouble, see you when I see you.'

He doffed his cap as he returned to the boat, looping the rope as he waded out and pushed off. 'Good luck with the fish. Bye, Essie.'

And with that he pushed the boat out into the waves and started the motor.

She watched him head out towards the horizon before steering to the right and disappearing around the headland. Essie. No one had called her that for years. He was a good man, Vincent Kennedy, solid. Minded his own business and nobody else's. A shame his boss and a few of the others around here weren't the same. If they thought that closing her access road was going to force her off the property, they could think again. She'd faced worse than that in her lifetime. Let them try their hardest. There was nothing they could do to make her forfeit her small patch of paradise. Not a thing. She licked the salt from her lips and, carrying a couple of grocery bags in each hand, started up the beach towards the track that would take her home.

Sydney

Miranda woke late from a restless sleep still with the same thoughts repeating themselves over and over: who was the woman in the photo and how could she find out more about her? She stumbled out of bed and checked her phone: a text from James. *Hey there, all good here. Miss you. See you tonight. x* She texted back: *Miss you too. Have fun. x* and fixed herself some brunch. There was no point mentioning her discovery to James. He'd just give her the same advice Belle had – ask your mother – which Miranda knew was completely out of the question. At least for the time being. It was impossible to explain to anyone else why she needed to get to the bottom of this – she hardly knew herself. But what she would do was take up Belle's suggestion about the Registry of Births, Deaths and Marriages.

So, where to start? Her mother's birth certificate was probably the easiest place. She switched on the computer and found the registry's website, clicked on Birth Certificates and hit an immediate dead end. Only the individual concerned or their parents could apply for a birth certificate, and that wasn't going to happen. There had to be some other way of finding out the names of Kathleen's parents. If Esther and Leonard had married perhaps she could locate their marriage certificate.

Again, she had no luck in the Marriage and Relationships section but when she hopped over to the Family History page she found it was possible to enter the couple's names and date of marriage and do a search. She entered the two surnames but had no clue as to the year – there was no date on the newspaper clipping to even give her a starting point. Kathleen was born in 1947 so if these two were her parents presumably they had married some time before that. She typed in 1937 to 1947 as the time frame but was then stumped again by the district so left that space blank. Her finger hovered above the enter button, butterflies swarming in her belly. Why was she so nervous? Or was it guilt? This was only a bit of family research, perfectly harmless. She hit the key and waited for the answer to appear on the screen.

Zero matches found.

Damn! She clicked on the search tips heading and scanned the page.

If you want to refine your search, also include the father's or mother's given names.

Why didn't they just say that in the first place? She typed Esther Wilson and Leonard Clarke in the appropriate boxes, then pressed enter. And there they were.

Registration number 5061/1946, Clarke, Leonard Charles and Wilson, Esther Rosemary, Paddington.

So her instincts had been right, they did marry! The sole survivor of the boating disaster and the girl who risked her life to save him had fallen in love and become man and wife. Miranda smiled and let out a sigh at the romance of it all. That was one piece of the puzzle solved. And to top it off her own middle name was Rose – an abbreviation of Rosemary. Was it mere coincidence or could her mother have chosen it as a tribute to *her* late mother?

The death records might reveal more information. It was possible to locate records of deaths up to thirty years ago so she typed in Leonard's full name, and gave a field of 1960–1970 for the years to be searched.

Yes!

30299/1967, Clarke, Leonard Charles
Father's given name: Charles William
Mother's given name: Kathleen Elizabeth
District: Paddington

This had to be him! It was the same district as the wedding and *this* Leonard's mother had the same name as Miranda's mother. If it was him he had died when Kathleen was twenty years old. How hard it must have been for her to lose two parents within a decade, one at the beginning of her teenage years and one at the end. Was that why she never spoke of them?

Now, on to Esther. From the tiny skerricks of information Kathleen had ever let slip Miranda knew that her mother had died when she was just eleven, which would make it around 1958. She clicked away at the keyboard, entering

Esther's name and the year and waited again, her fingers poised above the computer.

Zero matches.

Maybe that was the wrong year? She tried the ten years prior and the ten years following but found nothing. Very strange. *This* Esther Wilson might not be Kathleen's mother after all? And yet the evidence Miranda had collected seemed to point in that direction. There had to be some way of finding out more. Miranda knew that her mother had a brother but he lived in Queensland and the two of them had never been close so there was not much chance of finding anything out from him either.

Why don't you just ask your mother?

Yeah, right! She leant her elbows on the table, resting her head in her hands. The more she uncovered the more certain she became that she had to have all the information clear first. Otherwise her mother would just shut down and accuse her of stirring up trouble. At least now she had her grandparents' names – or she thought she did – and knew that they'd been married in Sydney.

It was probably a good idea to have a record of all this. She clicked purchase, paid for the two certificates and shut down the browser.

She closed her laptop feeling only partially satisfied with the day's detective work. Falling against the back of the chair she gave her shoulders a wriggle. Her head was spinning. That was about all she could come up with for now. It was Sunday afternoon, there was washing to do and some work to catch up on. James would be home soon and the weekend would be over. Tomorrow it was back to the treadmill.

Pelican Point

The afternoon had turned dull and windy. Woolly storm clouds were banking and there was a damp chill in the air. Down below the headland a slate-grey sea hissed and spluttered. A lone cormorant flew overhead buffeted by the strong breeze. The handful of mail Vincent had collected from the postbox yesterday was still sitting on the verandah table unopened. Esther plonked herself in the chair to take a look: an electricity bill, a bank statement and one from the local council. What the hell did they want now? She slipped her pinky under the fold of the envelope and ripped.

Dear Mrs Wilson,
It has been brought to our attention that the home you are currently occupying has fallen into a state of disrepair. Council has certain standards which must be adhered to for a dwelling to be considered habitable.

We will be sending a building inspector to investigate the situation further and assess whether the house is fit for habitation. As the occupier of the dwelling you are expected to comply with council regulations regarding the upkeep of properties in the area.

Could you please telephone our office to arrange for an inspection at a time that is convenient?

Sincerely,
Graham Patmore
Building Services
Mullawa Shire Council

Esther gave a snort, screwed the piece of paper up into a ball and tossed it on the ground. Who did these people think they were, telling her what she had to do with her own house? Graham Patmore – whoever he was – was nothing but a lackey. She knew what this was about – and who was behind it. The same person who'd organised to get the access road closed because it was supposedly in need of maintenance. That was weeks ago and not a thing had been done to patch it up. Now they were pulling this stunt. Let them try as hard as they liked – she wasn't going to budge. She had a pair of legs to walk into town and there was Vincent to help her out with the groceries. If they thought she was going to just roll over and let them take away her home they could go to hell. There was no way she was moving, not for love or money.

They'd already tried both. First that scoundrel of a nephew had come snivelling around pretending he was interested in her welfare – didn't think it was safe, an old woman living out here on her own, who knew what might happen? Said he'd help her find somewhere more comfortable where she'd have some company. But she wasn't falling for that baloney. The money angle hadn't worked either. What was she going to do with it? And where else was she going to go? No, she was staying put.

She stood and looked out across the bay at the brooding sky. It was going to be a cracker of a storm. Buster crawled under the chair as a rumble of thunder shook the air.

'You'll be all right, boy,' she said, giving him a rub on the forehead.

Fat drops of rain plopped onto the roof and within seconds the torrent began. It hammered onto the corrugated tin and fell in sheets, turning the yard into a river as she watched. There wasn't a storm that passed without her remembering. She closed her eyes and felt the fistfuls of mane between her fingers and the surge of the waves as she pushed the horse on, urging him into the depths, gripping her legs tight to his sides. The memory of that icy water sent a tremor through her body even now and brought her back to the present, to the pouring rain and the dog trembling by her feet. The night that had changed everything was never far from her thoughts.

Not for the first time she wished she'd let him drown.

How different her life could have been.

Sydney

The deep turquoise ocean stretched as far as she could see. There was no telling where the sea ended and the sky began. Sunshine warmed her back. She dipped her toes into the shallows and her bare skin tingled. Tiny fish swam around her feet, flashes of brilliant green and cobalt blue darting one way and then the other. She walked until the cool water came up to her waist before she dived under, a chain of bubbles floating to the surface as she slowly exhaled. Her eyes were open. It was so beautiful down here, swimming along in peace, until she felt something brush against her shin and then a sudden surge of pain as whatever it was took hold, wrapping itself around her leg, pulling harder, dragging her out to the depths where it was murky and dark. As she struggled, a second tentacle enveloped her body and then a third as she tried to kick her way towards the surface where she could see the sun still shining. Water began to fill her lungs. No matter how hard she tried to push herself upwards, the creature kept dragging her down.

Miranda sat bolt upright in bed, her heart racing, perspiration soaking the sheets. She heard James snoring in the dark beside her and leant her head back against the bedhead. The same old dream had woken her, the same one she'd been having on and off since she was a child. And more often just recently. She shook it from her brain and looked at the clock: 5.05 am. No point going back to sleep now. Even if she could. Dragging herself out of bed, she tiptoed outside, trying not to wake James. Why did she feel lonelier now that he was home than she had all weekend without him?

Coffee would help get rid of the fuzz. She filled the machine with water, taking care to be extra quiet. There was no point talking to James about her nightmares or her worries – she hadn't even told him about finding the necklace. He always wanted to get involved and fix things, and there were some things that just weren't that simple. Some things she had to sort out for herself. She flicked on the kettle, pulling her dressing-gown tighter against the frostiness of the morning and the residual fragments of the dream. Her diary was on the kitchen bench and she opened it to today: Monday 19 March. Work, late meeting. The rest of the week was pretty much the same. She let out a groan when she saw a meeting with the priest scheduled for Tuesday. They'd already done the whole 'are you prepared for marriage' course. James' parents were only part-time Catholics but had wanted them to marry in the chapel at his old school, the whole old-boy-ra-ra carry-on. It was a gorgeous traditional old church with stained-glass windows and timber pews, so Miranda had agreed, but this whole education thing was starting to wear thin. She knew

James wasn't into it either, but he just smiled and said a few hours with the priest wasn't going to kill them.

She picked up her phone and looked through her photos for the image of the woman in the wedding dress. There was a faraway look in the woman's eyes, as if she was actually somewhere else. Could this really be her grandmother? The only way to find out would be to ask her mother or find her birth certificate. Doing the cat-burglar prowl again didn't appeal, but the thought of questioning her mother was even worse. She remembered a time when she was at school and had to draw a family tree for homework. When she'd asked her mother to fill in her grandparents' names all she wrote was DEAD. In capital letters, just like that. The look of the word on the page, so stark and bold, had sent a shiver scurrying all the way down to Miranda's toes. After that she'd known better than to ask and had made up a name and a story to go with it. Her imaginary grandmother was an older version of Mary Poppins. She would sit Miranda on her knee and tell her tales about distant places, handsome strangers and mysterious old castles haunted by the ghosts of long-dead emperors. Her imaginary grandfather had ruddy cheeks and smelled like the sea. He took her fishing and told her stories of pirates that made her eyes pop in wonder. Perhaps because her paternal grandparents lived in England and she'd only met them once before they both died, this fictional couple had been as alive to her as any real family.

But fantasising wasn't going to get her anywhere. She gazed back at the photo. Maybe her father would know something, but broaching the subject without giving away that she'd been snooping was going to be tricky. Now they were both retired it was hard to see her parents separately but today was a golf day – she could call him on his mobile, if he had it switched on, and have a chat.

The sliding of a wardrobe door from the bedroom upstairs told her James was awake. Time for a shower. Racing to the bathroom she locked the door behind her. She was in no mood for an early-morning chat – or anything else he might have in mind.

⁓

Just after eleven Miranda excused herself from yet another meeting and ducked out for a break. The numbers dropped as the lift descended and she stepped outside the building onto the street. Suited women and men hurried by, most of them on their mobiles, some in pairs deep in conversation, undoubtedly about work. This was the business end of the city, full of movers and shakers, people who spent far too long at the office but were paid handsomely for their efforts. She manoeuvred around a crowd of smokers and took out her phone to call her dad.

He answered surprisingly fast. 'Hello, sweetheart. I wasn't expecting to hear from you this morning.' She smiled at the sound of her father's voice, warm and welcoming as always.

'Hi, Dad. I was just in between meetings and thought I'd give you a call. How was your weekend?'

'Good. We had a nice time. Your mother visited as many knick-knack shops as she could find and I got in a game, so everyone was happy.'

Miranda nodded as she listened to his jubilant tone. 'Never too much golf, eh Dad?'

'You've got it. Just finished up here for this morning. Bloody good game I played too, if I do say so myself.'

'I'm sure.' She paused, crossing her fingers behind her back as she fabricated the lie. 'So, I'm just filling in a couple of forms for the church and it asks for the grandparents' names. I know yours, of course, but Mum's never talked about her parents, and since it's sort of taboo with her, I thought I'd give you a call and ask.' She bit her lip and waited for his response.

'Jeez, love, I don't know if I'm much help. You know as much as I do about your grandparents. They were already gone when your mother and I met and she always refused to speak about them so I never pushed it. I'm not sure if we ever had to put their names on anything ourselves. I only ever saw Kathleen write *deceased*, if she wrote anything at all.'

Disappointment hit her like a sledgehammer, even though she hadn't expected anything else.

'Can't see why it matters – it's you and James they should want the details on.'

So much for that idea!

'Are you still there, love?'

'You don't think you could ask her about it again, do you?'

The long silence before her father responded answered the question before he did. 'I really don't want to trouble her, love. She's been so good for such a long time, I'd rather not upset the apple cart, if you know what I mean. Just tell them you don't know. I'm sure they're not going to refuse to marry you.'

'No, of course they're not. It's fine, Dad. Better get back to the meeting before they miss me. Have a good day.'

'You too, love.'

Miranda shoved her phone in her pocket and swallowed back her anger. If she was going to find out any more about Esther Rosemary Wilson she'd have to do it herself. It wasn't really her father's fault. God knows he'd had enough to put up with over the years, and he was right – on the whole her mother was doing a lot better these days. He evidently knew nothing about the outburst the other day. She marched back into the building, pressed the up arrow on the elevator and put on her best business face as she stepped in and watched the doors close.

The afternoon was a complete waste of time. Words blurred endlessly together as Miranda stared at the computer screen and chewed on the end of her pen. There were contracts to prepare and deadlines to meet – if only she could get her mind to focus she might actually be able to get some work done.

'Got a minute?' Todd Mulherin appeared over the wall of her workspace.

The pen fell from her fingertips onto the floor. 'Sure.'

As she followed him into his office she was well aware of the dozen pairs of eyes watching them. This could be it, the news she'd been waiting for. Everyone knew there were only two real contenders for the partnership. If she was successful she would be the youngest employee ever to make partner, and the only woman. Damien was her only competition in the Sydney office, but there were other possibilities too. Whoever was chosen would receive a hefty pay rise and benefits along with the prestige.

'Close the door, Miranda, if you wouldn't mind. Take a seat.'

She settled herself into one of the black leather swivel chairs, crossed her legs and clasped her hands around her knees.

Todd positioned himself behind his desk, picked up a pen and rolled it between his fingers. He was flawlessly dressed as always in a pin-striped navy suit, white shirt and a patterned tie, his salt and pepper hair perfectly groomed in short cropped waves. 'So, I guess you know why I've called you in here?'

'I assume it's about the partnership?' She curved her lips into what she hoped was a smile.

'Correct.' Todd had a formal manner but Miranda knew that a lot of that was about keeping up appearances. Since his father had started the firm in the 1970s – before Miranda was even born – it had become one of the most respected law firms in the country, and Mr Mulherin Senior was very picky about Todd maintaining his distance from the staff. But there were some employees he found it hard to be formal with and Miranda was one of them. He was only a few years older than her and they shared a similar sense of humour.

'It's been a tough decision. Candidates from Melbourne, Canberra, the Brisbane office as well as Sydney. You know I went into bat for you, don't you, Miranda?'

She nodded. 'I do. And I really appreciate it.' He was letting her down easy, she knew, beating about the bush because he didn't want to hurt her feelings.

'Whoever is given this partnership has to be someone who we feel respects the family values of the firm, someone who is dependable, who we know is going to put the interests of

our clients first and uphold the reputation of Mulherin's.'
He was dragging it out, like he was the host of one of those
reality TV shows where they withhold the announcement of
the winner until after the ad break. Any minute now there'd
be a drum roll.

Miranda ran her tongue across the roof of her mouth in
an effort to moisten it as she waited for him to continue.

'So, after much deliberation, I'm happy to announce that
the new partner is . . . Miranda McIntyre.'

'Really?'

'Don't sound so surprised. I know there was competition,
but you were the obvious choice – your work ethic, your
impeccable record here at the company, the way you deal
with the clients and with your colleagues. You shouldn't sell
yourself short, Miranda. So what do you say?'

She sat completely motionless in the chair while the room
started spinning around her. Todd was speaking again but he
sounded a long way away and she couldn't make out what
he was saying. When she opened her mouth to answer him,
nothing came out. The words stuck in her throat. Water, she
needed water. The room was spinning faster now, faster and
faster, like she was on that ride at Luna Park, the one where
you stuck to the walls and the floor dropped away from you
and you went round and round and round. The Rotor, that's
what it was called. She tried to stand, to reach for the water,
but the floor really was dropping away from her now and
she was finding it harder and harder to breathe. The more
she tried to inhale the sharper the pain in her chest became.
Tiny silver spots danced before her eyes as she began to sway
with the movement of the room. From somewhere far away

she heard Todd calling her, saying her name over and over again. Maybe if she closed her eyes his voice would become clearer and the ride would stop and she'd be able to get off. Her knees buckled beneath her as she felt herself falling.

It was an effort to even turn the key. She flicked on the light, glad that James was working back and she'd have a chance to compose herself after this afternoon's debacle at the office. Dropping her bag on the table and kicking off her heels, she headed directly to the bathroom. What she needed was a shower, a long hot one to clear the cobwebs from her head and help her think straight.

She stripped off her clothes and dumped them on the floor instead of hanging them up as she usually did after work, then turned the shower tap hard to the right so it was running as fast and as hot as it possibly could. Stepping in, she pulled the mixer back just far enough towards the cold to make it bearable and then closed her eyes as the water teemed onto her scalp and stung her skin. What the hell had happened to her today? One minute she was listening to Todd tell her she'd been given the partnership and the next everything was spinning out of control.

All she really remembered was waking up on the floor with Todd staring down at her while his PA, Jemima, held a wet cloth against her forehead. She'd mumbled something about not feeling well, dragged herself to her feet and rushed to the bathroom, where she dry-retched into the toilet bowl, relieved that she'd worked through her lunchbreak. Sitting there on the cold tile floor she'd tried unsuccessfully to hold back the tears of embarrassment. Jemima had followed her into the bathroom and she pulled herself together enough to have a conversation through the door.

'Are you okay, Miranda?'

'Yes, I'm fine.'

Clearly not.

'I've brought your bag in. Todd wants me to call you a cab so you can go home, or to the doctor's?'

'I'll be okay. I don't know what happened. All of a sudden I just felt faint.'

'All the excitement of the news, I expect.'

Miranda pulled a few sheets of paper out of the holder and wiped her mouth, flushed the toilet and opened the door. She forced a half-smile. 'Must have been.'

'Sure you're okay?'

She nodded and looked at herself in the mirror. Black blotches were smeared beneath her eyes and strands of hair had escaped from the bun she'd pinned them in so neatly that morning. 'God, I look a fright.'

'Todd was going to make an announcement and organise some drinks but he wanted me to see if you were feeling up to it. He's happy to wait if you'd rather – he wants you to be there when he tells everyone.'

Miranda looked back at her reflection. Could she really go out there in front of all those people looking and feeling like this? Maybe she was coming down with something, or maybe Jemima was right and the shock of being offered the partnership was just too much after all the build-up. Either way, it would be better to wait until she was looking the part before announcing it to the world.

'Can you tell him I think I'll wait, go home and have a rest, and we'll do it tomorrow?'

'Not a problem,' chirped Jemima. 'So would you like me to call you a cab?'

'No. I'll be fine. Really.'

She'd slunk out of the bathroom and made a dash for the lift, thankful that nobody had seen her disappear. And now here she was trying to wash it all away in the shower, still not even sure what had happened. Whatever it was had left her feeling totally drained. Not the way you should feel when you've just found out that the one thing you wanted more than anything, the thing you've been working towards for years, is finally there for the taking. Thinking about it now she couldn't even remember if she'd told Todd she accepted the offer. Maybe she was losing the plot, working too hard as her mother had told her.

Or maybe you don't really want what you thought you wanted after all.

She opened her eyes and pushed the tap off, flung the glass door of the shower open and grabbed her towel, wrapping her hair into a turban, then pulled another towel from the rail and rubbed herself dry. There was a perfectly logical explanation for her little meltdown and she wasn't going to listen to any bullshit the voice might say otherwise. So she'd fainted, passed out, whatever you want to call it. There was no use moping about it, trying to analyse the situation. It had happened and now she was fine. End of story. Time to pour herself a glass of wine, relax and get a good night's sleep.

Everything would be better in the morning.

Pelican Point

Esther twisted the rhubarb stalks one at a time, being sure to choose only the widest, darkest stems. They would probably be the last of the season, although the plants were healthy enough and sometimes a few kept growing year round. She collected the harvest and placed it carefully into the plastic bag she'd brought with her. The spinach was thriving, the glossy leaves growing larger by the day. And the last batch of carrots and potatoes would be ready to be dug up soon.

She poked around in the soil, still wet from the storm a few days ago, and nodded when she saw the light green tendrils of a crop of broad beans she'd sown last week just starting to shoot. All in all, the garden was looking good. There was a certain satisfaction in growing your own food, pushing the seeds down into the earth, tending them, watching them flourish. Like watching children grow to adulthood. The thought brought an ache to her chest and she buried it as fast as she could, picked up her bag and trowel and trudged back up the path towards the house.

Sydney

'But you never miss work. Are you sure you don't want me to call the doctor?' James held his palm against her forehead. 'You're a bit warm.'

'I'll be fine. I think I've just been overdoing it. A day in bed and I'll be back to normal.'

'Ring me at work if you need anything.' He bent down and kissed her cheek, the scent of his aftershave lingering as he stood.

'I will. Promise.'

Miranda snuggled back beneath the covers. He was right – she never missed a day's work – but then she never usually polished off a whole bottle of red by herself on a weeknight, either, as she'd done last night while watching *Breakfast at Tiffany's* for the zillionth time. A day off was probably just what she needed, a day to sleep, read and maybe even ponder the riddle of the family mystery a little more. Todd could wait to make his announcement – one day more was hardly going to matter.

Just as she was about to close her eyes again and will herself into a dreamless sleep, her phone buzzed a reminder: *Meeting with FD, 7 pm.* FD was Father Donelly – it was their last meeting with the priest before the wedding. Groaning, she dumped the phone back onto the bedside table, rolled over and pulled the doona over her head.

⁓

Miranda sat quietly looking up at the stained-glass windows of the church: Jesus on the cross against a backdrop of purple clouds, a haloed woman wearing golden robes kneeling at his feet, a disciple standing at her side, hand on his heart and head bowed. In an alcove beneath the window the pipes of an organ gleamed like giant silver teeth above the timber-framed keyboard. The elaborate fretwork of the roof arches and the honeyed stone walls finished off the traditional feel of the place perfectly. This was where she would soon be standing in her bridal gown saying her vows, promising to love, honour and respect.

Until death do us part.

The previous meetings had taken place in the office, but Father Donelly liked to see 'his couples' in the church itself, said it gave them a sense of the solemnity of the step they were about to take and helped them feel more at home in the surroundings, although the churning in Miranda's belly made her think those two things were completely contradictory. The priest sat in front of them at the makeshift desk he'd set up in front of the altar, resting steepled fingers against his lips. Thinking he was about to burst into prayer, Miranda bowed her head.

'So, James, tell me why you want to marry Miranda.'

Not a prayer at all but a question. She turned to James. His eyes gleamed as he squeezed her hand.

'That's easy. I love her.'

The priest nodded. 'And you understand that by marrying her before God and the church, witnessed by your parents, family and friends, you are undertaking to devote yourself to her for the rest of your life.'

'Absolutely.'

'And Miranda, why do you want to marry James?' Father Donelly's eyes were on her now. They were pale green and slightly bloodshot beneath his rimless glasses. From the corner of her eye she could see James looking at her, waiting for her response. The words swam in her head: I want to marry James because . . . because he's kind and he's sweet and . . .

And you turned thirty last year and time is running out.

'Miranda?' Father Donelly took off his glasses and raised his eyebrows.

'Oh, sorry. Because I love him too. Of course.'

The priest gave a slight nod, looking down at the piece of paper in front of him.

'Good. And you understand that in making that promise before God, the church and your family, you are agreeing to devote yourself completely to James?'

'I do.' A slight quiver beneath her ribcage as the words left her lips.

Father Donelly thumbed through his papers. 'Right, well just one more thing for you to sign. Must have left it in my office. Be right back.' The scraping of his chair on the parquetry floor echoed in the cavernous space of the church.

A muffled buzz. James pulled his BlackBerry from his pocket. 'Sorry, have to take this,' he said. 'Stuff going on at work.' He stood and moved a few feet away, leaving Miranda sitting gratefully alone. Her palms were clammy, her mouth as dry as sandpaper. She took a deep breath in through her nose and counted slowly as she exhaled, pressing her fingertips to her temples to try to stop the spinning in her head. *What the hell is wrong with me?* The dots that had flickered before her eyes in Todd's office were back, tiny silver balls bouncing into each other.

'Mindy? Shit, are you okay?' James was kneeling beside her, an arm wrapped around her shoulder, as Father Donelly returned.

'Is everything all right?' he asked.

'I just feel a little giddy,' Miranda stammered.

'Here, have a drink of water, babe.' James offered her the glass that had been sitting on the table. 'She was off work sick today,' he explained to the priest.

Miranda was too preoccupied with trying *not* to be sick to notice the priest's reaction. Her antics at the office had been bad enough but throwing up here in the church would be completely mortifying. She sipped at the water and tried to stay calm. James took his seat again and rubbed her back. As the dizziness subsided she turned and gave him a weak smile. His brows were furrowed in concern. Sunburn from the weekend cycling trip still tinged his cheeks and a five o'clock shadow darkened his jawline. He looked so dapper in his suit, his tie loosened now the official 'talk' was over. He was everything she'd always wanted: handsome, dependable, financially independent.

She thought back over the conversation the two of them had just had with the priest and at other meetings in the preceding weeks: their plans to work hard and pay off the mortgage before selling up and moving somewhere with a yard, probably north of the harbour, when they started a family; their assurances that the children would be raised as Catholics; their dream of spending a life together. James had been so certain about it all and she knew that deep down this was what he wanted. But was it really what *she* wanted? Or was she just trying to live out the fairytale?

Father Donelly's voice disturbed her thoughts. 'If you're feeling better, I just need one more signature each here.' He pointed to the bottom of the page.

Miranda signed where directed and passed the pen to James. 'You okay?' he whispered.

A nod was all she could muster.

'And I will see you two at dinner with your parents. Saturday week, if my memory serves me correctly?' said Father Donelly.

The idea of a family dinner with the priest sent yet another tide of anxiety washing through her insides. God knows how my mother will react to that.

'Thank you, Father – see you then.' James shook the priest's hand before taking her own and leading her past the rows of polished timber pews, along the aisle that she would soon be walking down in the opposite direction. She kept her eyes focused on the door, ignoring the voice that whispered inside her head.

Be careful what you wish for.

A few hours later Miranda lay curled up in bed gazing at the worn pages of *Pride and Prejudice*. How many times had she read it now? There were so many new books in her to-be-read pile but there was something about this story that kept drawing her back – the way Elizabeth and Mr Darcy appeared so nonchalant in each other's company and yet underneath it all they seethed with longing. Was such passion only possible in works of fiction or could it truly be found in real life? Passion certainly wasn't running high in her own relationship just now, right at the time when it should be. James had been so sweet after her turn in the church, brought her home and tucked her up in bed with a cup of chamomile tea. He was so good to her, she really didn't deserve him.

That's a cop-out, said the voice. *It's not that you don't deserve him. You don't want him, but you're too afraid to admit it.*

'That's ridiculous,' she mumbled to herself.

Is it?

The sounds of whistles and horns bleated up from the lounge room, where James was watching some European cycle race, interrupting her conversation with the voice. She snapped her book shut and shoved it on the bedside table. Maybe what she needed was a good night's sleep. After all, it had been a pretty chaotic few days, what with the wedding arrangements, her mother, the intrigue of finding the necklace, the excitement of the news at work. No wonder she was feeling a little overwhelmed by it all.

Footsteps on the stairs.

Unable to muster the energy for a conversation, she switched off the lamp and buried herself beneath the blankets. After a few minutes in the ensuite, James climbed into bed and moved close, knees bent behind hers, his hand firm against her stomach. Her body stiffened at his touch and she hoped he hadn't noticed. As he nestled his face against her neck she concentrated on lying completely still.

Why don't you just talk to him, tell him the truth?

But what was the truth? She wasn't sure herself, so how could she even begin to tell him? Was her apprehension about the overall pressure of the wedding itself? Or was it the prospect of marrying James in particular that was the problem? What she really needed was some time away from it all to get her head straight.

'James,' she whispered into the dark.

'Hmm.'

'I was thinking I might take a week off work and get away for a bit. Everything's been so crazy. I think I just need a break from it all.'

He shifted in the bed behind her. 'Not from me, I hope.'

'No,' she said, louder than she'd intended.

'That's good. But I can't take any time off right now, babe.'

'That's okay. It'd do me good to have some time on my own.'

'Where would you go?'

'Not sure, up the coast somewhere.'

Or down.

'Well, if you can get the time off, go for it. I'll miss you, though.' He tightened his hold around her waist and nuzzled closer. 'When will you go?'

'Tomorrow, if I can wangle it.'

'That soon?' he murmured. 'Well, I guess the sooner you go, the sooner you come back.'

Lying in the dark, eyes wide open, she pressed her hand against his and waited as his chest fell up and down in the regular rhythms of sleep. Visions of the past week carouseled around in her mind: drops of blood seeping across a creamy lace rose, a glass smashing on a tiled floor, a faded photo of a stranger, herself shrinking smaller and smaller as Todd gave her the news of the promotion.

Father Donelly's pursed lips.

James' tender smile.

Some time and space away from everything, that's all I need, she assured herself. And I know exactly where I'm going to go.

Part Two

Miranda

When the first light of morning peeked through the shutters, Miranda opened her eyes and threw the sheets back, her decision to get away now even firmer after a restless sleep. Making a mental list she hurried about the room pulling clothes from drawers and grabbing toiletries. She kissed James goodbye as he left for work, promising to let him know where she was as soon as she arrived, and then steeled herself for a call to the office. Jemima sounded surprised that she'd be taking time off, especially after the promotion, but Miranda explained that she'd seen a doctor after her fainting episode, was completely run-down and had been advised to take at least a week off. Well, that wasn't exactly a lie, even if it was self-diagnosis – she'd deal with the medical certificate problem later. She ran a brush through her hair, collected her phone from the bench and locked the door behind her. Before she knew it, she was heading south.

It felt strange to be driving away from the city on a weekday against the flow of the traffic. But here she was, nevertheless, her handbag thrown onto the front passenger seat, its contents spilling onto the floor: wallet, lipstick, deodorant, a jar of multivitamins, antiseptic cream, and a portable first-aid kit she'd grabbed from the medicine cabinet, just in case. Her clothes were shoved into the faded overnight bag that sat on the back seat of the car, nestled between *Pride and Prejudice*, a straw hat and her laptop tucked inside its burgundy crocodile skin case.

Sutherland, Helensburgh, Wollongong . . . the names flew past as she followed the grey ribbon of road, as suburbia gave way to bush and finally a rolling patchwork of hills embroidered with cows and horses. She pressed a button and the roof folded back, section by section, until the wind was blowing through her hair, streaming over her face. Reaching behind her head she pulled out the elastic that held her blonde waves in place and let her hair fly loose in the breeze. Crowded House were crooning a song about taking the weather with you and she sang along, feeling surprisingly and suddenly liberated. She leant into the curves with the car as she steered around one bend and then another. The road drew closer to the coast where the ocean shimmered in the glare of brilliant sunshine and she felt the dampness of salt on her cheeks and on her tongue. She found herself smiling, as she drove through seaside towns that reminded her of somewhere she'd been as a child or perhaps only longed to go, past beaches bathed in promises.

Her destination: Pelican Point. The place was the only real clue she had to the family mystery. If she could solve that puzzle she might be able to understand why her mother seemed to live her whole life in misery and why she herself had spent every minute of her childhood walking on eggshells. More importantly, the time away would give her some breathing space, help her clear her head and work out what she really wanted. But she wouldn't think about that right now.

Time to get back to the music: Track 6, 'Don't Dream It's Over'.

—⁓

'In 500 metres, turn left.'

Miranda edged the gears down and followed the TomTom's instructions. From what she could work out, Pelican Point was about six kilometres off the main highway. The vee dub glided over the neglected road beneath tall white gums, bark peeling in sheets from their dappled trunks, past the occasional house glimpsed between overgrown hedges, and through what seemed to be an invisible wall that divided this part of the world from everywhere else. Not one car had passed her for the past twenty minutes and she hadn't seen a single soul since she'd turned off.

She drove in silence now, delighting in the feeling of being alone. Her phone was in the glove box, turned off. If anyone was trying to contact her, they would have to wait. The road dipped, crossing a small bridge over Culnurra Creek, which meant she was almost there. It would be a relief to get out of the car and stretch her legs. Apart from a coffee stop just past Kiama, she'd been driving for just over five hours. A tremor of anticipation ran through her as she spotted some buildings up ahead.

The bush on either side of the road opened up to reveal a town – if that's what it could be called. In reality it was no more than a small collection of houses huddled together on a finger of land that pointed out towards the horizon. She cruised past the Shady Daze Caravan Park and across a one-way bridge, pulling up outside a grocery store. As she closed the roof and stepped out of the car she could hear the hushing of waves somewhere in the distance, but the only water that was visible was the inlet she had just crossed. Her heart sank just a little. She'd had an image in her head of a rural paradise with a long stretch of gleaming white sand and rustic cottages sprinkled across the hillsides – but Pelican Point seemed to be nothing more than a quiet backwater.

First thing was to find somewhere to stay. Looking around she doubted if there was a motel – the van park was probably as good as it was going to get. It was almost two o'clock and her stomach was seriously grumbling. Time to have some lunch and get a few things at the shop and then see what she could find accommodation-wise.

Outside the store a woman sat on a cushion-topped milk crate. In her hands a pair of knitting needles appeared to be making some sort of baby-wear in soft pink, completely of their own accord. The needles clacked furiously but the woman's eyes looked Miranda up and down as she approached.

'G'day, love,' the woman smiled. Her peroxided hair was coiffed into a beehive but that wasn't her most startling feature. Miranda wasn't sure what surprised her more, the tattooed-on eyebrows or the perfectly applied engine-red lipstick on a face otherwise free of make-up.

'Hello.' Miranda tried not to stare as she made her way into the shop. The woman stood and followed.

'Just stopping for a bit of lunch, are ya?'

Miranda nodded.

'Not much to tempt you with, I'm afraid. Don't keep hot food on in the summer months.'

'That's okay. I might just grab a drink and a snack.' Miranda headed to the fridge at the back of the shop and found a small tub of peach yoghurt and a ginger beer.

At the counter the woman held the yoghurt up to eye level. 'Just making sure it's in date. Wouldn't want ya keeling over or anything.' She chuckled as her fingers tapped away at the antiquated till.

'So you just passing through?'

Miranda handed over a ten dollar note. 'I was hoping to stay for a few days, actually. Can you suggest anywhere?'

'On holidays, are ya?' The woman smiled, revealing a smear of scarlet on her two front teeth.

'Sort of.'

'Good time of year. Avoid the crowds. Here on yer own?'

'Yes, just me.' Miranda picked up the plastic shopping bag.

'Well, if you're looking for something for a couple of days, your best bet's back over the bridge at the van park. Jean's got a couple of cabins there. Nothing flash but clean and plenty of room just for one.'

'That's great, thank you so much.'

'My name's Norma. If you need to know anything, just ask.' The woman grinned again as she headed back outside and resumed her position on the crate. Miranda could feel the woman's eyes on her all the way back to the car, even as she pulled the seatbelt over her shoulder and started the motor. When she did a U-turn to head back over the bridge she waved to Norma, now returned to her knitting, who dipped her head in reply.

Miranda groaned as the car bounced along the potholed road into the caravan park, then pulled up outside a neat yellow weatherboard building that she assumed was the office. The main door was shut but there was a buzzer that played 'Edelweiss' when she pressed it. She had a brief image of Captain von Trapp standing onstage in the spotlight fighting back tears before she heard footsteps and the door clicked open.

Miranda peered through the wire screen but couldn't see who was there. 'Hello, I was just wondering if you might have any accommodation for a couple of nights.'

'You lookin' for a van or a cabin?' a gruff voice replied, but the door remained closed.

'A cabin. If you have one available.'

The key turned and the door swung open. 'Come in.'

Miranda stepped inside to find a bird of a woman with permed hair and a blue rinse taking up her position behind the counter.

'How many nights?'

There was clearly no point trying to engage the woman – Jean, she presumed – in small talk, so she just answered the question. 'I'm not sure yet. Possibly five, maybe a week. Can I just pay for a couple of nights to start with?'

If the woman heard, she gave no indication as she filled out a form and passed it to Miranda. 'It's $130 for the two nights. Plus a surcharge if you need linen.'

'Yes, I will, thanks. Do you take credit cards?'

'Six dollars a night extra for the linen. Take cards but there's a 3 per cent surcharge.'

Miranda signed her name and handed across her credit card. If there was an evaluation form – which she doubted – she wouldn't be giving Jean a five-star rating for customer service.

The woman handed back her card and a key. 'Straight down the road and turn right. Cabin 8. Riverview.'

'That's lovely, thank you.'

'My name's Jean. If you need anything I'm in cabin 1. Next-door to the office.' Miranda thought she detected a flutter of a smile as she turned and let herself out.

She made her way to the far end of the park, which looked completely deserted, and followed Jean's directions. Number 8 was a small timber cabin like the others perched along the perimeter of the park, and she was right, it did have a view. It was soothing to be so close to the water, even if it was more the beach she was interested in exploring. But that was going to have to wait until tomorrow. This afternoon she would settle in and unwind.

If such a thing were possible.

⌐

After unpacking and checking her phone messages, Miranda sat at the table sipping peppermint tea and typed up a shopping list on the notes page of her phone: some muesli and milk for breakfast, crackers and fruit for snacks and hopefully chicken and salad for dinner.

She looked out the cabin window as she chewed on the end of her pen, then added an extra point to the bottom of the list: ask someone about Esther Wilson/Clarke.

She'd need an angle, a story about why she wanted to know. Revealing herself as a relative might not be the way to start. Maybe she could be an historian researching boating accidents, or perhaps a journalist writing an article? That might work.

It was nearly half past four. Where the afternoon had gone she had no idea, but there was a good chance the shop would shut by five, so if she wanted to eat tonight she'd better get a move on. Deciding to walk so she could get her bearings, she grabbed her bag and locked the door, giving the handle an extra tug just to be on the safe side.

Jean was sweeping the path out the front of the office. Miranda gave her a wave but got only a raised eyebrow in return. *Poor thing, she hasn't got much of a life, I suppose, stuck here cleaning all day and waiting for a customer to show up.*

It wouldn't kill her to smile, the voice countered.

Taking a left turn out of the park she made her way along the road to the bridge. The lake – Culnurra - was actually quite pretty on closer inspection. A couple of pelicans pedalled their way across the water, their beady eyes on the lookout for dinner. A kookaburra was perched on the branch of a dead tree that clung to the banks, and just as Miranda approached, it let out a roaring cackle that made her jump.

'You cheeky thing,' she said in reply. The bird ruffled its feathers and gave her a look before flapping its wings and vanishing into the bush.

As Miranda arrived at what she presumed was the centre of
'town' she stopped to scan the assortment of shops. There was
the grocer's, a knick-knack shop, a chemist-cum-newsagent,
a fishing shop and some sort of artist's studio. Further down
the road was an old picture theatre, now closed up and empty,
shingles falling from the rafters and paint peeling from its
bolted doors. Graffiti stained the side wall and weeds littered
the facade. It was sad to see such a lovely old building so
forlorn and forgotten. The whole village – it couldn't really
be called a town – felt tired. It was probably one of those
places that came to life in summer and then struggled to stay
afloat for the rest of the year.

Still, it had a quiet unpretentiousness about it that Miranda
liked. No fancy shops or restaurants, no fun parks. The
perfect place to disappear for a few days. The perfect place
to get lost – and hopefully find yourself again.

When she entered the store Norma was nowhere to be
seen. She headed to the freezer section and picked up a pack
of frozen schnitzel that would have to do for dinner, along
with a few vegetables that looked fresh enough, but most of
the items on her list were nowhere to be found. The counter
was still deserted when she returned.

'Hello? Is anyone there?'

A door banged. Footsteps approached and Norma appeared
looking more than a little dishevelled. 'Sorry, love, just having
me afternoon nap. Did Jean have something for you?' She
rang up each item, placing them in a bag as she went.

'Yes, thanks, she did. So have you lived here long?'

'Only all me life.'

'Nice and quiet.'

'Is now. Never used to be. Main road used to pass right through here before they put the bypass in about ten years back. Killed off most of the businesses. Still get a crowd of holiday-makers in the summer, but the rest of the year the place is like a cemetery. That'll be twenty-two dollars and sixty-five cents.'

Miranda picked up a postcard from the counter, her insides trembling as she asked the next question. 'So do you know if the Wilson family still live in the area?'

The woman snorted. 'Live in the area – they own most of it! Got a huge landholding that runs most of the way along the coast just south of here. Prime real estate. Richard Wilson owns the place now. Runs cattle and horses on it. Arrogant pig of a man, he is.' She paused, her hand rustling the plastic bag of groceries. 'You don't know him, do ya?'

'No, not at all. I . . . I was doing some research on . . . on courageous women, for an article I'm writing, and I came across a newspaper story about a woman named Esther Wilson who rescued someone from the ocean on a horse.'

The woman nodded. 'Before my time, but everyone around here knows about it. Her father originally owned the property. Richard Wilson is his grandson. He and the old girl can't stand each other.'

Miranda put her wallet away and picked the bag up from the counter. The tingle of excitement she'd felt earlier was back and building to a crescendo.

'So, do you know if she's still in the area?'

The woman folded her arms across her chest. 'Sure is. Planning on talking to her, are ya?'

Alive! Esther Wilson is still alive?

'Well, I thought I might try and interview her, yes. Do you know her?'

There was a sly smile on the woman's face that Miranda wasn't quite sure how to read.

'Depends what you mean by "know", I guess. I know who she is and I know she's lived out at the point on her own for donkey's years, and I know she's a mean old biddy who thinks she owns the beach. She comes in here to shop occasionally, but isn't exactly friendly. Good luck trying to get anything out of her. She hasn't talked to anyone around here for years.'

A cranky old recluse. Not exactly grandmother material. But the woman had the same name as the Esther in the photo, so there was a good chance she could be the one Miranda was looking for.

She made sure to keep a professional edge to her tone. 'So if I did want to talk to her, how would I find her?'

'There's an access road out to her place at the northern end of the beach, but it's in a bad way and they've blocked it off. You can park your car there and walk. Or if you're after the scenic route, you can drive to the other end and walk along the beach. Take the track up to the house about three quarters of the way along.'

'Great, thanks.' Miranda picked up her bags and turned to leave.

'Don't say I didn't warn you when she refuses to talk to you. And be careful. I hear the old bat's got a loaded gun out there.'

Miranda forced a brief smile. The woman's obvious dislike for Esther was disconcerting. 'Thanks. I will.'

She left the shop with a curious mixture of elation and apprehension running through her veins, and the prospect of meeting the woman who could be her grandmother occupying her thoughts all the way back to the cabin.

⌐

Four missed calls – one from Belle, one from Todd and two from James. As much as she really didn't want to talk to anyone, she knew she owed Todd an explanation, and she'd promised James she'd ring. She dialled his number first and he picked up almost instantly.

'Hi babe, everything okay? I was getting a bit worried.'

'Sorry, I meant to call, just getting settled in.'

'So where are you?'

'Pelican Point.'

He laughed. 'Where the hell is that?'

'Just a little place I stumbled across on the south coast.' She still hadn't told him about finding the necklace. Come to think of it, she hadn't really discussed much with him of late, apart from the wedding.

'Well, take care of yourself. I'll call you tomorrow.'

'I will. Bye.'

She pressed the end button. At least she'd bought herself a little time on that front. Now to tackle the harder one. She called Todd on his mobile and waited for him to pick up, with no idea exactly what she was going to say when he did.

Just stick to your original story.

'Miranda, hello. I just wanted to check you were okay. Jemima tells me you won't be in the office for a week.'

'Hi, Todd – sorry, but apparently I have some mystery virus and my immune system is shot. The doctor's told me to have a week off.'

'That's not good. I was hoping to announce the news, but I'll wait until you're back on your feet. I'll get Jemima to cancel all the meetings on your calendar. Anything urgent she can pass on to Damien. Take care of yourself. You'll be busy when you get back.'

Todd's tone was congenial but Miranda could sense an underlying frustration. Her sudden absence from the office would be more than a little inconvenient.

'Thanks, Todd – I will. Bye.'

More lies. She'd always prided herself on her honesty, but it was amazing how easily the truth could be bent once you started. She wouldn't have to keep up the pretence with Belle, but even the thought of another conversation was exhausting, so she sent her a text saying she'd give her a call tomorrow. Time to whip herself up a gourmet meal – frozen schnitzel for one.

⁓

After dinner she checked the cupboards and under the bed, then triple-checked the locks on the sliding door and all the windows and left the light on in the kitchen area before curling up in bed with a book. But she found herself reading the same sentence over and over. The place was so quiet – apart from the echo of distant waves – and the night outside was so black. This was the first time in her life she'd stayed anywhere alone, apart from occasional work conferences, where there was always a boozy bunch of colleagues to keep you company. Luckily she was completely knackered, so sleep shouldn't be a problem. It could have been the drive that had made her so exhausted, but she was more inclined to think it was the tangle of deceit she was knotting herself up in. She thought back to the discovery that had brought her here to Pelican Point, to the story of Esther rescuing the drowning Leonard from the wild sea, and imagined the two of them swooning into each other's arms, falling instantly in love. When she switched off the light and closed her eyes, an image of the young woman in the photo appeared beneath her lids. Esther's cheek lay against her new husband's shoulder, her lace dress swishing across the floor as they moved effortlessly together to the melody of 'As Time Goes By'.

Esther

The clouds that had curtained the sky for the last week had parted and the day was warm and inviting. It must be around nine o'clock, she thought, not bothering to check the clock – as good a time as any to go fishing. Inclement weather had kept her indoors but there was no reason to be sitting around idle now. She deposited the newest crop of vegetables into the fridge, along with the eggs she'd collected, grabbed a bag of bait from the freezer and pulled her wind jacket from the back of a chair. Buster was already one step ahead of her, wandering across the hill towards the track. He knew what was happening as soon as he saw the tackle box and rod in her hand.

He was a funny old bugger. Not that she knew how old he was. She'd found him on the beach a couple of years back, or rather he'd found her. Not a soul in sight and no one ever came to claim him, even after she'd put notices up in a few of the shops in town. He'd sat in the sand by her side that day and followed her home, curling himself up on an old towel on the verandah for the night. A southerly buster had hit and she'd thought that was as good a name as any. As much as she could've done without another mouth to feed, he was good company and they'd been inseparable ever since. She grinned as she watched him waddle along, a barrel on stumpy legs, his tail flipping from side to side as he led the way down to the beach.

Hopefully the fish would be running. It seemed to be either feast or famine lately but she could do with stocking up. What she couldn't eat in the short term she usually froze and if there was a surplus she'd pass it on to Vincent. He was about the only person she could be bothered with around here these days. All of the older ones, the ones she'd known in her youth before she moved to Sydney, were either dead or locked up in some nursing home. And most of the others, the ones she'd met since returning, weren't worth the time of day. Too busy telling stories or indulging in malicious gossip. Nope, they didn't need anyone, her and Buster, just themselves.

'A fishing line, a roof over our heads and enough food to keep the stomachs full, that's all we need. Isn't that right, matey?' The dog looked up when he heard her voice and Esther gave him a rub on the head as she stopped and got a better grip on her tackle box. She glanced back over her shoulder to the mossy slope of hill, to where her house sat just beyond the rise, out of eyesight. Her contentment souring at the nagging thought that it could all be taken away.

Miranda

The lapping of water just outside the cabin drew her from sleep. Whipping back the curtains, she filled her lungs with the briny scent of the early-morning air and for the first time in a long time her skin tickled with pleasure at the thought of just being alive. It wasn't that her life had been horrible, but it had been, what was the word? Confined. That's it, she thought, I've been living in a box, all neatly put together and beautifully decorated, but a tiny box that doesn't let me see what's outside of it, to feel the open spaces. Outside and in.

She stepped out onto the tiny porch and looked across the lake. The surface was completely still, apart from a series of ripples made by a pair of black swans that glided side by side, moving effortlessly one way and then the other in an impeccably choreographed waltz. Close to the bank an army of crabs soldiered across the sand, marching in battalions above the tideline towards a forest of mangroves.

A bottlebrush tree nearby was coming into bloom, sprays of brilliant red blossoms bursting from its stems, and a wattlebird balanced on one of the top branches, dipping into the flowers in search of nectar.

The knot in Miranda's shoulders loosened as she took it all in. As strange as it was even to be here, a sense of peace crept through her at the wicked pleasure of being alone. Lacing her fingertips, she lifted her arms above her head, stretching them as far as they would go, before venturing back inside to prepare for what she hoped would be a momentous day.

Esther

Despite the clear skies, that nor'-easter had a bite. It was a good thing she'd brought her jacket. A bit of rock fishing was on the agenda this morning and it could get a bit nippy out there when the wind got up. Buster had vanished – he was probably already down there tormenting the gulls. Before Esther had even made her way down the track and onto the beach, the dog had already covered himself completely in sand and found a nice patch of seaweed to roll in.

'Get over here, you mad galoot.' The dog raced towards her, jumping up, showering her legs with sand. 'All right, all right, no need to go entirely stupid.' Tongue dangling from his open mouth, he trotted along beside her as she made her way to the rock platform at the end of the beach. It was a juggling act carrying her rod, a tackle box and a bucket, but she'd mastered it after all these years. She took her time, making sure she got a foothold on the more slippery sections and avoiding the oyster-encrusted ones. Buster spotted a crab and dived at it, but it dashed into a crevice, too cunning for him.

'You'll be sorry if one of those things latches onto your nose,' Esther warned. He followed her out to the furthest point, where she deposited her load and looked out over the ocean. The tide was high, and a few small waves were breaking close to shore, but this spot looked safe enough, even with the southerly swell. Off the rocks here the water was already deep, a great spot to catch tailor and kingies as they came in to prey on the smaller fish among the weeds. She pushed her straw hat back off her forehead while she peeled a prawn and baited up her hook. Buster sat looking on as Esther lifted the rod over her shoulder and the line whirred out into the ocean. Water gulped and slurped at the edge of the salt-caked rocks. She pulled her hat down against the heat of the sun and settled in.

There was nothing more relaxing than standing here looking out to sea, waiting for something to nibble. Apart from playing the violin, of course. That was something she'd done all her life, learnt as a young girl, so it was as natural to her as breathing. And as necessary. Fishing was something she'd taken to much later, more out of need than want, but it had become part of her routine now, and since she'd always loved being so close to the ocean it fed her soul as well as her stomach.

As usual at this time of year the place was deserted. Sometimes she'd watch from her porch in the early morning or late afternoon and young Vincent would appear with that black horse of his, making the most of the empty beach and the end of the tourist season. It was a magnificent creature.

She'd stand on her porch and watch him flying along the sand, riderless, stretching his legs out like a racehorse, kicking his heels up. Vincent would wait at the far end of the beach, and before long he'd whistle and the horse would stop, turn and trot back, stopping right in front of his owner. Part of her wanted to go and have a closer look, touch the horse's neck, take in the smell of him, but she knew it was better to keep her distance.

A sharp tug almost pulled the rod from her hands. Esther jerked it upwards, refocusing her attention. Whatever was on the end of the line pulled back, and she wound her reel, slowly at first, focused now on the water directly in front, her body stiff with concentration. The blinding glare stung her eyes but she kept her grip on the rod and her gaze fixed. Just as the fish appeared above the surface, wriggling on the hook, a sudden surge of water sent Esther stumbling backwards. The rod dropped from her hand as she fell with a thud. Scrambling to get away from the errant wave she turned onto all fours and tried to stand, but just as she righted herself she slipped on the weed-covered rock and came down hard against something sharp. Pain tore through her leg and she fell onto her back, hands clasping her shin. The wave receded. She was soaked to the skin. Buster whimpered, licked at her face.

'It's all right, boy,' she told him, panting.

She pushed herself up to a sitting position. Her rod had vanished but the tackle box and bucket were still in one piece. Blood gushed from somewhere below her left knee, where a nasty gash tore the already blackening skin. She swallowed back the nausea that erupted from her belly as she tried to stand. Tiny black flecks clouded her vision. Had she banged her head when she fell? She needed to get out of the sun. If she could make it to the cave she could rest a bit before she tried to make it back home. With Buster by her side she dragged herself along the rocks inch by torturous inch. God knows what sort of muck was inside that wound. Oyster cuts were nasty, but she'd have to worry about that later. For now she just had to get to some shelter. Her chest heaved as she hauled herself the last few feet into the shadow of the cliff and then into the cave that yawned onto the rock shelf. Relief flooded through her limbs as she collapsed in the shade, the damp sand cool against her cheek.

She closed her eyes and everything went black.

Miranda

It was such a beautiful day she decided to start at the southern end of the beach and do the longer walk. Pulling the car into the bay by the side of the road, she grabbed her pack from the back seat and made sure to click the auto-lock before following her instincts along what seemed to be a track. Rocks slipped beneath her feet as the path twisted and turned downhill and she was glad she'd worn runners rather than sandals. The scent of the sea was on the breeze and the booming of waves echoed through the gums.

Miranda lost herself in the heady perfume of boronia, loving the feel of earth and rock beneath her feet. It had been a long time since she'd been on a bushwalk – she used to do the occasional one with Simon and her father in the Royal National Park when she was a child, back in the days when life had been simpler, before it became too hard to leave her mother alone. She'd loved striking off with her dad and brother, marvelling at the skinks that darted across their path. In the early days she and James had done some bushwalking but his determination to get where they were going and back again at top speed spoiled the whole thing. After a while he'd taken up cycling instead and that had been that. Another of the many things Miranda had given up or just plain forgotten about, like some of her old friends, for instance, or going to a movie by herself. Or doing anything by herself. She'd filled her life with busyness so she didn't have time to think.

Because thinking too much is dangerous?

When she rounded the next bend, Miranda stopped and stared at the vision before her: an empty arc of pure white against an infinite stretch of opaline blue. A series of rocky steps led down through towering grey eucalypts to the beach. She sped up, tripping a few times over the loose stones littering the track. Within seconds she made it to the bottom and stepped out of the shade into the dazzling warmth of glorious sunshine. She shifted her sunglasses from her head to her face and pulled a cap from her backpack. To the south the bush melted into a headland of vivid green pasture spotted with a few black cows. To the north was a cliff – but there was no sign of a house at either end of the beach. Miranda thought back over the directions Norma had given her. This seemed to be the only track out to the beach, so where exactly did Esther live?

She unlaced her shoes, tying them together and threading them through the strap of her pack, socks stuffed firmly inside. The sand squeaked beneath her feet as she made her way along the water's edge. A wave washed over her toes and she gasped. The south coast was renowned for its icy waters, which was why they'd always headed north on family holidays. But there was something about the isolation of this place, the sense of something wild and untamed that definitely appealed. Tiny shells, hundreds of rainbow-coloured cones, lay scattered across the sand. Mermaids' tears, her mother used to call them, she remembered now. They had combed the beach together when she was very young, cradling their haul in a swag made from one of her father's hankies. At home they'd count the shells and lay them out on the table according to pattern and size. She'd stored them in a glass jar that she still kept in her old room at her parents' house. Funny, the things we hang on to, she thought, the things we keep for whatever reason, and the things we leave behind. Crouching down, she gathered up a handful of the conical shells, wrapped them in a tissue and put them in her pocket.

The sound of a barking dog startled her to attention. He was running along the sand towards her. Something about the way he was bounding like a circus clown told her he was friendly. She'd always liked dogs, had a natural affinity with them, despite never having had one. Her mother had disliked their smell and the way they dropped hair all over the carpet, although Miranda had always wondered how her mother had known this, never having actually owned a dog herself.

As he barrelled up to her, Miranda knelt and stretched out her hand. He came right up and licked it. 'Hello there,' she said.

He tossed his head in the air and barked again before lying on the sand and crawling closer, commando style, then jumping up and dashing back off along the beach. He turned and barked again. There was something frantic about his bark that told Miranda she should go after him. By the looks of it she'd come out here on a wild goose chase, so she might as well follow a strange barking dog as turn around and head back to the cabin.

The dog raced off ahead but stopped and waited for her every so often, turning his head back in Miranda's direction, wagging his black tail and giving her a 'hurry up' sort of look.

'I'm coming,' she called. As she plodded on through the sand she glanced up towards the headland, but there was no sign of a house, just dune grass that merged into a wall of bush. She could have sworn she'd followed the directions, but maybe she should have gone further south. The dog sauntered on towards an outcrop of rocks just beneath the lip of the cliff. A wave snuck up and caught Miranda by surprise, grabbing at her ankles, making her falter in the wet sand. The dog waited patiently as she steadied herself. Miranda took out her water bottle, having a good few gulps before returning it and continuing on behind her new friend. I wonder what he wants to show me, she thought, as the sand squished between her toes and the cold water kissed her shins.

He stopped at the mouth of what appeared to be a cave, barking furiously.

'Keep your hair on, I'm coming,' Miranda called as she hoisted one leg and then the other onto the ledge that jutted out beneath the cave. She was no stranger to this sort of landscape. As children she and Simon would scramble over the rocks exploring the nooks and crannies, poking their fingers into the squelchy centres of pink and brown sea anemones, picking up starfish and flipping them over to watch their perfectly shaped suckers open and close before placing them gently back where they came from. They'd had fun together in those days, throwing seaweed at each other and squeezing the sponges that they secretly called sea penises (well, that's what they look like, she'd explained to her mother when she'd overheard her one day and threatened to give her the wooden spoon when they got home). Those days were long gone, though. It had been three years now since her brother had married an Irishwoman and settled in London, and the two had become virtual strangers. Her throat tightened at the thought and she took another swig from her water bottle.

The dog raced towards her from the shadows of the cave, then looked up and whined.

'Okay, boy, let's do it. What have you got to show me?'

Miranda followed the dog a few steps into the cave, pushed her sunnies back and waited until her eyes adjusted to the dim light. The roof of the cave sloped downwards as she walked further in, so that she had to stoop. She could hear a strange moaning noise and the back of her neck prickled. What if she'd been lured into the den of some axe-murderer, and the dog was his accomplice?

Don't be so paranoid, the voice prodded.

She squinted into the gloom and made out the shape of a person lying flat out on the sand about a metre away. The sight jolted her upright and she banged her head on the hard rock ceiling.

'Ow, shit!'

'There's no need for that sort of language.'

For a minute Miranda thought it was the voice.

'You'd be swearing if you'd smashed your head on hard bloody rock,' she retorted.

'Actually, I wouldn't, and I've done a good sight worse to myself today than crack my scone. Could you stop feeling sorry for yourself for one minute and give me a hand?' The stern tone coerced Miranda into submission.

'Oh, I'm so sorry, are you all right?'

'Obviously not. It's my knee.' The woman spoke in short bursts. 'I can't put any pressure on it. Came up here to rest it for a bit and must have fallen asleep. When I woke up, Buster was gone.'

'Buster? The dog? He came and found me. I was walking along the beach and he ran up to me barking his head off, so I followed him.' Miranda crawled towards the woman, dragging her bag along behind. 'Can I take a look at your knee?' She pulled out the small first-aid kit she'd thought to throw into her pack.

'I haven't much choice, have I?' the woman answered.

You'd think she might be a little happier to have some help.

The woman was obviously not feeling well, Miranda reasoned. She studied her more closely as she unravelled the bandage from its plastic wrap. Her hair was bundled into a loose arrangement on the top of her head. She wore a plain black T-shirt and pants rolled up above her knees. It was difficult to see her face clearly and so hard to guess at her age.

Miranda bent over the woman's leg with the small torch from the kit. Her knee had a lump on it the size of a grapefruit, and there was a deep cut beneath it oozing blood. As Miranda dabbed at the wound with an antiseptic cloth, the woman flinched.

Miranda smiled apologetically. 'Sorry. It's really swollen, and still bleeding. Best idea is probably to clean it up a bit and bandage it, then see if we can get you upright.'

'Do what you have to,' the woman snapped. 'Then we can both get out of here.'

Miranda wrapped the bandage carefully around the injured knee, chatting quietly to distract the woman from the pain.

'My name's Miranda, by the way – what's yours?'

No reply.

'Did you fall when you were fishing?'

'Are you going to finish that bandaging or not?'

Taken aback by the woman's gruffness, Miranda gave up her attempts at conversation, wrapped the bandage around a couple more times and secured it with a fastener.

'There, that should do it. Now let's see if we can get you up.'

It took a lot of moaning and grunting from them both, but Miranda eventually bent down low enough to get the woman's arm around her shoulders and haul her up onto her feet. The dog danced and circled around them as they struggled outside, clearly pleased that his owner had been rescued and was back in action. He barked excitedly, tail wagging madly.

'Get out of the way, Buster.'

At the mention of his name the dog wheeled about even more frantically. The woman almost smiled. 'You're a good boy.'

No one who loves a dog that much can be all bad, thought Miranda.

They made their way out of the cave into what was now the middle of an unseasonably hot day. Miranda glanced at the woman. Out in the light she could see that she was elderly. Lines crisscrossed her face and neck, and her white hair, come loose from the bundle on her head, fell in thick strands past her shoulders. Sweat beaded her brow.

'Are you sure you're all right to keep going? We might be better heading back to the cave where it's cooler. I could go into town and get some help.' The beach was deserted and Miranda knew there was no way the two of them could make it all the way to the car.

'We only have to reach that track up there.' The woman pointed to a spot just a bit further along the beach. 'That's where I live, up on that headland, not far. If you wouldn't mind just helping me get home, and then I won't trouble you any further.'

'No, it's fine, really.' Miranda's eyes widened beneath the smudges on her Ray-Bans. This woman was old and lived nearby. Could this be her?

'Do you live out here alone?'

'No, me and Buster live up there together, don't we, boy?' The dog wagged his tail dutifully as he ambled along beside them. The woman stopped and sighed deeply before continuing on. It was clearly difficult for her to walk at all.

'Let's get you back there then, eh?' Miranda was straining with the effort of bearing the woman's weight, but the idea that this was who she'd come in search of gave her the stamina to go on. They staggered together up the slope of the beach, soon finding a sort of rhythm. Waves hushed onto the shore beside them, salty tongues of foam that bubbled across the sand and then disappeared in an instant. She concentrated on the sound of each wave as it crept in and slunk out. The woman was making a valiant attempt to be as light on her feet as she could, but walking on sand wasn't easy at the best of times and Miranda knew that it was taking a lot out of her. Out of them both.

At the beginning of the path they stopped again. How the hell am I going to get her up there? Miranda wondered. As if she'd read her mind, the woman replied, 'I'll be right. It's not too far.'

They made their way slowly up the rocky track, Miranda focusing on one step at a time, trying to ignore the pain shearing through her shoulders, neck and back. Sweat dribbled down her temples onto her upper lip and she licked it away with the tip of her tongue.

After what felt like hours but was in reality only a few minutes, the trail opened up to reveal a timber cottage perched on the hillside, a wide slope of green pasture rolled out like a giant doormat in front. A verandah ran the width of the house, which had a brick chimney at one end and silver solar panels glinting on its corrugated roof.

Mustering one last burst of energy they made it to the house and launched themselves up the steps – thank god there's only two, thought Miranda. Somehow the woman was able to climb them using the verandah post for leverage. She collapsed into an old cane chair by the door, exhaling loudly in relief. Miranda bent forward, both hands on her knees, waiting for the feeling to return to her upper body. When she uncurled herself, her neck and shoulders were on fire, but it was the view that lay spread out below that literally left her breathless. A 180-degree panorama of bush and beach, ocean and sky. 'Magnificent,' she whispered. From the beach the house had been invisible, tucked away behind a screen of trees, but from here she could see the southern end of the beach, with the ocean tossed like a blanket in the background.

Lobster pots, fishing lines, buckets and piles of assorted shells and driftwood decorated the timber planks that formed the patio of the little shack. The house was made from wooden slats, with one window either side of the door, both fringed by faded floral curtains. One pane of glass was shattered and had been covered with a sheet of thick plastic.

'Do you think you could get me a drink from the tap over there?'

Miranda had been so busy taking the house in she'd almost forgotten that the woman was there. 'Yes, of course.' She took the water bottle handed to her and filled it from the tap by the steps. The woman swigged back half the bottle in one go before flopping back in the chair. Now that Miranda thought of it, her own throat was as rough as gravel, so she took the bottle from her pack, refilled it and drank thirstily.

'How's the leg feeling?' she asked, wiping wayward drops of water from her chin.

'It'll be fine once I've rested it.'

'You might need to see a doctor.'

'Not likely. Haven't been to a quack for well over ten years. A bung knee isn't going to get me there. I'll be right.'

'Well, at least let me unwrap it and clean it up properly.'

The woman replied with some sort of noise that Miranda took as a yes. She went ahead and opened up her first-aid kit once again before unravelling the blood-soaked bandage. Her mind was still racing with the possibility that this could be

the person she'd come looking for but at the moment tending
to the wound was more important. On closer inspection the
cut was only about three centimetres long, but being on the
curve of the bone it was gaping and angry. The knee itself
was the colour of an overripe fig and just as swollen.

'Sorry, this is going to sting,' Miranda apologised as she
dabbed at the wound first with water and then a wad of
cottonwool with antiseptic.

The woman didn't flinch. 'Just get on with it.'

'I'll clean it as well as I can, but I really think it needs
stitching.'

'It'll be fine.'

'Can I do anything else?' Miranda asked as she applied
a fresh bandage.

'Wouldn't mind a cuppa. Kettle's on the bench. A slice of
bread and jam, too. Help yourself if you're peckish.'

As she started into the house, Miranda almost tripped
over a violin case propped against the side of the chair. The
black leather was smooth and shiny and the clasps gleamed
like stars. Bizarre, thought Miranda, as she stepped around
it and swung open the door.

'By the way,' the woman's voice came softly from behind
her. 'My name's Esther.'

Esther

It was an effort, but she reached down and picked up the case after the girl had gone inside. Slipping the violin carefully from the red velvet interior, she positioned it beneath her chin, willing the pain away with the music. It was always at times like this when he came back to her, when she was at her most vulnerable, his calloused fingers warm against her cheek. That first time she'd felt his touch had been in the stable when she was unsaddling Duke. He'd walked straight up and introduced himself, held out his hand in greeting. His palm was hot on hers and she'd known right there and then, just as he did. She looked into his eyes, black as molasses, with a smile behind them that could melt your insides. Unable to speak, she nodded and waited until he broke his gaze and turned away. Alone again in the quiet of the stable she heard nothing but the drumming of her heart. Just as she could hear it now whenever she thought of him, all these years later, as she played.

Miranda

She let the flyscreen door bang behind her as the words reverberated inside her head.

By the way, my name's Esther.

Esther, the woman in the newspaper story, probably the woman in the photo and quite possibly her supposedly dead grandmother. This was unbelievable! She wanted to rush back out there and hug her and find out more. But this Esther – unlike the grandmother in her daydreams – wasn't exactly huggable. Miranda needed to work out how to broach the subject to make sure she didn't screw the whole thing up. In the meantime she'd make the tea.

The interior of the cottage was sparsely furnished: a formica table with two orange vinyl chairs, a sideboard with a sliding glass door, a leadlight dresser and an old burgundy couch with a checked tartan picnic rug thrown across the back of it. The tiny kitchen had a two-burner stove, a sink with one tap, and an overhead cupboard that housed a few basic necessities in the way of plates, cups and utensils. There was a relic of a fridge that looked like it might have come out of the ark. Miranda opened it to find it practically bare. She took out the jam and a small tub of butter, found a loaf of bread on the benchtop that was surprisingly fresh, and began buttering, feeling suddenly hungry. Then she heard a noise, a faint sigh at first which built into the louder and unmistakable sound of a violin. She dropped the knife and turned, listening to the sweet-sad sighing of the notes that wafted in through the wire door.

Moving quietly to the doorway, sandwich in hand, she watched the old woman playing the violin. The sound of waves striking the shore below and the gentle snoring of the dog harmonised with the music. Esther's face softened as her body relaxed deeper into the chair and the song. After all the drama of finding her in the cave and carrying her back up here, the idea that this woman could be her grandmother was suddenly overwhelming. She slumped against the wall and peered through the wire door. Miranda studied Esther's face now, trying to find some resemblance to the photo as she sat with her eyes closed, the bow gently traversing the strings. There was no obvious similarity but there was something about her that felt familiar, something Miranda couldn't quite put her finger on.

Or perhaps you're just wishing there was.

A shrill whistle from the kitchen behind her reminded her about the tea. She let it shriek a little longer while she listened to the melody, her eyes filled with tears.

The last thing she really wanted to do was go traipsing back to the rocks, but Esther had asked her to collect the tackle box and bucket, so she could hardly say no. It was quiet on the walk back down, except for the occasional scurry of an animal in the bushes and the cracking of twigs beneath her feet. The path wound down the hill, and even though it was much easier than the trek up had been, she still had to concentrate on where she was going – no point in twisting her own ankle, one invalid was enough.

It was almost midafternoon. The last couple of hours had evaporated by the time she'd done the first aid, made the tea and sandwiches and helped Esther into her bedroom for a rest. If you could call where she slept a bedroom. The whole shack was really just one single room, and the bedroom was separated by a partition, with a dust-laden navy blue curtain instead of a door. How could anyone live in such a tumbledown house, and honestly, why would you want to? Esther really was a mystery.

Miranda wondered again why the woman in the shop had been so antagonistic when she mentioned Esther's name. What possible harm could a lonely old woman living on her own in the middle of nowhere do? Probably better not to bring up the grandmother issue just yet, she thought, better to wait until I know more about her, be certain before I go asking questions.

The beating of the waves as they pounded on the sand grew louder and the wind whipped clumps of Miranda's hair across her face. This morning's sun had disappeared behind a bank of grey clouds as she emerged onto the deserted beach. She paused a minute to stop and look. Really look. This was a spectacularly beautiful place. The beach was gently curved, with rocky outcrops to the north and south, like bookends, forming a secluded cove. But the ocean itself, earlier a deep iridescent turquoise, was now a murky indigo, dark and uninviting. Just as she was about to continue on, something in the water caught her eye. It was moving around the rocks to the south. Maybe a whale or a pod of dolphins? She'd left her glasses at the house so she shaded her forehead with her hands to get a better view.

No, it can't be!

Protruding from the surface was what appeared to be a horse's head, neck raised, mane tousled by the wind, moving through the water at a furious pace. Miranda's eyes were glued to the animal as it came closer and closer to the shore. If it stayed on its current course it would emerge right in front of her. What the hell am I going to do when it gets out? she thought.

The horse reached the shallows, bounded through the breakers and stopped on the sand, shaking first its head, then its whole body. Beads of water sprayed into the air as Miranda watched, mesmerised. Tall and sleek, black coat shining, it arched its neck and lifted its muzzle. Miranda thought it looked in her direction for a second or two but if it did it gave no indication that it had seen her. Then it took off at a gallop, mane and tail flying, clearly relishing the freedom. Miranda watched, awestruck. She'd never seen anything like it. The nerves she'd initially felt when she saw the horse were replaced by sheer wonder at the majesty of the creature as it raced along the sand, bucking with delight every now and then, until it screeched to a halt at the far end of the beach.

There was another movement in the water. This time it was a human form: a man swimming overarm around the rocks, his gaze fixed on the horse, which was now rolling on its back in the sand, legs kicking the air.

Feeling as if she'd fallen down a hole and entered some other dimension, Miranda watched as the swimmer climbed out of the water. He was tall and well built – a girl couldn't help but notice – and wearing cut-off jeans and no shirt. Just like the horse, he glanced in her direction but made no acknowledgement. Perhaps this whole thing was one of her crazy dreams and she was merely an invisible observer?

Fingers either side of his mouth, the man gave a piercing whistle. The horse turned its head, ears pricked, and charged. The man let out a long, hearty laugh before he called to Miranda, 'Hi, how are you doing?'

She lifted her hand in a wave, still unsure whether this was really happening, as he walked up the beach towards her. She noticed an earring in his left ear, and his hair, still wet of course, had fallen into a mop of ringlets. There was a pirate look about him that seemed fitting, considering what she had just witnessed. He held out his hand, realised it was wet and dropped it again.

'Vincent. And this is Flint.' The horse trotted up and stood beside them, dipping its head and letting out a gentle neigh, as if to say hello.

She took a step back. 'Miranda. Nice to meet you. Both.'

'What brings you here on this cloudy afternoon, Miranda?'

There was a faint lilt to the man's voice that suggested some kind of accent. English, perhaps? She considered telling him about her morning but thought better of it. If he was a local, there was a good chance he wouldn't have a high opinion of Esther. 'Just doing some walking. And I presume you're taking your horse for a swim?'

Vincent laughed again as he rubbed the horse's withers, a deep throaty laugh that brought an instant smile to Miranda's face. 'And a run. We live around the headland and he likes to swim, so on days when I don't think there'll be anyone around we come over here for some exercise.'

'I have to say I was surprised to see a horse coming through the water out of nowhere.'

'Sorry if he frightened you. He looks intimidating but he's a friendly guy. Do you like horses?'

'I used to love them when I was younger, but I haven't been around one for years.'

'You can pat him if you like. He's completely harmless.'

Miranda stood stock-still and stared at the horse. She hadn't ridden since she was a teenager – one of the things she'd given up on to concentrate on her studies and then completely forgotten about. Looking at this one right now she felt a combination of awe and fear – such a huge, powerful creature, so unpredictable.

Just pat the thing, it's not going to bite.

'Okay.' She took a careful step forward and held out her hand. The horse sniffed at it and then lowered his head. Miranda rubbed his cheek, moving closer to scratch behind his ears.

'He'll be your friend for life if you keep that up.' Vincent grinned.

She scratched the horse's neck. He was dark and strong, yet seemed so gentle. His glistening coat was flecked with sand. When she dropped her hand, he gave it a nudge, as if to say *more, please.*

'He likes you.'

Miranda's trepidation began to wane as she stroked Flint under the chin. 'I used to go to riding camps when I was a kid.'

'Well, if you're in the area for a while and feel like trying a ride, our place is just around the headland.'

'I don't have to swim there, do I?'

Vincent laughed. 'No. You head south out of town and take the first turn on the left. The name of the property is on the gate. Garewangga. We breed stockhorses, but we do lessons and beach rides as well.'

'I might even do that.'

There was something so disarming about the guy's manner that Miranda was seriously thinking she would take him up on his offer. Wasn't it about time she got back to doing some of those things she loved?

Vincent nodded. 'Well, we'd better be getting back. Work to do. Nice meeting you.' And with that he swung himself onto the horse and cantered off into the water. The horse didn't hesitate, charging straight into the sea, Vincent hanging on to his neck with one hand and turning to wave with the other. Miranda watched them swim out to the point and vanish around the rocks. She waited for a minute, blinking at the spot where the man and horse had just been.

'What the hell was that?' she asked aloud.

That was a dream come true.

A rumble of thunder made her jump, and brought an end to her reverie. Esther might be wondering where she was and she still had to retrieve the tackle box and bucket. She trudged up the beach under the darkening sky pondering just how much more extraordinary the day could get.

Esther

Eyelids shut, she heard the door click. It was good of the girl to go and collect her fishing gear. If it was still there. If another freak wave hadn't come and washed it away the same way she'd been bowled over. Bloody nuisance of a thing. Still, she had no one to blame but herself. Should've kept her wits about her and not been daydreaming. The painkillers had taken the edge off, but when she tried to roll over it felt like someone had tied a boulder to her leg. She groaned and heard Buster murmur in response. When she dangled her arm down the side of the bed, his rough tongue licked the back of her hand.

'Good boy,' she whispered.

All she needed was a bit of sleep and she'd feel better. The waves thumped on the beach below, slow and regular, as they hit the sand and then sighed away again into the shallows, a steady chant, in and out. She tried to focus on their movement so she wouldn't notice the throbbing in her knee. Slowly the beat changed into an old familiar rhythm. Hooves pounding across the paddocks, her body moving in time with the horse, the feel of muscle and blood and strength beneath her as they surged into the wind together. For as far as she could see there was only grass and sea and sky, flashing past her in a blur. She was young and strong and alive and nothing could stop her. This was all she would ever need, the only place she ever wanted to be.

Miranda

Lightning splintered the sky. Miranda turned up the track, the ocean hissing and snarling behind her like an angry beast. A few footsteps more and the rain started to fall. Bucket in one hand and tackle box in the other, she hurried to the top of the hill as the sky above her opened and ran as fast as she could to the shelter of the porch.

She brushed a slick of wet hair back from her face, water dripping down her bare arm onto the verandah at her feet. The wind had picked up, screaming through the trees bordering the cottage, bending their branches into impossible angles. Rain hammered onto the tin roof and gushed from the gutters, and she folded her arms against the sudden chill.

All seemed quiet inside. Esther must still be asleep. No sign of Buster out here either. When she had helped the old woman into bed the dog had lain down beside her, resting his head between his paws. The locals might not be able to stand her but the dog was certainly a fan.

The door creaked as she pulled it open. She hunched her shoulders and continued more slowly, tiptoeing to the corner of the partition and peeking around. Esther was lying on her side, her chest rising and falling, her face looking pained even in sleep. Miranda bit her bottom lip and looked around. The light inside the house was faint now that the storm had set in and the day was coming to an end. She scanned the walls but there didn't seem to be any light switches. There was a solar panel on the roof and the fridge was running, so there must be some form of electricity. Surely the woman didn't sit here every night in darkness?

On her way to the kitchen Miranda stubbed her toe on the leg of the chair. 'Shit.'

'I heard that,' a hoarse voice came from the bedroom.

'Sorry. Just kicked my toe.'

'Did you find my gear?'

Miranda winced and clung to the table. 'Yes. I did.' She hobbled back to the bedroom. 'How are you feeling?'

Esther shuffled up a little higher in the bed.

'I'm all right. Sounds like that rain's set in.'

Miranda nodded. 'Certainly has. I was looking for a light switch but can't seem to find one.'

'Everything in the kitchen is connected to the solar. There's a lamp out there and a box of matches. Another at the end of the kitchen bench,' said Esther.

Miranda had assumed the lantern on the table was for decoration. She gave her toe a wriggle, walked over and lifted the glass cover. When she struck a match and lit the wick the lamp spluttered to life, shedding a warm glow over the place. The sharp smell of kerosene permeated the room.

'You'll have to bunk down here for the night. Too late to be walking back in the dark and wet.' Esther's invitation was more grudging than heartfelt, but when Miranda glanced out the window she realised she was right. It was almost completely black out there now. The idea of walking along the bush track – or the beach – with only her tiny torch for light didn't exactly thrill Miranda. And staying here for the night might give her a chance to ask Esther a little more about herself.

'If that's okay with you,' she said meekly.

Esther gave a grunt in reply.

Lighting the kitchen lamp Miranda called, 'Can I get you anything?'

'Might have a bite to eat. Toast and cheese will do me. Some sausages in the fridge if you want them. Or a tin of soup in the cupboard. And could you throw some of that meat into Buster's bowl?' Miranda could hear the rustle of sheets as Esther spoke from behind the wall. 'Look out, Buster.' Then the uneven thumping of feet on the old timber floor.

'Is everything okay?' Miranda called.

'Yes, yes.' The dog appeared around the corner wagging his tail at the smell of food and Miranda gave him his bowl filled with meat scraps she'd found in the fridge.

The noise behind the partition stopped. 'I might need a hand getting to the bathroom,' Esther called. Miranda could tell by the irritation in her voice that it was killing her to ask for help.

'Of course.' She went around to find the old woman bent over, clinging to the end of the bed. Miranda stood beside Esther, who put her arm around her shoulder, and together they made it to the back door and then on to the outside toilet. It was pitch-black and pouring with rain.

'I'll give you a call when I need you,' said Esther and shut the door.

Miranda blushed and hurried back inside. As much as part of her wanted Esther to be her grandmother, the other part was slightly scared that this cranky old hermit might really be related to her. She busied herself in the kitchen, deciding to stick with toast and cheese. The toaster was one of those old-fashioned stainless steel contraptions with doors that flipped down. She sliced two pieces of bread and deposited them in each side. Before she had time to turn them over, Esther called from out back. It was a battle to get her up the single step into the house, and when they did get back inside smoke was pouring from the toaster.

Esther scowled.

'Sorry.' Miranda deposited Esther on a chair at the table and opened the doors of the toaster to find the two pieces of bread charred black. 'Better try that again.' She half-smiled at Esther but got only a blank look in return.

It's going to be a very long night.

❧

The only sound at 'dinner' was the crunching of toast and the slurping of tea. Esther resisted any attempts at conversation and Miranda felt increasingly awkward.

'Early to bed, early to rise,' Esther said soon after. 'If you wouldn't mind giving me a hand.'

Miranda leant down and Esther pushed herself up to stand. Each time the woman put her foot to the ground, Miranda could see the pain wash across her face, but luckily it wasn't far to the small bedroom.

'Would you like a hand getting changed?' Miranda asked.

Esther shot her a look. 'I might be temporarily incapacitated, but I'm not an invalid, thank you very much,' she said.

If she was any pricklier she'd be a porcupine.

'Of course, no problem.'

'Right. Well, goodnight then. You'll find some blankets in the cupboard.'

'Thanks. Goodnight.'

And that was that.

A little gratitude might have been nice.

Miranda found the blankets, itchy old woollen things that smelt of mothballs and looked like they needed a wash. After switching off the lamps, she tried to settle in on the lounge. It was shorter than she was so her knees were bent, her head jammed against the faded flowers of the armrest. The lumpy cushion beneath her neck was almost as bad as the broken spring sticking into her backside, forcing her to move to the edge of the lounge and practically hang over it. The temperature had dropped considerably and the brick fireplace held only a blackened stump of wood. She pulled the blankets up around her chin and closed her eyes. Within a few minutes the house was filled with a chorus of snores, coming from behind the partition. Miranda wasn't sure who was snoring louder – Buster or Esther – but between them they were a regular symphony. She gave up even trying to sleep and lay staring into the shadowy space above her. Wind whistled through the cracks in the floorboards. The place was positively primitive. Why on earth anyone would live here with so few creature comforts was way beyond Miranda's comprehension. The cabin back at the van park was small but at least it had hot running water and reverse aircon. Compared to this place, it was a veritable palace. Hmmm, it was a mystery all right, but then so was Esther. It was one thing to be the quiet, private type but another thing altogether to be flat-out unfriendly.

There was the tapping of claws on floorboards as Buster wandered out and plonked himself down by the lounge. She reached out and stroked him. His fur was sandy and smelt of the sea and there was something soothing in the regular rhythm of his breathing. Soon he was snoring again.

Miranda flipped the cushion and rolled to face the back of the lounge for the millionth time. When she'd been a little girl and her racing mind kept her awake, her father had always told her to turn the pillow over and roll the other way, and it usually worked. Well, it wasn't working now. She closed her eyes and concentrated on the sound of the waves as they crashed against the shore, drowning out the snoring and lulling her into an uneasy sleep.

⁓

Waking early the next morning, Miranda felt like she'd been battered all over with a meat mallet. She tried to uncoil herself quietly but a few groans and sighs escaped as she stretched out her legs and sat up on the couch. She gave herself a shake and rolled her shoulders, twisted her head from side to side and heard her neck crunch.

There was no sound coming from the bedroom. At least she's stopped snoring, Miranda thought as she stood and padded to the door, grabbing her jacket from the table. Some fresh air might help loosen everything up. I must look a fright, she thought as she wound a band around her tangled hair, pulling it back into a ponytail. She crept out, leaving the door slightly ajar. Buster was beside her in a second and darted straight onto the grass, rushing about to inspect what Miranda assumed were his familiar haunts.

Everything was crisp and clear after last night's storm. The waves had calmed to a gentle roll. Miranda felt the knots in her shoulderblades soften as she sank into the porch chair and stared out across the water to where a fine thread of mist cobwebbed the sky. Being near the ocean was something she missed. For ages now she'd wanted to rent a beach house with James, just sit and relax, but he'd always wanted the adventure holiday. She'd tagged along but found no real pleasure in it.

James – it had been a whole twelve or fifteen hours since she'd thought of him. Perhaps he'd been trying to call her or send a text? Her phone was in her jacket pocket, but when she pulled it out there was nothing but a blank screen. Dead. And the charger was back at the cabin. Calling James would be her first priority when she returned – she knew he'd be worried. He was that sort of guy.

A brief vision of another sort of guy – the horse owner from the beach yesterday – flickered through her mind, along with a tiny fizz of excitement deep inside her. She shifted forward, shaking the image away. Don't even think about it, she warned herself.

Why not?

Buster raced up the stairs from around the corner of the house, a stick twice the length of him clamped between his teeth. He deposited it at Miranda's feet before sitting back and looking up at her.

'You're a nut case.' Miranda shook her head, smiling. She broke the stick in half with the ball of her bare foot and wandered down onto the lawn, then threw it as far as she could. Buster leapt after it, bringing it back again and again until Miranda's feet were numb with cold on the still-wet grass.

'That's enough, boy.' She headed back indoors, leaving Buster to his own devices, steeling herself for Esther's mood this morning and hoping against hope that it might be better than it had been the night before. At some point she wanted to raise the possibility of them being related, but she had to wait for the right moment.

The cottage bristled with silence. She crept inside and took a few steps closer to Esther's room.

'Hello, Esther, you awake?' She remembered what the shop lady had told her about Esther threatening trespassers with a gun. What if Esther had forgotten she was here, thought she was an intruder?

Seriously? Get a grip!

Shaking the idea from her head she took another step and poked her head around the partition.

'Of course I'm awake,' Esther grumbled from beneath the covers. 'If it wasn't for this damned knee I'd be out there catching my breakfast.' She pushed herself upright against the wooden bedhead, long silver hair falling around her shoulders, her face pinched and worn.

'So it's still sore?' Miranda realised the stupidity of the question even as it left her lips.

'Of course it is.'

'Can I take a look?'

Esther threw back the quilt and shifted herself to the edge of the bed. 'So you didn't tell me what you were doing in these parts.'

Miranda wondered if she should just blurt out her true intentions but thought better of it. 'Oh, you know, just taking a break. Change of scene.' She kept her eyes on the bandage as she unwrapped it.

'Don't touch it,' Esther snapped.

Miranda drew her hand away. 'No, I wasn't going to,' she lied.

'You live in Sydney?'

'Yes.' Miranda grimaced at the angry gash beneath Esther's knee. It was redder than yesterday and the skin around the cut was blackening. The knee itself had blown up like a balloon. 'I really think you need to see a doctor.'

'Doctor, schmocter. I haven't been to a quack in donkey's years and I'm not going now. A few days' rest and I'll be good as new. I've had worse in my day and survived. Just wrap it back up. It'll be fine.' Esther wasn't budging an inch. 'What brought you here?'

Miranda patted the wound with the last of the Dettol. 'Well, I'm getting married soon and I've been really busy, so I just thought I'd treat myself to a little road trip. Clear my head.'

'What's he like?' Esther asked. 'The fella you're marrying.'

Miranda pondered. 'He's smart, good-looking, thoughtful and works hard.'

'And you're madly in love with him?'

'Of course. I wouldn't be marrying him otherwise, would I?' She felt unreasonably offended by Esther's question.

'People marry for all sorts of reasons other than love.'

Miranda studied Esther's face. Was she speaking from experience?

'You're sure you don't want me to call a doctor or anything?'

'No need for that. The swelling will go down in a day or two.'

Was there no end to this woman's stubbornness? The knee was badly damaged, the pain must be intolerable, and yet she was prepared to lie here and wait for it to mend itself.

'What made you choose this part of the world to run away to?'

The question caught Miranda off guard. 'Sorry?'

'Why did you end up here, at Pelican Point?'

Here's your perfect opportunity – tell her the truth!

'Just got in the car and drove south.'

Miranda rewrapped the leg, being as gentle as she could. There'd be time for true confessions later. 'Will you at least let me go into town and get you some more antiseptic and dressings?' she said, as Esther pulled the sheet back over her leg.

'I suppose so,' said Esther, her voice softening. 'If you haven't got anything better to do. I wouldn't mind some toast first, and a cuppa to wash down the panadol.'

'Coming right up.' Miranda headed to the kitchen and fossicked around for the tablets, put the kettle on the cooktop and sliced a few chunks of bread. Surely Esther lived on more than just bread and jam? She did say she fished every day, but even then she'd need fruit and veg, and other groceries. How on earth the woman survived out here on her own, even when all her limbs were fully functioning, was a complete mystery – let alone how she would get by now.

Buster appeared at the door, wet, sandy and panting.

Miranda greeted him. 'Hey there, what have you been up to?'

'No good, I'll warrant,' called Esther.

At the sound of her voice Buster raced into the bedroom.

'Hello, my gorgeous man.' Miranda heard the laughter in Esther's voice. 'If you're very nice to Miranda, she might throw some breakfast crunchies in your bowl.'

Esther was so much better at communicating with the dog than she seemed to be with humans.

'I certainly will,' Miranda called out. 'Where will I find them?'

'Out in the laundry beside the tub.'

When Miranda walked out to the back of the house her jaw dropped. It had been too dark to see anything clearly out here last night but what she saw now was a veritable oasis. Six raised rectangular garden beds were crowded with spinach, herbs and a whole range of vegetables, all green and healthy amidst the scrubby grass. They were surrounded by an orchard of trees covered with a net. Further down the yard was a wire chicken coop inhabited by a collection of brown and white chooks.

My god, how did she do all that way out here?

Miranda ducked into the laundry, a tiny shed with a single rusty tub, a couple of buckets and an assortment of fishing rods and tackle. She found the dog food, scooped a cupful into the bowl and put it down just outside the back door. Buster came bounding out when she opened the door and proceeded to wolf down the contents of the bowl in less than a minute while Miranda stood and watched.

The dog was fed, now for the humans.

'Thought you must have left already,' Esther grumbled as she came back in.

'Tea's on its way.'

'So's Christmas.'

The kettle had boiled and the bread was already done. Miranda grabbed an old tin tray from where it sat propped behind the sink. She laid out the plate of toast beside the mug of tea, braced herself and ventured back into the bedroom.

'Here we go.'

Esther took the tray from her without a word of thanks. 'Help yourself to something if you like,' she said. 'Not much to offer, though, I'm afraid.'

'I don't really do breakfast – thanks anyway.'

Esther looked her up and down. 'No wonder you're so skinny. Suppose you're a vegetarian as well, are you?'

'No. But I try to stay healthy.'

Esther grunted and chewed another mouthful of toast.

'Your vegetable garden is fantastic,' Miranda said. 'How did you ever build that all the way out here?'

Esther swallowed a few more mouthfuls. For a while

Miranda thought she mustn't have heard her, but then she replied.

'Took a while. Built them up one by one. Gathered timber and rocks bit by bit and filled each bed up with compost. Planted the seeds and just let them re-sow themselves each season. Not a lot to it, really.'

'I've never planted a thing in my life,' admitted Miranda.

'Does you good to get your hands dirty, dig around in the earth.'

The thought of dirt caked beneath her manicured nails made Miranda squirm. 'So what supplies can I bring you from town?'

Esther rubbed one weathered hand across the other. 'If you get me a pen and paper from that drawer over there I'll write a list. My shopping bag's in the cupboard.' She began scribbling a few things down while Miranda retrieved the bag – a khaki rucksack. 'Right, that should do it. A local fella delivers for me when I need it but since you're offering I may as well get a few basics.'

Ah, so she does have some contact with the outside world, Miranda thought. She stuffed the list into the front pocket of the bag, grabbed her wallet from her own pack and swung the rucksack over her shoulder, considering her options for getting to and from town. She'd have to walk back along the beach to get the car but it would be closer to park on the access road when she returned, and easier than trudging through sand with a heavy bag.

'I'm not sure how long I'll be,' she said.

'No hurry, I'm not going anywhere.' The old woman threw Miranda a grin, the first one since they'd met. It altered the whole appearance of her face and Miranda thought she caught a glimpse of the young girl in the photo. Or was she just imagining it?

'Well, I'll see you a bit later then,' she said. 'And you too, Buster,' she added, giving the dog a pat as she headed around the corner and out the door.

The day was ridiculously hot for late March. Miranda found herself rushing back up the beach.

Slow down – you don't have to kill yourself!

True – what was the rush? She slowed her pace, dodging around piles of mustard-coloured kelp that had been dumped overnight. Waves wriggled onto the shore, licking at the edge of her runners, forcing her onto the higher, softer sand that squeaked beneath the soles of her shoes.

As she walked, her thoughts kept returning to Esther. *She's an enigma all right. There must be someone in town who knows something about her, though. Or maybe some clues in the house itself?*

Curiosity spurred her on and she picked up the pace again. The quicker she got back to the car, the faster she'd be back at Esther's and have the chance to find out more about the mysterious old woman and her past.

Esther

sther hauled herself to the edge of the bed and grabbed the stick that was leaning up against the wall. The girl had left it there in case she needed it and even though the painkillers were starting to wear off she was buggered if she was going to lie around in bed all day like a geriatric. The sun was out and she needed some fresh air. She manoeuvred herself across to the partition by hanging onto the bed with one hand and using the stick to support her with the other. From there she used the kitchen chair and then the back of the lounge, until she made it to the front door. She was puffing like a billy goat and by the time she got to the chair on the porch she felt like she'd run a marathon.

Silly old cow, she thought to herself, fancy doing this much damage to yourself just from a stupid fall. She hadn't had an injury or an illness for as long as she could remember, hardly even a cold, and now she felt like a cripple. Fear slithered across her scalp as she imagined the possibilities: crutches, an operation, a walking frame or even a wheelchair. They're not getting me into one of those things, she decided. Nope, all she needed was a few days' rest and she'd be back to normal, walking and fishing with Buster. He was sprawled out beside her now, soaking up the sunshine, his favourite pastime apart from chasing the gulls. Esther smiled and shook her head at the sight of him. She always thought she'd wake up one day and he'd be gone, just like that, but it was four years later and he was still here. They looked after each other, him and her, respected each other's space.

'If it wasn't for you, old boy, I'd probably still be flat on my back in that cave.' Buster and the girl – Miranda. What a trick she is, carrying a first-aid kit around with her. Lucky for me she does, I suppose. No, she's a decent young thing. Doesn't pry too much, minds her business. Good of her to put herself out the way she has, but if she thinks I'm going to be seeing any doctor she's got another thing coming.

Picking up her binoculars, she sat forward in the chair, adjusted the focus and gazed out over the treetops to the sea. It was smooth as glass today, hardly a wave breaking. A cormorant swooped down, spearing through the surface and shooting back out with a fish squirming in its beak. This was what she loved – the continuing cycle of life ebbing and flowing, ever-changing but always the same. This was how she spent her days: watching the colours of the ocean, the patterns of the clouds, the quality of the light, the birds and whales and dolphins as they went about their business unaware of the silent observer hidden away in the bush.

For a while after she'd moved back to Pelican Point she'd missed the noises of the city, missed the bustle of the shops and the roads and the crowds that allowed you to be completely anonymous. But out here she soon embraced a new kind of existence, one where nobody bothered you, where you could be alone with your thoughts and your memories. She'd become so used to the solitude – addicted to it, you might say – that she sometimes even resented the sight of people on the beach, invading what little space she had left in the world.

As the sun warmed her face she closed her eyes and drifted off to the sound of the sea, an orchestra of whispers, crescendo and diminuendo, carrying her far, far away.

Miranda

Back at the cabin Miranda plugged in her phone. Another missed call from Belle. And three from James. Shit! Her thumb hovered over the green voicemail icon. He'd be wondering where she was, why she hadn't called. Should she tell him about Esther? She pressed the button and listened to the three messages, all asking where she was, why she hadn't rung, each one more frantic than the last. Dialling his number, she tried to collect her thoughts, but he answered before the phone even rang.

'Miranda, thank god, I was getting worried. Are you okay?'

'Yes, yes, I'm fine.'

'So why haven't you called?' He sounded wounded rather than mad and Miranda was once again guilt-ridden.

'There's no mobile reception where I'm staying. Sorry. I've come for a drive today, that's where I'm calling from.' Did that sound believable?

'Right. So how's it going?'

'Oh, you know, quiet, sleeping a lot, reading, walking on the beach, that sort of thing.'

James laughed. 'Sounds pretty boring to me.'

She smiled. 'Yeah, you'd hate it. Look, I might just hang out at the cabin for the next few days, so if I don't call, don't worry, okay?'

'I'll miss the sound of your voice,' he said softly. 'I miss you.'

'I know, but it won't be that long until you see me again. Better let you get back to work.'

'Okay, babe, enjoy.'

She hung up with a huge sigh of relief. Telling James she had no mobile reception had been a stroke of genius. It would give her some time to herself to really think, without feeling any pressure to go home. And then there was the Esther issue. The riddle of her grandmother had only deepened, and she wasn't going anywhere until she found out more.

Time to report in to Belle. Should she tell her about the niggling doubts she was having about the wedding?

'Hi, Mirry – I was wondering if I'd ever hear from you again! What's happening?'

'Well, I'm in Pelican Point.'

'Where the hell is that?'

'About five hours south of Sydney. I found Esther.'

'As in Grandma Esther?'

'Yes. Only I haven't exactly found out if she's my grandmother yet.'

'Okay. I'm confused.'

Miranda told Belle the whole story, starting with the panic attack at the office and ending with her discovery of Esther and what had happened since.

'Shit. So how are you going to find out if it's really her?'

'I thought I'd wait until I get to know her a bit better, until she's back on her feet.'

'So James is okay with you being away?'

'He's fine with it.' She heard the tremor in her voice and knew Belle would be hearing it too.

'And he knows why you're there?'

'Not exactly. He just thinks I've come for a little R and R. I never told him about finding the necklace or looking up the births, deaths and marriages register.'

'Why not?'

That was a good question. There were a lot of things she hadn't told James about lately, and when she thought about it she really had no idea why. 'I don't know. I just wanted to find out the answers for myself, I guess.'

'Hmm. You sure you're not having second thoughts about the wedding?'

'No, definitely not.' Realising she sounded a little too vehement, she softened her tone. 'Once I get this grandmother business out of my system, I'll be back on track.'

'If you say so. You take care of yourself down there. And keep me posted.'

'I will. Bye, Belle.'

The phone calls over, she stripped off her clothes, stepped into the tiny shower cubicle and washed away any more worries about what might be happening at home. Right now sorting out things with Esther was her top priority.

The dirt access road stopped abruptly in front of a black and yellow striped barrier and a sign that read 'Road Closed Due to Slippage'. She pulled the bags from the car, locked it up and followed the dirt track that ran along the roadside. A rustle in the bushes made her jump before a large lizard poked its head from under a piece of bark and then shrank back at the sight of the stranger. She found the path that led onto the back of Esther's property about fifteen minutes later, just as she was about ready to collapse. Passing the chicken shed and gardens, she marvelled once again at the old woman's self-sufficiency.

'Esther, hello, it's me, Miranda.'

Buster appeared at the door, tail wagging, but there was no other sound.

Miranda opened the wire door and took a tentative step inside. 'Hello?'

The dog headed back across the lounge room and into Esther's bedroom.

Still no sound.

'Esther?'

A moan, so quiet she wondered if she'd heard it at all. Miranda dumped the bags on the bench and, following Buster's lead, peered around the corner.

Esther's face was ashen. She looked straight at Miranda but didn't seem to be aware she was there.

'Esther, Esther, can you hear me?'

Miranda went to the bedside and held the back of her hand to Esther's cheek. It was burning. She picked up the glass of water on the bedside table and, dipping her fingers into the glass, dabbed them against Esther's face.

There was another moan and the old woman's eyes closed then began to flutter.

'Are you okay?'

Esther's voice was croaky and thin. 'I'm fine. Just having a nap.'

'Here, have a drink.' Miranda held the glass to Esther's lips, which were parched and cracked. 'You're really warm. I think you have a temperature.' This didn't look good. 'I'll grab you some more panadol and change the dressing on that knee.'

Esther didn't say a word, so Miranda returned to the kitchen and unloaded the meat and chicken from her bags into the fridge. She wet a tea towel – the only cloth she could find – and went back in and placed it on Esther's forehead. Again, no grumbling. She popped a couple more headache tablets from their silver packet and placed them in Esther's hand.

'Do you think you can swallow these?' she asked, handing her a fresh glass of water.

Esther nodded and took the pills as instructed.

'Can I take another look at your knee? Put a clean bandage on?' Miranda asked.

Another nod. The lack of argument from Esther was a worry. Miranda had only met her yesterday, but she knew enough of the old woman to know she didn't like being prodded or poked – or told what to do. As Miranda lifted the injured knee and unwrapped the bandage, she saw Esther's face wrinkle with pain. 'Sorry.'

The bare knee looked like an eggplant, shiny and swollen, and the cut beneath was red raw and oozing pus. Miranda reeled a little at the sight of it then rallied. 'I'll need to clean this up, Esther – it looks infected.' Back in the kitchen she pulled some clean gauze and antiseptic from the backpack. She'd never really been good at this sort of thing, always felt squeamish at the sight of blood, but there was no one else here, so she was just going to have to suck it up and get the job done.

'Don't bother saying it,' Esther told Miranda as she cleaned the wound. 'I'm not going to a doctor.'

Though Esther's voice was weak, Miranda could tell there was no point arguing. She chewed on her lip and shook her head.

'Buster needs a run. He gets all tetchy if he doesn't get out.' The old woman was more concerned about her dog than herself.

Miranda shrugged. 'Sure.'

She headed to the door, where the dog was already sitting, looking up at her with pleading eyes. I swear this dog has ESP, Miranda thought as she headed outside. The clouds had thickened into the same threatening pattern as yesterday and the sun had completely vanished. Buster ran ahead of her down the trail and onto the beach. The stretch of sand that had this morning been so inviting now looked lonely and desolate. Not that the dog seemed to mind. He raced off towards the rocks and Miranda followed. Nothing like getting a bit of exercise, she thought.

⟋⟍

It started to drizzle just as Miranda caught up with Buster. They were at the end of the beach, not far from where she had found Esther. Was it really only yesterday? As the rain got heavier she climbed over the rocks and headed for shelter. She sat on the floor of the cave, resting against the wall, and the dog dropped beside her, panting. Miranda let out a heavy sigh as she looked out at the rain sprinkling the surface of the ocean. Buster licked her hand.

'Thanks, boy, I like you too.'

The cave was like a small room, its ceiling arched and the ground covered in sand. Blackened logs and lumps of charcoal sat in a pile further back, remnants of an old fire. An etching on the wall opposite drew Miranda's eye. It was the rough shape of a heart with two sets of initials carved inside. Time had worn them away so the letters were hard to decipher. She ran her fingers over the rough surface of the rock. One letter could be an S, another possibly a W, but she couldn't be sure. She wondered where the lovers were now, if they were still together, or if their romance had just been some adolescent fling, doomed to come to an end with the onset of adulthood. Her own first love had been her friend's older brother, two years her senior, and for a year and a half she'd been completely smitten. So smitten she'd lost her virginity to him. She'd thought it was love, but after a while they both seemed to lose interest, and that was the end of that. There'd been a few others along the way, but work had been her priority and then she'd met James.

A dull ache in her chest brought her back to reality. The rain had eased enough for her to venture back to the house. Buster gave her a lick, on the leg this time, as if he too was keen to get going.

By the time they arrived at the cliff top rain had veiled the sea in a light mist. There was a quiet beauty to it that

Miranda couldn't help noticing, despite the fact that her T-shirt clung to her skin and beads of water dripped from her hair. She followed Buster up onto the porch and inside the house.

A steady wheezing sound signalled that Esther was asleep. Miranda crept in to check. Her cheeks were pale, her mouth partly open. Hopefully the tablets would do some good, but Miranda was worried. With no phone reception out here and no way of getting Esther back along the track by herself, she had serious concerns for the woman's health. That knee was definitely infected, not to mention the bruising and swelling, and a few doses of paracetamol were not going to perform a miracle. There must be someone she could contact, someone Esther knew who could help out. It was time to have a good hunt around.

Where to start? There was an old dresser against the side wall, as good a place as any. Miranda lifted the latch and froze as the door squeaked open. She stopped and listened – still the same regular inhalation and exhalation from Esther's bedroom. Inside the cupboard was an assortment of odds and ends – a pile of old fishing magazines, a collection of photos and albums, pages of crosswords torn from newspapers, some pieces of chipped crockery – but nothing resembling a telephone book. She closed that door and opened the next: a battered doll, one of the ones with the china heads that Miranda had always found slightly creepy, some books on astronomy and a cane basket containing a collection of what looked like old diaries. Miranda picked one up and ran her fingers across its worn leather cover. It reminded her of Esther herself, shabby at the edges but with an indefinable air of dignity. She opened it, glancing around to make sure no one was watching. The writing was like calligraphy, flowing and even, the tails on the y's and g's curled perfectly. She flicked through the pages which were filled with sketches of the beach, seagulls, a kookaburra, a horse – not just sketches but works of art. It seemed Esther was an artist, on top of everything else. The more Miranda learnt about this woman, the more intriguing she became. A surge of adrenaline rushed through her veins. Last weekend she'd been creeping around her parents' house like a cat-burglar, and now here she was about to read a stranger's diary. What was she even thinking? She replaced the diary, pushed the basket back onto the shelf and closed the door, reminding herself she was supposed to be looking for a phone number or contact, someone who might be able to help her with Esther. Rummaging through the remaining drawers she found the usual third-drawer-down type goods – sewing gear, string, sticky tape – but nothing else. Great!

Miranda slumped onto the lounge, wiping her now damp hair back from her face. It had turned to frizz after the rain, but for once she didn't care. She had more important things to worry about. A plan, that's what she needed. Not much she could do for now – she couldn't leave Esther here in this state alone. She'd cook up some of the sausages, help Esther get settled for the night and reassess the situation in the morning. If things were no better she'd hotfoot it back into town and find some way of getting a doctor. Of course there'd be an argument, but for once in her life Miranda was not going to take no for an answer.

Esther

L ying in bed with her eyes closed, she could hear the girl clattering around in the other room. The dresser door opened. Why would the girl be looking in there? She tried to muster the energy to call out and tell – what was her name – to stay out of her business, but it was too much effort to open her mouth. Pain flared up her leg like fire every time she tried to move. Chills trailed like icy fingers up her spine. Her eyelids were heavy as lead weights.

She lay back and willed her mind elsewhere, tried to conjure the feel of the violin resting beneath her chin, recall the sound that always relieved and transported her. But all that came was the jagged seesawing of the bow against the strings as the burning in her body deepened and her temples throbbed in time to the erratic beat.

Miranda

The next morning Esther was no better. Miranda did the best she could to jolly her along, but the old woman was groggy and seemed unsure of where she was. It was a struggle to get her to the bathroom but somehow Miranda did it and then helped her back into bed. She made her a hot cup of tea sweetened with sugar and propped her up on some pillows. Now was as good a time as any to sort out a plan.

'Esther, you're not getting any better,' she ventured, speaking slowly, enunciating each word in case the fever had affected Esther's hearing or powers of comprehension, 'and I really think we need to get you to a doctor. Somehow. Or get one to come out here.' She paused and waited for the woman's reaction.

'I may be sick, but I'm not deaf, and I haven't lost my marbles, so you can stop speaking to me like I'm three years old.' Although Esther spoke in quiet bursts she certainly hadn't become any pleasanter as a result of her illness.

'Isn't there anyone around here I can go to for help?'

Esther shook her head, put her half-full cup down on the table beside the bed and drooped against the wall. The conversation had taken it out of her and Miranda could see she was already drifting back into sleep. What if she passed out – or worse? 'How about that neighbour you mentioned, the one who delivers your groceries?'

'Vincent,' Esther mumbled. 'Vincent Kennedy. At Garewangga.'

Vincent? Wasn't that the name of the guy with the horse? 'Right. I'll be as fast as I can.'

Esther gave a slight nod of her head and closed her eyes.

There was no point wasting any more time. When they'd spoken on the beach Vincent had said he lived south of town. She gave Buster a rub on the head, told him to be a good boy and look after his mum, and dashed out the front door, not quite sure whether the hammering in her chest was a result of her worry about Esther or the prospect of seeing Vincent Kennedy.

Esther

Fingers tight around her wrist. Muffled voices calling her name. The faint noise of crying. If she concentrated very hard she would be able to move her lips and speak, tell them she was all right. Her lids were too heavy, as if someone had stitched them together, fastened them shut. A single voice, closer now, but the words scrambled inside her brain. It was no use. Better just to rest for a while, stop struggling, and soon enough she would wake up and the voices would be gone.

Miranda

Back at the car Miranda paused to think a minute. Where had Vincent said he lived?

South out of town and take the first on the left.

Garra something . . . *Garewangga* . . . that was it. She turned the key and after a six-point turn steered the vee dub along the bumpy road. As she drove her mind drifted over the strange events of the past few days. She'd come here in search of her missing grandmother. Now that Esther was so ill, when was she going to get the opportunity to find out if they were really related? There was a strong likelihood that the news wouldn't be taken well.

She slowed the car down as she approached the turn-off to the main road, then turned left. She was heading further and further away from home, when that was exactly where she should be right now. In her other, real life. She seemed to have entered some kind of parallel universe, where she glanced across at her original self every now and then, gave a cursory wave as if to a complete stranger, and then continued on in this new world where she felt strangely at home. It was all very bizarre.

Right, she had to keep her wits about her. The road was flanked by gigantic gum trees, their limbs arching into the centre, forming a kind of tunnel. Shadows flickered on the grey asphalt and Miranda took off her sunglasses in an effort to see more clearly. As she rounded the next bend a dirt track appeared on the left and she had to brake suddenly to make the turn. There was no street sign but she assumed this was it – a narrow road, lightly gravelled, that twisted and turned until finally it straightened out and the bush was replaced by folds of mellow green hills dotted with slow-moving cows. Around the next corner she pulled the car to a stop in front of a pair of wrought-iron gates set in a stone wall. The title of the property, Garewangga, was written across them. Praying they weren't locked, she pulled on the handbrake and hopped out to investigate. She was in luck: the padlock that hung from the latch was undone. She slid the bolt across and drove through, hopping out again to shut the gate. Her earlier sense of being in another dimension only increased as she drove further onto the property. Lush paddocks speckled with horses unfurled on either side as the car wound up and over the hill. As the road crested the next rise Miranda hit the brake and stared in open-mouthed wonder. Opening up before her was an expanse of verdant pasture rolling right out to the sea. Nestled among it all was a two-storey colonial-style home complete with French windows and a wraparound verandah. So in awe was she of the beauty of the place that as she continued on, coming to a stop at the bottom of the drive, she'd forgotten why she was even here.

Vincent, that's right. Getting help for Esther.

The bang of the car door jarred the quiet. There didn't seem to be anyone around. Opposite the house was an old stone building that backed onto some horse yards. That was probably where he'd be if he was here.

'Hello?' she called.

The only reply was the whinny of a horse in a stall by the stable. It was a grey, with soft dark eyes, and as Miranda approached it came to the corner of the pen and lowered its head.

She rubbed the horse's cheek. 'Aren't you beautiful?' The horse bent forward and pushed its nose against Miranda's hand.

'She is, isn't she?' The gravelly voice startled Miranda and she turned to find a man standing within arm's reach behind her. 'Richard Wilson,' he said without a smile. 'And you are?'

'I'm . . . hi, Miranda McIntyre,' she stammered as she took in the man's portly frame and balding head. Definitely not who she came here to find. There was something about him that unnerved her, and then she remembered where she'd heard his name. This must be the Richard Wilson the shopkeeper had told her about, the one who owned half the area and who was some relation to Esther.

'Can I help you with anything?'

Miranda thought fast. The shop lady had said that he and Esther were bitter enemies, so it probably wasn't a good idea to ask him for help. 'Actually, I was looking for Vincent. I met him the other day and told him I was interested in horses, so he suggested I come out for a ride.'

The man sniffed. 'He's not here right now. We only do rides by appointment.' He pulled a business card from his coat pocket. 'You can phone and see when it would be convenient.'

'Okay. Thanks.'

The horse stuck its head over Miranda's shoulder and inspected the card between her fingers. She stepped back and gave it another pat.

'By the way,' the man said, 'how did you get in? The gate should have been locked.'

'The padlock wasn't closed. I'm sorry if I've intruded.'

He didn't reply and Miranda got the very clear message that it was time to leave. As she drove back out she checked her rear-view mirror and saw him watching. Urgh, what a creep. Something about him made her skin crawl. So much for that plan. She'd just have to find a doctor herself. She stopped at the gate and opened it, then drove through. As she went back to close it a black ute rounded the corner and pulled up beside her car.

'Hello there.' Vincent stepped out of the car. 'So you did find time to come out for a ride?'

As he came towards her Miranda felt suddenly conscious of her dishevelled hair and lack of make-up. 'Not exactly. I actually came to ask for some help.'

'Ask away.' He folded his arms and leant back against the front of the ute.

She tried not to notice the way his jeans were slung low on his hips, or the way his biceps curved beneath his black T-shirt. 'Well, I'm not really sure where to start, but you know Esther, right?'

'Esther who lives in the cottage on the hill?'

'Yes, that's right. I, um, I found her on the rocks the other day, she'd fallen and hurt herself, and I took her back up to her house, but she's in a bad way and I need to try and get her to a doctor.'

'Are you a friend of hers?' Vincent asked.

Miranda hesitated. She couldn't very well confess to being a blood relation when she wasn't even sure it was true. 'No, I was just walking on the beach and found her, like I said.'

'What's she done to herself?'

'She's got a bad cut in her knee. It should probably have been stitched and I think it's infected. Her temperature is soaring and she needs to see a doctor. Today. But I have no idea how to get her there. She said you deliver her groceries for her.'

Vincent ran a hand through his thick, dark curls and scratched the back of his neck. 'Yeah, I do. On the quiet. My boss would crack it if he knew. But that's another story. She's not much of a people person, old Esther.'

'No, I gathered that.'

'She must like you to let you anywhere near her. She generally threatens to shoot anyone who comes by her place. I'm sure it's all bluster, though.'

Miranda was getting impatient. 'Well, she didn't have much choice. Look, I don't know anyone around here, so do you think you can help?'

'I can't really ferry her out of there by boat. The only thing to do would be to call an ambulance and go in and get her.'

'But the ambulance couldn't get through to her house.'

'Paramedics could get in there and carry her out. I expect she'll probably try to fight them off.'

Miranda laughed. 'Believe me, she's in no condition to fight anyone.'

'She must be in a bad way, then. I'll organise something. It's good of you to take the time to look out for a total stranger.'

There was a genuine tenderness in his voice that impressed Miranda. Surprising that a guy like him would take the time to help out an old woman. 'I'll head back out and wait with her,' she said.

'Are you sure? You don't have something else you need to be doing?'

'Well, I could be going for a horse ride, which is what I told your boss I was here for – I presume he's your boss, the short bald guy who told me I should call to make a booking?'

Vincent threw back his head and laughed. 'That's him. If you still have time when we've fixed Esther up I'll book you in.'

Miranda smiled and nodded as she got back into her car. 'Oh, and I apologise in advance – I think I might have got you into trouble – the gate wasn't locked so I let myself in. Your boss wasn't impressed.'

'Don't worry about it,' he called back. 'I can handle him.'

She drove back along the road feeling a whole lot lighter than when she'd arrived. And it wasn't all to do with sharing the burden of her concern for Esther.

⁓

Walking the now familiar track, a growing sense of trepidation plagued Miranda. The image of Esther lying on the bed, her skin clammy, her breathing shallow, kept creeping into her

mind. What if she'd taken a turn for the worse? What if . . . ?
She hastened her step at the thought, marching through the
bush like an army cadet in training. The sound of the ocean
grew louder. Miranda emerged from the track and made
her way across the paddocks to the house. She stepped onto
the porch and waited. Not a sound. In the silence she could
almost hear her own heart thumping as she imagined the
worst. Her feet felt like two lumps of cement and it took all
her courage to move towards the doorway of the bedroom.

'Esther?' She walked to the bed, hand pressed against the
base of her throat. Please don't be dead, please don't be dead,
she thought, blinking away the welling tears.

'What took you so long?'

Oh thank god. The woman might be sick but she was a
long way from dead.

'Sorry. I came back as fast as I could. I found Vincent
and he's going to organise some help. How are you feeling?'

'About as good as I look, I imagine.'

Esther's eyes closed again and Miranda wasn't sure what
to do next. She busied herself out in the kitchen and took
Buster outside for some fresh air. He charged down the steps
and stood at the top of the path down to the beach looking
back at Miranda.

'Not right now, boy, we're expecting some visitors.' As if
he knew exactly what she was saying, he did the rounds of
the yard, waddled his way back up the hill and deposited
himself down by her feet in the sun. The sea was flat today,
a sheer sweep of bottle-green, and once again the beach was
empty. Not a soul in sight – horse or human. She sat for a

while, lost in the view, until a figure appeared around the corner of the house. It was Vincent.

Buster greeted him in his usual exuberant manner as Miranda jumped from her seat. 'Hi. Again. I wasn't expecting you.'

'Thought I'd come out ahead of the ambos and check on the patient. So, where is she?'

'Just inside here. Not much better, I'm afraid.'

She showed him into the room and waited at the foot of the bed.

'I hear you're not feeling too well, Esther.' Miranda melted at the gentleness of his voice.

'I've been better.' Esther tried to push herself up but he placed a hand on her arm.

'Stay there. An ambulance is on its way.'

'I don't need to go to a bloody hospital,' she said, her voice hoarse but fierce.

'The paramedics will take a look at you and decide if you need to or not.' He laid his hand against her forehead. 'You certainly have a temperature.'

Esther tried to sit up but collapsed back against the pillows. Vincent raised an eyebrow and followed Miranda out into the other room.

'She doesn't look too good,' he whispered. His head was bent close to hers and she had to resist the temptation to reach out and stroke his cheek.

What the hell is wrong with me? Focus.

Before she could answer there was a knock at the door. 'Ambulance,' a voice called.

Miranda showed the two paramedics into Esther's room and stood beside Vincent as they examined her. She hugged her arms across her chest while one of the men unravelled the bandage. The knee looked even worse than before, red streaks spidering down her leg. Esther flinched as the medic pressed on the surrounding skin.

'Hmmm, very nasty. An oyster cut, I presume?'

Esther gave a vague nod.

'Looks like there could be some dirt trapped under the skin causing an infection. It really needs to be cleaned up. Properly.'

The second man had been taking Esther's blood pressure. He looked at his partner and raised an eyebrow before he turned back to the patient. 'We need to get you into the hospital and have you looked after for a few days.'

Just as Esther was opening her mouth, undoubtedly to protest, Vincent jumped in. 'There'll be no arguments. You're sick and you can't look after yourself and that's all there is to it.'

As the ambulance officer finished cleaning the wound and wrapped a clean bandage around it, Esther lay there quietly. Probably plotting her escape route, thought Miranda. At least if she's in hospital she'll get some decent care.

The older of the two officers signalled to Miranda and Vincent and they followed him outside. 'Sepsis,' he said in a hushed voice. 'Bacteria's gotten into the bloodstream from the cut.'

'But it came on so suddenly. One minute her leg was a bit sore and the next minute she had a raging fever,' said Miranda.

'It can happen like that. Especially with the elderly. We're going to have to get her out of here on a stretcher. I'm worried she's going to deteriorate rapidly. Her blood pressure is a real concern. Can one of you fill out some paperwork for me?'

'I'll give it a shot,' said Vincent. He turned to Miranda. 'Can you organise a few things for her to take to hospital?'

Sepsis? Wasn't that blood poisoning? It all sounded very serious and Miranda's throat constricted at the thought that she should have cleaned the wound better or gone for help sooner. She tiptoed back into the room and over to the chest of drawers. They'd given Esther an injection, some sort of painkiller to help settle her down, otherwise she'd probably be yelling at Miranda for rummaging through her things. She pulled out some underwear and what looked like pyjamas and put them in a bag along with a few toiletry items she collected from the bathroom out back.

The two ambulance men lifted Esther onto the stretcher with some help from Vincent. Luckily they were a couple of burly men, but even so the way back along the track carrying Esther's not-so-light frame was going to test their fitness. Her eyes were closed and she seemed only vaguely aware of her surroundings. Miranda had to look away as they pulled an oxygen mask onto Esther's face. Buster sat by Miranda's feet, watching everything that was happening. He gave a little whimper and she bent down and rubbed his head. The sound roused Esther from her haze and she lifted her hand to the mask.

'Just leave it there, love,' the taller of the two officers said. 'It'll help steady your breathing.'

Esther shook her head and mumbled something as she ripped it from her face and beckoned to Miranda.

'They're going to look after you, Esther.' Miranda could hear the quiver in her voice and swallowed hard to stay calm.

'Buster.'

The dog's tail thumped on the floor at the mention of his name.

'I'll take care of him. Don't worry.'

'Right, we'd better get moving.' The ambulance officer went to place the mask back on Esther's face but she held up her hand to stop him. Miranda leant in close.

'Don't let them take my house,' she whispered. The old woman's eyes were awash with tears, her brittle shell cracked. Miranda took Esther's hand and felt the dampness of her palm. More than anything she wanted to tell her who she really was, let her know that there was someone in the world who cared about her, but this wasn't the time.

'Everything will be all right, I promise. I'll stay here and look after Buster. And the house.'

'We really have to go.' The officer replaced the mask and this time Esther didn't resist. Miranda watched as they carried her out the door, across the hill and then disappeared into the bush.

'She'll be okay.' Vincent's hand was on her shoulder. For a few moments she'd almost forgotten he was there but now she was acutely aware of his presence.

'That fucking access road should have been fixed by now,' he said. 'An old woman can't be expected to live out here on her own without any way in or out other than her own two feet. But I expect they know that.'

'Who?'

He rubbed his jaw with his palm. 'There's been a war of sorts going on for years between Esther and her nephew. Who happens to be my boss. They're related, but you wouldn't know it. His father, who was Esther's brother, left her this place in his will, with a caveat that it be left to Richard when she dies or moves away. He owns half the land around here and has a lot of influence with the local council. That's why the road hasn't been fixed.'

'I'm not sure I understand.'

'This land is worth an absolute fortune. A developer's paradise. Richard wants her out of here sooner rather than later.'

'But that's criminal. If people know about it, why don't they do something to help Esther?'

Vincent shot her a wry smile. 'She's not the most liked person in these parts. People aren't going to go out of their way to help her, I'm afraid.'

Miranda was speechless. The thought that people would deliberately try to force an old woman off her land in such an underhanded way was appalling.

'No wonder Esther never wants to leave the place.'

Vincent turned to her and for a few moments neither of them spoke. Miranda cleared her throat and shifted her gaze. It was midafternoon now and a gentle hush had fallen across the ocean.

'Are you sure you're okay to stay here and look after things?' he asked.

Miranda stared out over the water. It was hard to make out where the sea ended and the heavens began. She thought of Esther being loaded into the ambulance, frightened and alone. And she thought of the brave young woman in the newspaper report who had risked her own life to save a total stranger from the sea. How is it possible that they are one and the same person? she wondered. And how is it possible that you can start out in life as one person and end up as someone completely different?

'I'm happy to stay,' she said quietly.

'In that case I'll book you in for a ride.' Vincent smiled. 'Tomorrow?'

The urge to reach out and touch his face threatened to overwhelm her.

Just do it.

She moved slightly away from him as she returned his smile. 'Sounds good.'

He wandered down the steps. 'See you then.'

Miranda stood on the porch and watched him leave, wishing that he'd turn around and come right on back. She pressed her fingers against her temples. What the hell is wrong with me?

Nothing. You're just finally coming to your senses.

Buster's rough tongue rubbed against her shin.

'It's just you and me for a while, eh boy?'

He followed her inside and she shut the door against the day.

Esther

Patches of white flashed through the treetops, blinking like eyes. Her arms were pinned to her sides. She tried to wrestle them loose but there was something holding her down. There was no use fighting. She'd tried before and it never worked. Better just to go along with it, wait for the right time to make your escape. For now she was moving, floating through the bush like a dandelion, weightless, bouncing into the light. Like riding a horse again, hurtling across the paddocks, soaring over the hilltops, galloping into the sky.

Miranda

As night wrapped itself around the cottage she busied herself tidying up, feeding Buster, fixing herself a sandwich, and trying not to think about Vincent. The place was certainly no home beautiful but there was a quaint charm about it that a lick of paint and a lot of de-cluttering would undoubtedly improve. With Esther in hospital for a few days she could at least spruce it up a bit.

Time was ticking away – it was already Saturday – her fourth night away from home. Away from James. Hopefully her story about the lack of reception was buying her time. And it wasn't entirely a lie. There really was no reception out here at the point. Tomorrow she'd head back into town, check out of the cabin and try calling him. But what she was going to tell him she wasn't quite sure.

Just try telling him the truth.

That of course was completely out of the question, since she didn't know what the truth actually was and her main concern right now was Esther – and finding out if she was her grandmother. And this was the perfect time to do it. She made a beeline for the dresser and found the basket full of diaries she'd stumbled across. Was that really only yesterday?

One, two, three, four . . . in total there were nine diaries in varying states of wear and tear. She pulled out the oldest looking one and flicked through the pages, huddling over as if to hide it from view. The thought that anyone might read her own diaries mortified her, but this was the only way she was going to find out what she needed to know. The first entry was dated 21 February 1937. Some of the handwriting had faded and it was difficult to read, but from what Miranda could make out it was mostly about horses.

If I could spend my whole day riding then I would be deliriously happy. Duke is the best horse I have ever had. I wouldn't dare tell Dad but yesterday I took him down to the beach on my own and we flew along the sand. It was the best feeling in the world.

The voice seemed to be that of a young girl, perhaps twelve or thirteen. Miranda thumbed the yellowing pages, scanning them for anything about Esther's family. There were references to violin practice and school and complaints about doing chores, but nothing of major interest. She slid the volume back in its place and pulled out another at random. The first line of the first entry made her shift forward in her seat.

Something happened today. Something I want to remember as long as I live, so I am writing it down in minute detail. But where to start? At the marvellous end? No, I will start at the beginning so I can relive the whole experience all over again.

This entry was dated 7 October 1942. It was an older voice and there was the promise of a much more interesting story. Miranda sank back into the lounge, folding her legs beneath her, and settled in for a longer read.

I woke late and opened my curtains to a day filled with cloud, long thin wisps of it that hung like gossamer threads across the sky. Somewhere out there beyond the far hills was Samuel. He'd gone out to check on the cattle and the fences at the furthest end of the property. If I could get through my chores and practice early enough, I planned to surprise him on his way back and we could ride home together. Just the thought of seeing him made my body quake. In my mind I could feel his smooth dark skin beneath my fingertips and his soft curls against my cheek. I knew he would be thinking of me too. There was nothing surer.

Mum had gone to a CWA meeting and Dad is away in Sydney on business, so there was no one to please, only myself. I worked my way through the list of chores I'd been left – hanging out the washing, putting the bread on to bake, collecting the eggs from the henhouse – before racing through my violin practice, my bow skipping across the strings, thinking the whole time of him.

Once it had passed two o'clock I went out and saddled up Duke. He nuzzled at my pocket for the sugar cubes he knew I had waiting for him. When we were out the gate I let him have his head and we cantered across the first hill and then the second until we made the headland, where I could see far into the distance. Duke was eager to keep going but I pulled on the reins and held him back.

'Not yet,' I said, 'wait until we see him, it shouldn't be long now.' I searched beneath the white pintucks of my blouse and pulled out grandfather's fob watch.

I sat astride Duke scanning the tops of the far hills where I knew he would appear anytime now, and as I waited I thought about the last time Samuel and I had been together. It was in the stables where he'd been tending the horses. I snuck in when he was working and crept up on him. When I jumped out from one of the stalls I swear he squealed like a mouse. It was the funniest thing. He broke into peals of laughter as he wound his arms around me and drew me against him. My insides turned to water as his black eyes looked into mine, as if he could see into my soul. We lay down right there in the stable and kissed long and hard, his body on mine, pressing into me. I wanted to keep going but Samuel pulled away. 'Not here, Essie,' he said, 'it's too dangerous. Someone could come in.' He stood and walked to the other end of the stable and I knew he was right, even though every cell in my body wanted to chase after him and tell him he was wrong.

But today would be different. Today we had a plan and he said he was prepared. I raised my hand to my eyes as something moved in the distance. The speck grew larger and soon I realised it was Samuel galloping towards me. He let out a loud cooee as he came closer, tearing his hat from his head and swinging it through the air. I laughed out loud at his antics. Any minute now he would be here and then . . . and then . . .

'Come on, let's meet him halfway.' I turned Duke's head in Samuel's direction, pressed my heels against his flanks and we were off, thundering across the paddock and making our way down the hillside. The ride only served to heighten my anticipation of what was to come, my blood pumping faster and faster through my veins.

Samuel stopped at the bottom of the rise and waited for me, a grin stretched wide across his face, and I knew what he was thinking. How wonderful to have that effect on a man! But not just any man. He truly is my sweetheart. And I know I am his.

When I reached him he had already dismounted, his horse wet with sweat and the gleam of perspiration on his own forehead. I drew to a stop and jumped as fast as I could from the saddle and into Samuel's arms. His lips were on mine in a second, rough and strong, his tongue searching the roof of my mouth. I kissed him back with equal fervour and it was some minutes before Samuel broke off, laughing.

'Anyone'd think you were pleased to see me.' He squeezed his arms around my waist. 'Did ya miss me then?'

'I might have,' I teased as I settled into his arms. 'What took you so long anyway?'

'A few of the cows got through the fence on the far side of the property. Had to climb through and chase the buggers back. Then I had to try and fix the fence. I'll have to go back there tomorra and do it properly.'

'I might just have to come with you, then.'

Samuel laughed. 'Yeah, and your dad's going to allow that, do you think?'

'Who says he has to know? It's not like he knows everything we get up to now, is it?'

'And isn't that just as well, my Essie.' We kissed again, more gently this time, but no less passionately. And then he asked the question I'd been longing to hear. 'Why don't we leave the horses here for a bit and head down to the cave?'

My hands shook as I secured Duke's reins to the saddle to prevent him treading on them and doing himself damage and Samuel did the

same to his horse. Neither of us spoke. We left them to eat grass
and turned towards the beach, arms entwined. Others would say
it was wrong – immoral even – what we were about to do, but
to me it was the most natural and beautiful thing in the world.

As we walked across the sand I swear my heart was thumping
so loudly he must have heard it over the sighing of the waves.
Together we scrambled over the rocks that marked the entrance of
the cave. I took Samuel's hand and followed him into the darkness.

It is impossible to describe what happened next, only to say
that I entered the cave as a girl and left as a woman. My heart
and soul have long belonged to Samuel and now my body does also.

Was the girl telling this story really the same woman she'd
seen lying on a stretcher just hours ago, her face lined with
years and frozen with fear? It seemed impossible that the
young, vibrant Essie whose secrets lay between these pages
could possibly have become such a cantankerous, lonely old
woman. Miranda turned the next page and read on.

16 October 1942
The last week has been so busy with recitals, visitors from Sydney
and my mum insisting that I help around the house – I have hardly
even seen Samuel let alone been able to spend any time with him.
Farmwork is keeping him more and more busy now that our manager
Charles has gone off to the war. So far Dad has been able to keep
Samuel from enlisting, saying he is an essential worker, which of
course he is. He does more work around here than anyone, Dad
included, and the place would fall to pieces without him. When
Mum went into town this morning she left strict instructions for
me to make a batch of scones. Mrs Pratt was coming for afternoon

tea and bringing her dreary son, Clarence. I know exactly why she invited them. What in the Lord's name makes her think I would be remotely interested in a boy like him? Does she honestly think I would marry a weedy bore like that?

Anyway I was too busy daydreaming and looking out the window in the hopes I would see Samuel that I forgot whether I'd put two cups of flour into the mixture or three. I dug through the bowl with the wooden spoon trying to estimate what was already in there but flashes of our time at the cave last week kept creeping into my mind. The warm touch of Samuel's palm against mine as we walked together into the darkness, the way his eyes glimmered in the half-light, the fire spreading through my body as he undid the buttons of my blouse and ran his fingers over my breasts. That same heat spread through my thighs again as I stood there in the kitchen, just at the thought of him. I heard a moan, and realising it was me, opened my eyes! I turned but luckily no one was there. Thank god!

There was no use trying to guess at the measurements – if I made a mess of the scones I would be strung up – so I dumped the entire contents of the bowl into the bin, dusted my hands on my apron and started again.

We had afternoon tea in the 'good' room, as my mum likes to call it. She only uses it when she's trying to impress. Clarence sat annoyingly close to me. I could barely breathe for the stench of his body odour. Dark sweat stains had spread across his shirt from his armpits. Does he really think that is the way to impress a girl? I tried to move over as far as I could but I was already squeezed against the end of the lounge. Mum and Mrs Pratt sat opposite, absorbed in talk of what was happening in town, the outrageous prices the new draper was charging for thread and yards of fabric, *and the sudden engagement of the Bolton girl. The latter topic sent them into a frenzy of whispers, but though I tried, I couldn't pick up a word of what they said.*

'So, what are your plans now your schooling is complete, Esther?'

It took me a minute to register that Clarence was talking to me, so intent was I on hearing the conversation. I had no clue what he he'd said, so I pursed my lips into a sweet smile in reply.

'Now that your studies are over,' he said, 'will you be staying in the district?'

'Yes, as a matter of fact, I will. I plan to help my dad with the horses, expand the stud and improve on our breeding program.'

'Not exactly a suitable occupation for a young woman.'

'I can't see any reason why it wouldn't be.'

Clarence fidgeted at my reply.

'And you, now you're eighteen, will you be enlisting?' I knew it was wicked of me to even ask but I couldn't help myself. The Pratts had been broadcasting around the entire district that their son would of course sign up if only the army would overlook his asthma. I'm sure the army wouldn't want a weakling like him in the ranks anyway!

Mrs Pratt immediately stopped her own conversation and butted in to ours before her son could splutter an answer. 'Why don't you two youngsters go for a walk outside and get some fresh air?'

'What a lovely idea,' chimed in my own mother. Clarence stood dutifully while I attempted to argue but Mum only glared at me and insisted I show our guest the orchard. I almost burst out laughing at the ridiculous grin on Mrs Pratt's face. I swear the two of them were already planning the wedding as we left the room.

Clarence stuck far too close to me as we made our way out into the garden. I made sure to keep a few steps ahead so I wouldn't have to endure another conversation with him. After a walk around the orchard I turned to find him right behind me. He grabbed me by the shoulders and planted his chapped lips directly onto mine. It was like kissing a dried prune, if you could even call it a kiss. I wriggled out of his grasp and ducked under a branch loaded with bright yellow lemons, flinging one of them out of the way and 'accidentally' bumping him on the forehead. But Clarence is as thick as two planks and didn't get the message. He suggested we continue on down to the beach, so I made the excuse of having a headache and returned to the house, with Clarence following behind like a puppy dog. I deliberately took the longer route back past the stables where Samuel was busy shoeing a horse. He looked up long enough to raise an eyebrow and flash me a grin. I rolled my eyes and he grinned again. We both know what Mum is up to but it doesn't matter. Let her try her hardest. Nothing will come between Samuel and me. And no one. Certainly not Clarence Pratt!

Miranda blinked her eyes, fighting off sleep, desperate to read more. If Esther was her grandmother then she certainly hadn't married Clarence Pratt, but then she hadn't married this Samuel either, despite what seemed like a passionate love affair. Things were getting more and more interesting.

24 October
Last night I had the dream again.
*   There was nothing that seemed to trigger it, no wind outside to speak of, the only sound a tawny frogmouth hooting in the coral tree. I had gone to bed feeling uneasy, thoughts of Samuel swimming in my head, my body aching for him. I closed my eyes, remembering the way he had run his hands over my bare skin, feeling the same*

*rush of excitement I had felt in the cave as we lay down on the
sand and he took me in his arms.*

*I don't know how, but at some point I must have drifted off
to sleep, and there was the boat again, water swamping its decks,
waves thrashing against its sides smashing the hull to pieces. The
night was so black I could hardly even see the boat through the
lashings of rain. But then a light appeared through the gloom,
pulsing like a failing heartbeat in the darkness. The silhouette of
a man appeared, a smudge pressed against the heaving mass of
ocean, materialising as the battered boat crested a wave and then
vanishing as the vessel plunged back into the depths. Lightning
sparked, illuminating the man's face. Terror filled his eyes as he
uttered a soundless scream.*

*I have no clear idea what happened next, only snatches of
images: waves swirling around my feet, Duke surging through
the water, the man's hand grasping mine so tightly that when I
woke the first thing I did was rub my wrist, convinced it would
be black and blue.*

*None of it makes any sense and I'm sure it doesn't mean anything,
but it left me feeling so disturbed I thought it might be a relief to
write it down. Hopefully putting the images into words will bring
an end to it and it will be the last time that particular nightmare
disturbs my sleep.*

'Oh my god.' Miranda sprang upright, dropping the diary
onto the floor. This was the exact same story detailed in the
newspaper clipping she'd found. She knew the details off by
heart now, but this entry recorded a dream and not the event
itself. How could that be possible? She retrieved the diary
from the floor next to her feet and read on.

28 October

I cannot begin to explain how completely exhausted I am tonight after the muster. Every muscle in my body aches. It's all I can do to lift my pen and move it across the page. But if I leave it until tomorrow to record the day's events all the small, beautiful details will be forgotten.

The day began in darkness. I looked out and saw the light come on in the stable. Samuel would be just waking, tossing back the covers and folding his strong lean body into his work clothes, the horses restless in their stalls waiting for him to throw them a biscuit of hay. He would brush them down one at a time, talking to them quietly about the day to come, calling them by name as if they were people, taking special care to have Duke's coat shining and his mane and tail immaculate. Then he would saddle them up, being sure to be ready as soon as the light began to break, as my dad had instructed.

I spent so long daydreaming at the window, imagining his every move, that I hardly had time to dress and ready myself. By the time I pulled on my coat and raced downstairs the stockmen were already mounting.

'Where the hell have you been, Esther?' Dad, already on his horse, scolded. 'Didn't I tell you that if you wanted to come you had to be up and ready on time?'

'Sorry,' I said meekly. As I took the reins from Samuel our fingers brushed and a now familiar yearning ran through me. Ever since our time in the cave I've barely been able to think of anything else. Just remembering it now it's all I can do to stop myself from sneaking there with him again. But the stockmen are all downstairs drinking after the long ride today and the risk of being caught is too great.

So, back to the ride. We were heading to the far end of the property, which can only be accessed from the beach and then the tracks over the headland. The cattle had been left to graze on pasture far to the north and it would take the whole day to round them up and drive them south and back to the farm.

Dad only allowed me to go because he is shorthanded. Three of our farmhands have enlisted recently following the lead of Charlie Hoskins, the overseer. Since Darwin has been bombed panic has set in and more and more men have signed up now that our own shores are under threat. Samuel has been given special dispensation not to join, supposedly on the grounds that Dad couldn't run the farm without him. Of course it's really because of his colour. Even those who are only half black like him are being discouraged from going to war. Not that they'd say but the government are ashamed to have them as soldiers, which makes my blood boil. Samuel would make an excellent soldier, but the thought of him going off to war makes me giddy with fear. Luckily there's no chance of that now that he has been given more responsibility as a result of Hoskins leaving. It is a job he is more than up to and it will allow him to prove how capable he truly is. I even heard Mum talk of allowing Samuel to have Charlie's old cottage at the far end of the point so he can keep an eye on things at that end of the property. My heart sank when I first heard it as he will be further away, but I sparked up when I realised it will give us more chance to be together away from prying eyes.

Anyway, the muster. We set out across the paddocks, walking and trotting at first but then letting the horses have their heads and breaking into a gallop. A steel-cold wind had sprung up with first light but I braced myself against it and made sure that Duke and I kept up with the men. Samuel was up front, having been told to lead the way. A few of the riders are casual hands and so need direction. I flushed with pride as I watched him taking charge, knowing that one day in the future it will be our own farm he'll be managing. We made our way down through the bush track and along the beach. The sea was smooth as a turtle shell further out but with frothy waves building close in and then punching like fists against the shore. Duke loved it as always. I dropped back at one stage and allowed him to paddle in as far as the breakers before Dad turned and yelled at me to get a move on. I could see Samuel grinning at my antics, which made me show off even more. I dropped my heel back and turned Duke in a circle, water spraying up over my boots and legs, before cantering out of the water and along the beach. Dad tried to look cross but I know deep down he's proud of my stamina. He always says that I'm such a tomboy it's like having two sons. Since Martin has been away at the war he's let me help out more around the place. I'm sure he'll agree to my plan to stay here and work on the farm rather than sending me off to study at the Conservatorium as we'd originally planned. As much as I adore playing the violin I couldn't stand to be separated from Samuel.

But I just can't keep my mind on the story! We rode for another hour or so, as the going was rough on the other side of the point, and it was a while before we found open spaces again. When we finally arrived at the place where the cattle were supposed to be, there were only a few dozen instead of the three hundred or so that we were expecting to find. Samuel dismounted and went in search of them and then all hell broke loose.

'Over here, boss,' I heard him call.

My dad rode to where Samuel was standing. He cupped his hands around his mouth and called back to us. 'The fences have been cut.'

Sure enough, when we reached the perimeter there was a gaping hole in the wire. Dad cursed and stamped his foot. 'Damned bloody rustlers. I'd heard there were a few around. God knows how many head they've taken.'

'Looks like a pretty amateur job, boss,' Samuel tried to reassure him. 'Probably just some local fellas after a bit of grub.'

'A few of your mob, no doubt,' chimed in Ted Weatherby, our neighbour, who had come along to help. I gritted my teeth at his remark. Why Dad had even asked him to help was beyond me.

'Could be anyone, Ted,' Dad said. 'No use pointing the finger. But if I catch the beggars they'll be sorry. Better see what we can find of the cattle.'

It took hours to find them all and round them up. Sadie and Beau earnt their dinner tonight, sniffing their way through the scrub and barking wildly whenever they came across stray cows, then chasing them back out into the open. With all the commotion I hardly got to see Samuel and it was well into the afternoon before we could head for home. When Dad asked Samuel to stay at the back and move along any stragglers my heart leapt. We rode along side by side, finally able to speak.

'You'll be sleeping well tonight, Essie,' he said.

'I would be if I was sleeping with you.' I flashed him a wicked grin as he looked around nervously.

'Essie, you can't talk like that. Someone'll hear and then we'll be for it.'

'And who's going to hear us all the way back here?' I laughed. 'The cows, Duke, Betty?'

Samuel leant forward and covered the mare's ears. 'I've told you before she's almost human, so don't be surprised.' Betty glanced sideways at him as he rubbed her withers. He edged her closer until the two horses' shoulders were touching. 'I know what you mean, though,' he continued, almost in a whisper. 'I lie in bed every night wishing you were there with me.'

Our eyes locked as we rode along, neither of us watching where we were going, trusting the horses to follow behind the cattle, and I knew he was wishing as I was that we could ride away from all this and find somewhere to be on our own, to explore each other's bodies as we had in the cave that day. It was only a few weeks ago, but it seems like an eternity.

A sudden movement in front brought us to our senses as one of the cows slipped and fell. I watched in horror as the poor creature went careening down the embankment, tumbling over itself as it tried to get its footing and then lay at the bottom of the drop, its body twisted and one of its legs clearly broken. Samuel jumped off and scuttled down the hill. He knelt over the animal, placing his hand on its neck. His shoulders drooped and he shook his head before he stood and climbed back up, the cow bleating in agony.

'It was an accident,' I said. 'Things like this are bound to happen with this many head of cattle.'

'It shouldn't have bloody happened. I should have been watching what I was doing. Come on. We'd better catch up. I'll have to get one of the men to come back and shoot the poor bugger.' He gathered his reins and pushed Betty forward, me following behind, the ridge too narrow now to ride side by side. Wounded by his remarks, as if it was my fault that the cow had fallen to its death, I fell into a sulk.

The path wound around the hill for a few more miles. It was slow going, moving so many cows through the bush this way, but the meat was needed for buyers in Sydney and Dad had insisted the whole mob be moved together. Samuel didn't turn and talk to me once. I tried to tell myself he was upset for the poor animal, as

I knew he was, and worried too probably about what Dad would say when he found out. Samuel is too honest to lie. Except about us, of course. When he rode off ahead to break the news, my anger cooled, knowing how dedicated he is to his job. Dad just shrugged, saying these things happen, and rode back to put the poor creature out of its misery.

At the beach the cattle spread out and Samuel was able to drop back with me again. I knew he was there of course but didn't acknowledge it, looking out at the ocean instead. It was dusk, and sunset had painted the sky a vibrant canvas of pinks and oranges. The sea had calmed, and although the wind had dropped since we ventured out this morning, there was enough of a breeze that the strands of hair that had fallen from my braid were blowing across my face. I left them there, determined not to shift my gaze in his direction.

'You won't be able to see where you're going in a minute,' he joked.

I flicked my head back. 'You'd do better to keep your own eyes on the job,' I replied.

He was silent and I knew my sharp words had wounded him. 'Sorry,' I said as I looked across at him, his face hidden in the late-afternoon shadows.

'I deserved it. I'm sorry too, Essie.'

I wanted to reach across and throw my arms around his neck and feel his lips against mine. And more. But as the light faded and night began to fall we contented ourselves with riding side by side along the sand and back over the hills to the home paddocks, where the cattle were safely contained.

Back at the stables there were more than a few groans as the men dismounted and went inside for a drink and a meal, leaving Samuel to unsaddle and wash down the horses.

'I'll give him a hand,' I said to Dad as he headed inside.

'No you won't, young lady. Your mother will be wanting help in the kitchen.'

'I'm sure Sambo can do it himself,' added Ted, snickering at his own remark as he wandered into the house with his mates. I wanted to run at him and punch him and pull at his hair and tell him that he was not half the man Samuel was and that he was just a pig-headed ignorant bastard, but I bit my tongue and placed my hand gently on Samuel's arm instead. He gave me a tender smile but I knew the comment had stung. I tied Duke to the hitching post and waited until all the men had gone inside. A light shone through the kitchen window but there was no sign of my mum. The horses shielding us from anyone who might happen to be looking out, I turned to Samuel and held his face between my hands. His breath was hot against my mouth. Our kiss only lasted a few brief seconds but it was enough to wipe away the malice of Ted's comment and any lingering bitterness from our earlier quarrel.

'Esther, are you there?' Mum called from the doorway. I swept my lips once more across Samuel's before darting out from behind the horse.

'Coming.'

Before I closed the door I turned and looked back to see a hand raised in farewell in the darkness.

Miranda held the diary up to the light and ran her finger back up the page to the neighbour's reference to Samuel – Sambo, he had called him, and incurred Esther's wrath. Earlier, she had talked about Samuel's smooth, dark skin. Not only was she having a secret affair with the station hand, that station hand was Aboriginal. Miranda desperately wanted to read more but was too tired to go on.

It didn't feel right to sleep in Esther's bed so she rearranged the cushions on the lounge, pulled the blankets up and closed her eyes. An image of the beautiful young girl in the diary – Essie – came to her. Her blonde hair fell in waves around her shoulders as she walked hand in hand along the beach with a handsome young man, their fingers clasped as they stepped into the shadows of the cave and carved their initials inside a heart.

Esther

The sickly sweet smell of disinfectant caught in her throat before she'd even opened her eyes. Her stomach lurched as she tried to push herself up but her arms wouldn't work. She tried to focus, to see what was holding her back – a tube was stuck into the back of her hand, connected to the drip stationed by the bed. Everything around her was a haze of white and stainless steel that was frighteningly familiar. Voices outside the room boomed and receded like waves attacking the shore and then retreating. Someone laughed. They were laughing at her. She had to get out of here. Now. She dragged herself up to a sitting position, gritting her teeth against the shard of pain that stabbed at her knee. The room spun around her so she sat completely still waiting for the queasiness to pass. With one swift tug she ripped the tape from the back of her hand and yanked out the drip. Blood trickled from the cut and dribbled onto the starched sheets. It spread outwards through the cotton threads into the shape of an eye. An eye that was watching her. That's why she had to get away. She shuffled to the edge of the bed and heaved her legs to the side. If she concentrated on the grey streak in the centre of the white linoleum square she would be all right. Feet planted on the floor, hands on either side of her, fingertips pushing away from the mattress, she raised herself a few inches off the bed before a swarm of tiny silver spots clouded her vision. Her head fell forward as she lost her balance and the last thing she heard was the clanging of the metal tea trolley as it crashed to the floor beside her.

Miranda

As soon as her eyes opened the next morning, two thoughts hit her simultaneously: finding out how Esther was and revisiting Garewangga. And it wasn't just with the aim of seeing Vincent again – although that particular idea did bring a smile to her sleep-rumpled face. After reading the diaries, she had a longing to see exactly where it was that Esther had grown up. But first things first. If she was going to stay here and mind the place, she'd have to collect her gear from the cabin. She raised her elbow and sniffed at her armpit. Errgh! Definitely time for a shower.

'Okay, Buster, let's get this show on the road.' The dog looked up at her adoringly and then raced to the door, keen for his morning jaunt.

Miranda shivered as she stepped out onto the back step, towel in hand, in nothing but her T-shirt and knickers. The cottage was completely surrounded by a dense curtain of mist, so thick that when Buster ran down the steps into the yard she lost sight of him completely. Goosebumps prickled her thighs and she wrapped her arms across her chest. There wouldn't be much point going anywhere until the fog cleared. And it was way too cold for an outdoor shower. She whistled for the dog, who came charging up the path panting like a madman, and headed back inside. Maybe there was time for another scan of the diaries while she polished off some vegemite toast.

⁓

Draping a blanket across her knees, she flicked through the next few entries about days on the farm and Essie's passion for Samuel, which had only increased after a few midnight trysts in the stable. The opening words of the next page caught her eye. Popping the last piece of crust into her mouth, she brushed the crumbs from her fingers, picked up the diary and settled back on the lounge.

13 November 1942

How can I even write of last night's events? How is it possible that something that has happened time and time again in my dreams could actually happen in reality? But dream is the wrong word – nightmare is more appropriate, and this time the nightmare was real. Or was it? Perhaps I am still sleeping and only dreaming that I am writing this down even now?

But no. The whole catastrophe was too terrifying to have been merely imagined.

It began some time shortly before midnight. I lay in bed reading, listening to the rain teeming down, trying to keep my mind on the story, but of course my thoughts kept drifting to Samuel. The shrieking of the wind in the trees was so strong that I'm sure the house shook in fright. It was too noisy to sleep so I climbed out of bed and went to the window. With not even a skerrick of moonshine on the water, the land and sea had become one mass of solid darkness. The only light shone from the stables, where I knew he would be reading, making his way through the pages of *Seven Little Australians*, which I have been reading with him when we can snatch a moment. But as I peered through the window a strange sensation overcame me. A feeling of having stood in this exact same place before at this exact same moment. And then somewhere far off in the distance a pinprick of light appeared and as I watched it darting like a firefly a burst of lightning illuminated the ocean and I could see clearly a small boat listing, a flare waving frantically from side to side. It was too far off to see who held the flare but I knew from my dream it was a man and I knew how his eyes bulged with terror as he clung on for dear life.

And I knew what had to be done. I pulled my nightie over my head and dressed, pushing my arms into the sleeves of my oilskin coat. Whether I was acting on instinct because I had lived this scenario before in my dreams I don't know, but for some reason I decided not to wake Mum and as Dad was away at the stock sales I headed straight for the stables.

The yard was flooded and I was already soaked to the skin by the time I burst through the stable door.

Samuel looked at me in amazement. 'Essie, what are you doing? What's wrong?'

I could hardly speak the words. 'There's a boat, I saw it out my window. It's the same as the one in the dream I told you about.'

'What are you talking about?' He looked at me as if I had lost my marbles.

'There's a man out at sea, his boat is going down, we have to do something.'

Within seconds he was up and pulling on his trousers. We hurriedly bridled up Duke and Betty without a word and rode out bareback into the night. The rain had eased slightly by now but the wind screeched through the trees, flaying the branches and tearing strips of bark from their trunks. Feeling Duke's hesitation, I patted his neck and spoke softly to him.

Samuel led the way out onto the hills and within minutes we were on the beach, horses and riders totally drenched. I shielded my eyes from the rain with my hands as I peered out to sea. For a few seconds there was no sign of the light I had seen from the window but then I spotted it again. As the damaged boat rose with the swell, something flickered in the gloom.

'Out there,' I pointed.

Samuel tried to push Betty forward but the mare reared and he was thrown into the shallows as she raced away from him and vanished into the darkness.

'I'll swim out.' He was at my side, holding my leg, shouting up at me.

'No, it's too dangerous,' I called back. 'The swell is too strong. You'll be drowned. I'll go on Duke. He can do it.'

'Don't be a fool, Essie.'

If he said anything else I didn't hear it. Lifting the reins I gave Duke the mightiest kick I have ever given a horse in my life and he plunged through the water and out towards the breakers. Within a few feet he was swimming.

'That's the boy.'

As I spoke to him I sensed a shadow rise before me. I leant forward and clung to Duke's neck as the wave engulfed us. The force was so great it knocked me from my seat. I tumbled and fell, swirling through the water like a piece of flotsam. My lungs burnt as I held my breath, hotter and hotter until I knew I could hold on no longer. This was not the way it was meant to be, not the way my dream had unfolded. As my head began to spin, something gripped my hand and my arm was yanked upward until I broke the surface, choking and spluttering. The shock of the air sent me reeling backwards.

'It's all right Essie, I've got you.' Samuel pushed me through the water and up onto Duke's back. Somehow he had swum out and found us. He climbed up behind me, cradling me in his arms as he took the reins. We were out beyond the breakers now, and although the sea was seething, Duke swam on, out towards the stricken vessel. We were closer now and could see more clearly. The boat was almost completely submerged, but clinging to its railing, his back towards us, was a man.

'Hello there,' I called, not knowing if any sound would even come from my mouth. But he must have heard because he turned, his eyes white with fear.

'Oh god, please save me, please.' He let go of the rail and immediately began to thrash, sinking beneath the surface.

'Come on, Duke.' Samuel and I willed rather than pushed the horse forward to where the man had gone under. A hand seized my wrist, so ferociously that had Samuel not been holding me firmly around the waist, I would surely have been pitched back into the sea. The drowning man erupted from the depths, babbling, his words incomprehensible. We both jumped into the water beside him and heaved him onto the horse.

'Hold on,' Samuel instructed, but the poor fellow was only partly conscious, so between us we wrapped his arms around

Duke's neck before we both clambered up behind him, myself in the middle and Samuel perched at the back, enveloping both the man and myself in his arms. I held the reins and turned Duke back towards the shore.

Although I thought myself completely numb already, as I held the man in front of me the iciness of his body seemed to seep into mine. My teeth chattered uncontrollably until the noise of them banging together drowned out the fury of the ocean and the wailing of the wind. Samuel gripped his legs around mine as we let the force of the tide carry us forward, Duke's shoulders rolling beneath us. The man made no sound, save for a faint moan as we were lifted by the motion of the waves.

Somehow we made it to the shallows still clinging to the horse and to each other. When his feet found the sand, Duke hauled himself out, stumbling but righting himself again as we fell sidewards. Samuel and I stood, each grabbing one of the man's arms and dragging him up above the tideline before we fell into a heap beside him. I closed my eyes and felt the firmness of the shore beneath my feet and heard myself laugh. We were safe. Alive. I rolled over and took Samuel's hand, forgetting for a moment about the man we had rescued, not caring whether or not he was alive. Caring only that we had survived the tempest. I lay my head on his chest and felt it heaving beneath my cheek before I crawled across the sand to where the man lay motionless.

Was he dead? Had we almost lost our own lives to pull a body from the sea rather than a living human being? Feeling my way in the dark I turned his head and rolled his torso sidewards. A groan was followed by a cough and then a gush as he spewed mouthfuls of salty water onto the sand. I sat back and waited for the fit to end, relieved that our efforts had not been in vain. Samuel lay there, still panting.

'He's alive,' I whispered.

The man pushed himself up onto one elbow. 'You saved my life,' he croaked. 'Thank you, thank you.' He began to sob and I let him be. In reality it had been Duke who saved the man and I looked around for him now but could see nothing through the coal-black night.

'Please god, let him have taken himself home.' I blocked out the thought that the ordeal had been too much for him and he had gone off to die as animals sometimes do.

I don't know how long we sat there on the beach in the darkness, wet to the bone, but at some point Samuel stood.

'We can't stay here all night,' he said, 'we'll catch our deaths of cold if we haven't already.' He crouched beside the man, who had not spoken a word since his sobbing fit ceased. 'Do you think you can stand, mister?'

The fellow turned over and pushed himself onto all fours in reply as Samuel and I each put a hand under one of his arms, lifting him to his feet. The journey uphill to the house was the longest and hardest I can ever remember. My frozen feet had lost the will to move and my sodden clothes were like a coat of armour. Samuel urged us on but we stopped every few minutes to rest and adjust the man's arms around our shoulders. He helped as best he was able but the effort of the walk after the trial he had just been through in the ocean made the going hard.

At the house we dragged ourselves into the lounge room. I left Samuel with the man while I ran upstairs to wake my mother.

When I rushed into her room she sat up in bed, fumbling with the lamp switch. 'Esther, my lord, what's the matter, you're dripping with water, where have you been?'

Water streamed from my clothes and pooled onto the floor around my feet. In a jumble of words I tried to explain what had happened. 'There's a man, downstairs, with Samuel.'

'Samuel, in the lounge? But that's not allowed.'

'Oh Mum, for god's sake just come now. Please!'

She jumped from bed and pulled a robe around herself before following me downstairs, where I rushed to the linen press and grabbed some towels. To say that Mum is not good in a crisis is putting it somewhat mildly, but she could see that Samuel and I were almost frozen solid, as was the man, so she pulled herself together enough to take charge.

I must have glazed over a little at that point for the remainder of the night passed in a blur. I remember Mum helping me out of my clothes and wrapping me in a blanket. Whether she changed the man into some of Dad's clothes or instructed Samuel to, I can't recall. I remember sitting in the kitchen sipping hot tea, Samuel in the chair beside me, for the first time in his life being permitted to stay in the house for an hour or two while he thawed out. I have a vague memory of Dr Fisher arriving and looking into my eyes with a small torch before sending me off to bed with a hot water bottle. At what point Samuel left or how I made it up the stairs, I do not know, but I woke well after lunchtime to a bowl of chicken soup on a tray and Mum's hand on my forehead.

'I'm fine,' I said, opening my eyes and smiling.

She sighed with relief. 'I've brought you something to eat.'

'How is he?' I asked, meaning Samuel.

'He seems fine, although he's weak and shaken. His business partner was on the boat with him. The police have sent out a boat to search for him with no luck.' She settled the tray on my lap as I looked out the window. The storm had passed but clouds still

*bruised the sky. 'He wants to speak to you as soon as you feel up
to it. To thank you for saving his life.' Her voice began to shake.
'Esther, you could have died. What were you thinking?'*

*I thought for a moment of telling her of my dream but I knew
she would think I was mad. 'I don't know. I just knew that I had
to save him. If it wasn't for Samuel, we both would have drowned.'
The memory of Samuel pulling me from the ocean just as I was
about to give up made my chest ache all over again. 'Is he all right?'
I tried to keep my voice light, to hide my desperation.*

'He's fine. Strong as an ox, that boy.'

'And Duke?'

*'Very weak. Refusing to eat. But Samuel is keeping an eye on
him. Your dad's on his way back from Sydney. Now eat up, and
when you feel better, get dressed and come downstairs.'*

*Despite my layers of blankets I was still chilled to my core but
perhaps it was more the thought of the icy sea than anything else.
The soup warmed me a little, at least enough to be able to pick up
my pen and write.*

*My mind is whirling with the strangeness of it all. How is it
possible for a dream such as this to come true?*

Miranda stared at the page even after she read the final
words. It was true, Esther had saved a man from the sea
on horseback, just as the newspaper clipping had described,
and just as she'd dreamt she would. This same woman was
somehow connected to her mother and in turn to herself
– why else would her photo be hidden away in the closet?
Miranda was getting closer to piecing together the puzzle.
It took all her self-restraint to place the red ribbon marker

between the pages and close the diary, but she had to find out how Esther was before the day grew any older.

⁓

The fog had cleared, leaving the sky a fresh cornflower blue. Buster followed her out to the bathroom and sat by the door, ears up, watching her every move as she dressed and grabbed her bag.

'You can't come this time, matey,' she said. He wandered over to his bed and sat down with a grunt.

All the way back to the car, Miranda's mind buzzed with possibilities. If Esther really was her grandmother, why did her own daughter think she was dead? What had happened to Samuel? When had Essie married Leonard? And more urgently, what if Esther died now, before Miranda had a chance of finding out? Questions tangled themselves into knots as she drove back into town and cruised into the caravan park. It had been five days now since she'd arrived in Pelican Point and she had no intention of leaving just yet. Certainly not while Esther was in hospital. If she could just have a few more days here, she'd be able to sort things out, including herself. It wasn't the ideal time to be taking more leave from work – she felt sick at the thought of telling Todd his wunderkind wouldn't be back in the office for a few more days. But she simply couldn't leave until she'd gotten to the bottom of the Esther mystery. And there was nothing stopping her from telling James she needed a little more time.

Other than your own cowardice.

Back in the cabin she picked up her phone. A list of messages appeared, obscuring the photo of her and James clinking champagne glasses. Three of the texts were from him. She read the first one: *Hi babe, guess you have no reception. Call me when you can.* The second: *Hope everything is okay. Call me.* And the third: *I know you said you'd be resting for a few days but can you try and find some reception and phone me so I know you're okay?* He was right – she should call him, he was probably worried, but she knew he'd be asking her when she was coming home. As cowardly as it was, she decided to send him a text. *Hi, all fine here, please don't worry. Will be home in a couple of days. x*

At least that would buy her some extra time. But right now she needed to find out how Esther was doing. She took a scrap of paper from her pocket and dialled the number the ambo had scribbled on it yesterday.

As she waited for someone to pick up, she watched an ibis poke around on the shoreline of the lake, its long, curved beak dipping in and out of the sand.

'Southern Region Hospital. Can I help you?'

Miranda gave the woman Esther's name and asked how she was.

'Are you a relative?'

'No, but I'm a close friend.'

Sort of.

Classical music filled her ears while she waited for the woman to return to the phone. The ibis had found a worm and tipped back its head, gobbling the creature down whole before moving further along the bank to continue foraging.

'Mrs Wilson isn't doing too well, I'm afraid.' The nurse had a singsong voice that was obviously well cultivated. 'She tried to get out of bed this morning and had a fall. They've settled her back down but the doctor has a no-visitors order – other than immediate family.'

Miranda flattened her lips and glared at the ibis. 'She doesn't have any relatives, so can't I come and visit?'

'I'm afraid not. But feel free to call again to check on her progress.' There was a click as the line went dead.

'Urgh!' She kicked at the railing on the tiny verandah and the bird, which had come right up to the edge of the grass in front of the cabin, spread its wings and shot up into the sky. Miranda had stopped short of saying she was Esther's granddaughter in case the hospital staff mentioned it to her. She had to be absolutely sure before she said anything but now Esther's condition was making the whole thing more urgent. Dropping into the plastic garden chair on the small verandah she put the phone on the table and gazed across the rippled surface of the water. Things were not going well. What was she even doing here anyway, running around on some wild goose chase to prove that someone she had never met was her grandmother? Why did it even matter?

It matters because you want to 'fix' your mother.

She gave a wry smile at the voice's wisdom. It was right. All her life she'd wanted to mend not only her mother but their relationship. Kathleen's unpredictable mental state had always been a wedge between them. There were times when they could actually sit and have a decent conversation without Miranda being constantly worried about saying or doing the wrong thing, but they were rare. And when her mother was at her worst, days would go by where she would walk around in a daze or lock herself in her bedroom. As a child those had been the times when Miranda would sit by herself in the kitchen and cry with longing – the longing to have a mother who loved her and who she could love back. It was only her father's steady constancy that had saved her, and school became her escape. Things had improved slightly as she grew older, and she'd hoped the wedding preparations would bring them closer together. If anything, they'd made it worse. Her mother had withdrawn and come up with any number of excuses not to be involved. And then there'd been that argument that had brought the isolation and confusion of her childhood rushing back. If she could prove that Esther was really her grandmother, if she could reunite Kathleen with her lost mother, maybe there was a chance that those old wounds could be healed. For all of them.

She sighed and stared out at the smoky lake. Since she'd come here the world back at home seemed like a distant planet, one that she'd journeyed away from and had no real desire to return to. Despite the dramas with Esther, there was a sense of peace here that was missing from her life in the city. And although she hated to admit it, she hadn't missed James.

The phone rang and she almost jumped out of her skin. She looked at the caller ID on the screen. Belle.

'Hey, Mirry – what's happening?'

'Hi, Belle, it's good to hear your voice.' Where to start? 'Well, Esther, the woman I found at the beach, has gone to hospital – long story – but I think I'm getting closer to finding proof that we're related.'

'So what have you found out, Sherlock Holmes?' Miranda pictured Belle grinning and smiled herself.

'I think she's definitely my grandmother.'

'Seriously? Did you ask her?'

Guilt bloomed like a rash across Miranda's cheeks. 'No. I found a whole pile of old diaries in her house. There was an entry about the sea rescue, the same as in the newspaper clipping I found.'

'Shit. Why don't you talk to her about it?'

'She's too sick. I want to find out more first. I'm going to stay on here for a bit, see what else I can find out.'

'Oh, okay. And you've told James?'

'Yeah. Well, I texted him and said I'd be home in a few more days.'

'Right. But you didn't ring him or tell him what you're up to?'

'No, I didn't.'

'Are you sure it's only this thing with your grandmother keeping you down there?'

'Absolutely. Look I'd better go. I need to check out of here – I'm going to stay out at Esther's and mind her dog.'

'While you dig up some more dirt, right?'

'Maybe.'

'You take care, my friend, and keep me posted.'

'Will do. Bye.'

The conversation had brought more of those niggling questions to the surface. Was Belle right? Was she using Esther as an excuse to stay away? Was her apprehension about the wedding more than just bridal nerves? That last thought made her stomach flip. Shoving her phone in her pocket, she went back inside, packed up her things and deposited them all in the car. She needed to stay focused. The sooner she could prove she was Esther's granddaughter, the sooner they'd allow her to visit. There was someone else who might want to know how the patient was doing, and that's where she was heading right after she checked out.

⟶

This morning's fog had cleared to a day of perfect autumn sunshine. The sound of the ocean echoed in the distance as she drove out of town. She pressed the button for the roof and thrilled at the sudden rush of cool air. Her hair was pulled back in a messy sort of ponytail and she wasn't wearing a scrap of make-up, but even so she felt fresh and alive. Perhaps it was the scent of the sea or the sense of space.

Or the prospect of seeing Vincent again?

She had to admit, once again the voice was right. Since they'd first met on the beach, that disarming smile and those coffee-coloured eyes had popped into her head more than once. And yesterday, he'd been so sweet and gentle with Esther. But there was no point getting carried away with some schoolgirl crush. After all, she hardly knew the man. And she was really only driving out there to let him know about Esther.

Before too long she found herself back at the gates of Garewangga. Would they be locked? She pulled up and peered over the dashboard. No padlock today, but there was a buzzer on the post and her finger hovered over it uncertainly.

For god's sake, just press the damned thing.

Before she could argue back she pushed her finger against the buzzer and the gates creaked open. Oh well, no point looking a gift horse in the mouth. She drove on through and made her way once again through the paddocks and down the hill. The place really was spectacular. She pictured Esther here as a girl, riding with Samuel, laughing, young and in love.

The tyres crackled over the red gravel drive and she pulled up by the small stone cottage to the side of the main house. This was probably the old stable, where Samuel had stayed, where he and Esther had first kissed. Again there was no one around. Miranda made her way across to the yard, where the grey horse was still standing. It greeted her with a whinny as she approached.

'Hi there, sweetie, do you remember me?' The horse nuzzled against her hand as she patted it. Its earthy smell took her back to her years as a teenager navigating the trails at the riding school with her friend Rochelle. She'd loved just sitting back and letting the horse meander down the rocky hills, sloshing their way across the creek and then giving the horse its head as they cantered along the home stretch. That intoxicating cocktail of fear and exhilaration rushing through her veins was one she hadn't experienced for such a long time. When Rochelle moved schools in Year 10 and Miranda became more focused on her studies, horseriding became something that she used to do once upon a time. Funny now to think that she'd ever dreamt of one day owning a horse herself.

'Looks like you've got yourself a friend there.'

She jumped at the sound of Vincent's voice. 'Oh, hi. What's his name?'

'It's a her. And her name is Zena. She's had a slight bout of colic, hence her confinement. But she's fine now.'

Miranda gave the horse another pat, conscious of Vincent's proximity as he stepped up beside her.

'Have you heard how Esther is doing?' There was an authentic concern in his voice that made her feel at ease.

'Yeah, I rang the hospital. She's not too good. Tried to get up this morning and had a fall. They've sedated her and said no visitors.'

Vincent shook his head. 'Stubborn old girl. Still, I guess she's in the best place.'

'They said only relatives are allowed in. Is there anyone other than your boss as far as you know?'

'Nope. He's it, I think. And there's no love lost between them, so he won't be paying her a visit any time soon.' He frowned and gave her a curious look. 'You're pretty concerned about her, considering you hardly know her.'

Miranda gave an exaggerated shrug. 'Just sad to think she's all alone in the world.'

'It is when she's sick like this. Normally she likes her isolation. I don't know the story but I get the impression that whatever has happened in her life has made her pretty wary of people.'

'So, anyway, I just wanted to let you know how she was doing and thank you for all your help yesterday.'

'Not a problem. What are you up to now?'

'Not much. I'll probably just head back to Esther's and hang out with Buster.'

Vincent smiled. 'Well, I'm about to go for a ride.' He gestured towards the yard, where a bay horse was tied up to the railing. 'Getting this horse back in training for a client. I need to do a bit of groundwork with him, then I'll be saddling him up. Zena here could do with a bit of exercise, if you're interested.'

Miranda looked at him and then at the horse. 'It's been a long time since I've ridden.'

'Like riding a bike,' he grinned. 'I promise.'

Just do it.

'Okay. Why not?'

'I won't be long with Levi. Come watch if you like.'

Vincent sauntered over to the fence and unfastened the horse's lead rope from some baling twine. Miranda's eyes drifted to his hips and the way his butt filled out those jeans so perfectly.

He led the horse out into the centre of the yard, held up his left arm and pointed as he swung the end of the rope with his right hand. The horse moved off slowly, circling around in what could barely be called a trot.

'Up,' Vincent called, spinning the rope a little faster, and the horse took off, tossing his head and kicking his feet out behind him. 'This is his way of saying he doesn't want to do anything.'

'Really?'

'His owner lets him get away with it. Stops as soon as he starts pig-rooting. Best thing is to just push him through it.'

Vincent stood firm and strained against the power of the horse, who was charging around the circle, throwing in a buck every now and then for good measure. The whole process was making Miranda feel dizzy, so she focused on a spot directly across from her where a white cockatoo was pulling small pieces off a pine cone it had dragged from one of the trees. Gradually the beating of hooves against the black sand slowed as Levi calmed down and fell into a more regular pace.

'Good boy,' Vincent called, lifting his left hand again.

The horse came to an abrupt stop and turned to face the centre of the circle.

'Right-o, other side.' Vincent repeated the process, the horse putting up less of a fight this time and once again halting on command before turning to his trainer, head low, and licking his lips. 'That's more like it. Come on then.'

Vincent stood completely still as the horse took a few steps toward him, and then followed close behind as he turned and walked the length of the arena.

'Wow, that's amazing.' Miranda caught up with the two of them back at the fence, where Vincent was now hauling a saddle onto Levi's back.

He laughed. 'Not really, just basic groundwork. You have to get them listening to you. Make sure you're the one giving the orders, not the other way around. Horses are honest – they tell you how they're feeling if you listen carefully enough. We need to be just as honest with them.'

And with ourselves.

She blinked the voice away and watched as Vincent finished getting the horse ready, slipping the bit into his mouth and securing the bridle, all the time talking to him and giving him the occasional rub.

'Here you go.' He handed her the reins and headed back over to where the grey horse waited patiently. 'This one doesn't need any lunging. She's pure sugar, aren't you, my girl?'

'I hope so,' laughed Miranda.

'You'll be fine. Zena here will look after you.'

Within a few minutes the horse was saddled up and ready
to go. Vincent tipped his head and waved his hand in a bow.
'Your steed awaits, madame.'

They swapped horses and Miranda sidled up next to the
mare. She put her foot in the stirrup and counted silently to
three before she tried to pull herself up, but only succeeded in
losing her balance. Vincent grabbed her around the waist as
she toppled backwards and broke into a fit of giggles. 'I told
you it's been a while.' His hands were resting on her hips
and she could feel the warmth of his palms through the light
cotton of her shirt. Her knees shook as she straightened up.

'I'll give you a boost,' he said, and before she knew what
was happening he'd bent down, grabbed her lower leg and
hoisted her up into the saddle. She picked up the reins and
gave herself a shake. It was a relief to be seated and have a
chance to pull herself together.

'Ready?' Vincent asked, settling into his saddle.

She nodded and squeezed her legs against Zena's sides.
The mare responded by gently moving off behind Vincent
and Levi, out past the yards and across the hill. Miranda
thought again of Esther and Samuel. Neither she nor Vincent
spoke and it felt completely natural to be in the middle of
nowhere, riding a horse for the first time in years with a
virtual stranger. She let her body move with the horse's gait
and looked out at the scene before her. It was as if there was
no division between the earth and the sky and the sea, and
she and Vincent and the horses were a part of it all. The hill
began to fall away and a rough track appeared. Miranda
shifted her weight back, letting Zena find her own path
down the steep descent. As they wound their way towards

the beach, the hum of the ocean grew louder. She closed her eyes for just a few seconds and let it vibrate through her entire body until every fibre of her being was buzzing. When she opened them again, the horses had stepped onto the sand. Water gurgled onto the shore and Zena followed Levi into the shallows, where the two horses and their riders sat and looked out towards the horizon.

'It's beautiful,' whispered Miranda. Was this where Esther had crashed through the waves to rescue Leonard?

'It is that,' Vincent said. 'Feel like a canter?'

There was a devilish look in his eye that sparked Miranda's courage. 'Why not?'

They turned the horses around and loosened the reins. Zena moved gently at first, and then picked up speed behind Levi. Miranda sat deep into the saddle, giving herself up to the movement of the horse, remembering what it felt like to fly.

Esther

Escape. That's what I need to do. Make myself so small they won't see me and then I can run, far away where they won't find me. Duke, I need to get to Duke. Climb on his back and gallop away as far as we can go, down the hills, across the sand, splash through the waves, foam bubbling at our legs. Moving together faster and faster away from them. Don't look back, don't turn around, don't look them in the eyes or they'll lock you back in the room, tie you up so you can't move, so you can't even breathe.

That's all you have to do. Remember to breathe.

Miranda

It was late afternoon. Miranda walked the track back to Esther's. The insides of her thighs were already feeling the effects of the ride, so there was a good chance she wouldn't be able to walk tomorrow, but she smiled again now as she thought of the afternoon, of the euphoria of cantering along the beach and, she had to admit to herself, of Vincent. As corny as it sounded, she felt like she'd known him for years rather than hours. They'd hardly spoken a word while they were riding and yet there was a feeling of easy companionship between them that she couldn't explain. Not to mention the way her skin tingled when he'd brushed against her or the way her pulse had raced when he hoisted her onto the horse and helped her off again. No, she certainly wasn't going to think about any of that – Vincent was the sort of complication she really didn't need right now.

Or maybe he's just the sort you do need?

She trod her way along the path, doing her best to ignore the dispute playing itself out in her brain. At the bottom of the hill she stopped to rest and gazed up towards the cottage. As run-down and weathered as it was, there was something about the old place – a real estate agent would probably call it rustic charm – that made her want to spruce it up and give it some TLC. Just as she wanted to do with Esther. The thought of her lying in that hospital without a person in the world who cared about her fired Miranda's indignation. It was time to get on with proving who she really was. And that meant reading more of the diaries.

Buster leapt from his bed and charged towards her as soon as she stepped through the door.

'Hello there, my friend. It's good to see you too!' He really was the sweetest thing, cute in an ugly sort of way. He rolled onto his back, legs in the air, and she gave him a good rub all over before letting him out for a run. A rumbling stomach drew her to the fridge. There certainly wouldn't be a three-course meal on the menu tonight, but there were enough bits and pieces to fill a hole – cheese, tomatoes, some leftover soup and a loaf of slightly stale bread that would be perfectly fine once it was toasted. She hummed as she made herself an early dinner, the sound of the ocean in the background harmonising with her untitled song. This must be the upside of living on your own, she thought, eating whenever you please, suiting yourself, enjoying the peace and quiet, answering to no one. As Esther did. But of course there would be the loneliness to contend with. Could I do it? she wondered, leaving the question hanging while she called Buster back inside and sat down to devour her gourmet meal.

Diary time. Where had she gotten up to again? The rescue, of course, how could she forget? She pictured the young lovers Esther and Samuel, wishing that their story would have a happy ending, even when she knew it hadn't. A sudden chill rippled through her body and she grabbed her cardigan from the back of the lounge, pulling it around her shoulders as she started to read.

15 November 1942

I am SO angry, more than angry. I am furious! The South Coast Times published the story today and there was not even a mention of Samuel. They refer to him only as 'the station hand', even though I told the reporter his name more than once and tried to get him to speak to Samuel in person. Dad discouraged it, saying he was too busy working. The way the story is written makes it sound like I was solely responsible for the rescue. If it wasn't for Samuel both Mr Clarke and I would have drowned. Are they stupid? How hard is it to get the facts right?

When Mum first showed me the paper this morning I was completely speechless. They make me out to be some kind of saint and mention nothing of the true hero. I tore the page from the paper and walked out the door, slamming it as hard as I could, my mother's remonstrations echoing in the kitchen behind me. Samuel was at the shoeing shed.

'Essie, what's wrong?' he called.

If I had been thinking more clearly I probably wouldn't have told him about the report. He knew the paper had visited and taken photos, but as he wasn't interviewed he took no more interest in the whole affair, other than to ask after Mr Clarke's welfare. When I spoke to him about his own fearlessness he shrugged and said simply that he did what any man would have done and that was that. When he saw me march out into the yard in such a state he took the paper from me and read the headline out loud.

'Courageous Young Woman Rescues Storm Survivor on Horseback.'

He continued on, reading quietly to himself while I patted Archie, the horse tied up waiting to be shod, and watched his face for a reaction. His expression didn't change.

'Well, they got one thing right.' He smiled at me. 'You are a beauty. And brave too.'

'But aren't you mad that they haven't even mentioned your name? It should be you receiving that award, not me! I don't want their stupid medal.'

He took a step towards me as he folded the page in half. 'It's enough for me to know I did what I could, Essie. That a man was saved from dying and that you're alive and well. Getting a medal isn't going to make any difference.'

'It's just not fair, the way they treat you. This place would fall apart without you and they know it. Dad should have had the guts to tell that reporter to interview you and to insist that you be awarded too but he's no better than the rest of them.' My eyes watered at the injustice of it all. I lifted my hand to his face but a noise behind me made me start.

'Esther, I need you in the house.' The voice was soft, yet stern.

I took the paper from Samuel and spun around to face my mum, who gave me a questioning look before following me back inside.

'I hope you're not encouraging Samuel in the wrong way,' she said as the door clicked shut.

'What do you mean?' Of course I knew exactly what she meant, but I wanted her to say it, not speak in innuendo.

She met my eyes and her tone changed, became gentler. 'I've seen the way you two look at each other, Esther. Don't lead him on. He's a pleasant young man and a good worker, but you know as well as I do that there's no possibility of anything more than friendship. I think it would be better if you spent less time out with the horses and more time concentrating on your music.'

The whole time she spoke I stared straight at her, my chest heaving with anger. I wanted to blurt out that it was too late, that I was already in love, that nothing would stop Samuel and me being together, but I knew it was better to play the game, at least for now.

'I don't know what you're talking about,' I said, forcing myself to speak calmly. 'I just don't think it's right that the newspapers and the police – and you and Dad – aren't giving him the recognition he deserves. The colour of your skin shouldn't make a difference, especially if you've saved someone's life.'

I flounced out of the room and up the stairs, deciding not to risk further argument and the possibility of my emotions getting the better of me.

Once this whole rescue drama is out of the way, I need to make some sort of plan. If there is no hope of my parents allowing Samuel and me to marry, then we will have to find another way to be together.

29 November 1942

Today Mr Clarke returned, looking a great deal better than the last time he was here. It was a shock to answer the door and see him standing there beaming down at me. He was wearing a suit and looked quite dapper. Apparently Dad was expecting him, as he rushed downstairs and threw an arm around his shoulder, shaking his hand and welcoming him like a long-lost friend. He asked me to put the kettle on and bring the two of them some tea.

I really could have done without it, having planned to take Duke out for a ride. For the last few weeks my mum has been doing her best to keep me busy and away from any sort of work on the farm. Of course I know why, but it hasn't stopped me sneaking over to the cottage a few times in the late afternoon when Samuel has finished work. Those few times have been brief but nonetheless blissful. I can't describe the way he makes me feel and the desire that ignites inside me every time I even think of him.

I gazed through the window as I made the tea. The sea was a solid sheet of indigo beneath a sky the exact colour of the hydrangeas in our back garden. Duke and the other horses grazed in the front paddock, their coats gleaming in the morning sunshine. It was such a waste to be indoors playing kitchen maid. What was Mr Clarke doing here anyway? I arranged some cake on one of the good platters and loaded up the tray. As I was just about to step onto the verandah I hesitated, listening through the part-open door to the men's conversation.

'Arthur, I wouldn't be doing it myself if there wasn't a need for it. People can't get what they want through the government channels. You know how strict they are with the rationing. There's a market out there for good-quality meat and people prepared to pay for it.' The tip of Mr Clarke's cigarette glowed.

'I know what you're saying, Leonard, but it goes against the grain. The country is at war, my own son is away at the front suffering god knows what sort of hell. It seems wrong to be making a profit out of the whole situation.'

'You wouldn't be hurting anyone. In fact you'd be making their

*lives more comfortable. You have a good supply of beef and there's
people out there who want it. It's as simple as that.'*

'And it's against the law.'

*Mr Clarke laughed. 'Only technically, my friend. The police turn
a blind eye to it. Most of them are profiting from it themselves,
don't you worry.' He lowered his voice, and for a minute I thought
he must have suspected I was listening, so I took a step back, still
straining to hear. 'Look, Arthur. I'm indebted to you. Your daughter
saved my life and I want to do something to repay the favour. You
can make yourself a good deal of money out of this venture without
having to lift a finger. No one will get hurt, people will have their
stomachs full, and your wallet will be a lot fatter.'*

*'Well, I'll have to think about it. But it does sound bloody
enticing when you put it like that.' A chair scraping on the tiles
brought me to attention. 'Where's that daughter of mine? Esther!'*

*'Coming.' The cups rattled as I hurried onto the verandah. Mr
Clarke stood and took the tray from me. As handsome as he is,
there's something that unnerves me a little about him. I could feel
his eyes on me as I poured the tea, and when I looked across at
him and smiled, the corner of his mouth twisted a little before he
looked away.*

*'I have something for you, Esther,' he said, reaching into the
inside pocket of his jacket and pulling out a rectangular velvet box.
'A small token of my sincere thanks for what you did that night.'
An ember of anger smouldered inside of me as I held the box in my
hand, thinking of Samuel's forgotten part, but I knew this was
not the time to let it blaze, so I accepted his offering. When I saw
what was inside I was completely dumbstruck. A string of pearls
with a small pendant in the shape of a horseshoe nestled between*

amethysts, and what looked to be a diamond suspended from the middle.

'Oh my god, that's it, the necklace.' Miranda tapped her finger against the pages of the diary. 'Leonard gave it to Esther as a gift!'

'Do you like it?' he asked as I stood there, my mouth gaping.

'It's beautiful. But I can't accept it, I really can't.' I closed the lid and held the box out towards him.

'Nonsense. I insist,' he said, opening the box and unfastening the necklace. He stood then, and before I could protest further, placed it around my neck. The clasp snapped shut. 'A beautiful necklace for a beautiful woman. I thought the horseshoe was a perfect thank you.'

'That's very generous of you, Leonard,' said my father. 'What do you say, Esther?'

'Thank you, of course. You really shouldn't have. It looks so . . .' I stumbled, trying not to appear rude but completely flummoxed by the gift.

Mr Clarke laughed. 'Expensive? Never you mind about that. I got it from a jeweller friend of mine I ran into down at the wharves. He gave it to me for a very good price, but it is a fine piece, I must say, and it looks particularly good on you, Esther.'

I could feel myself turning red at his compliments. The diamond rested just at the top of my cleavage and felt cool beneath my fingertips.

'You can wear it at the recital tonight,' said Dad. 'You must stay, Leonard. Esther's playing her violin at a concert the women have organised for the war effort. You'll be impressed.'

'Brave, beautiful and talented. I'm impressed already.' Mr Clarke stubbed his cigarette out in the ashtray on the table, the smoke spiralling into the air.

'I'd better go and practise,' I said, seeing an escape route. 'Thank you so much, Mr Clarke, it's very kind of you.'

'My pleasure, Esther. And please, call me Leonard.'

I left the two men to drink their tea, relieved to step back inside the house.

'Must've cost you a pretty penny,' I heard Dad say.

'Nothing I couldn't afford. You'll find that out if you come in on our little venture, Arthur.'

I raced upstairs to my bedroom and looked in the mirror. It has been a long while since I've had anything new, times having been tough these last couple of years, and I must admit it felt good to be wearing something so stunning. I touched the diamond again and turned towards the window, where it caught the light. Mr Clarke – Leonard – was certainly not going to hear of me refusing the gift and Dad seemed very pleased at his gesture.

I'm not exactly sure what they were talking about when I overheard them this morning. What sort of scheme is it that Leonard is involved in that allows him to make so much money? Whatever it is, I hope Dad knows what he is doing. But if there's money to be made I'm sure he won't say no.

12 December 1942

These last few days have been the worst of my life.

I arrived home from my Christmas shopping trip to Sydney on Thursday desperate to see Samuel. As soon as I could I made an excuse to get out to the stables, ostensibly to check on Duke, but as much as I adore him, it was someone else I was looking for.

The yards and the stable were empty, so I assumed he was out on the property somewhere working. It was already after three o'clock, so although it felt like I would burst if I didn't see him soon, I knew that he could be anywhere and it was better to wait until he returned.

Just as I was walking from the yards my dad appeared. The look on his face stopped me in my tracks. Thinking it must be bad news about Martin from the front I stopped and waited for him to speak. How wrong I was!

'If you're looking for Samuel, you won't find him,' he said, his tone sombre.

'What do you mean? Where is he? Has he had an accident?' My questions fell over each other as I rushed to comprehend.

'He's enlisted. Left the day before yesterday.'

I heard myself laugh. 'Enlisted? In the war?'

Dad nodded.

'But you secured a dispensation.'

'He came and saw me the day after you left, said he felt he had to do his duty and asked if I would give him my blessing, which I did.'

A storm of disbelief brewed inside me but I had to remember this was my father I was speaking to and I chose my words carefully. 'I don't believe it. He wouldn't go without saying goodbye, without telling me. We were . . . we were friends.'

Dad took a step towards me. 'From what your mother tells me, you were more than just friends.'

My mouth was dry as dirt and I couldn't speak.

'It's for the best,' he continued. 'Now he's gone you can get rid of any foolish notions you might have had about him. Concentrate on your music and find yourself a decent fellow to settle down with.'

At his last words something exploded inside me and I couldn't hold my tongue. 'I don't want to find a nice young man, or any other sort of man,' I screamed at him, anger sparking my nerve. 'I'll wait for Samuel and when he returns we'll be married.'

The force of his hand across my cheek almost knocked me sidewards. 'Don't you ever let me hear you say that again. And don't you dare tell anyone outside this family of your ridiculous infatuation. No daughter of mine will be marrying a black. I should never have let you spend all that time teaching him to read, or riding out with him as often as you did. I only have myself to blame but I've fixed the situation now. Don't bother mooning around waiting for him. There's a good chance he won't even return from the fighting, and if he does he certainly won't be coming back here.'

He turned towards the house, leaving me standing in the middle of the garden, numb with confusion. But as his words sank in, I realised his meaning.

'You forced him to enlist, didn't you?' The spite in my voice shocked me as much as him. He wheeled around.

'There was a recruitment drive, and I suggested that if he wanted to sign up, I wouldn't stop him. And that is the last I want to hear of it.'

I'm not sure how long I stood there, hunched over the rail of the horse pen, but at some point I began to shake with cold as the afternoon shadows fell across the yard. Even though I knew deep inside that what my dad had told me was true, that Samuel had really gone, I had to see it for myself. I stumbled to the stable and found Duke, lifting the bridle to his mouth, focusing on every movement to keep myself from thinking. Not bothering to waste time on a saddle, I hoisted myself onto his back and within a few seconds we were galloping out of the yard and into the paddocks.

I rode across the hills as I had done so many times before, but now it was dread that pumped the blood through my veins, not excitement. Duke knew the way so well that I didn't have to direct him. At the cottage I jumped from his back, looping the reins around his neck, then staggered up the steps and flung open the door. The neat emptiness of the place made me falter. The bed was perfectly made, as it always was, but there were no coats hanging on the hooks and no boots lined up beside the dresser. Already knowing what I would find inside the wardrobe, I pulled it open and stared in horror at the empty shelves. My hand flew to my mouth as I stifled a cry.

I knew he'd wanted to go to war, to be a man – he'd told me a hundred times that if they would just let him go and do his duty, he would do it proudly. But how could he just leave like this without telling me? My dad must have done more than give him his blessing, he would have arranged the whole thing, forced him to leave immediately.

I slumped to the floor and lay there in the dying afternoon light until finally I uncurled myself and stood.

That's when I saw it, sticking out from the pocket of his work-coat hanging on the back of the door, a flash of white. I pulled the envelope from the pocket and held it up, squinting to read in the dim light one single, lonely word: Essie.

I traced each carefully written letter of my name as I heard his voice whispering it over and over, until I thought my heart would break.

I rode home in the almost dark, the letter pressed against my breast. My dad tried to speak to me on my return, and my mum too, but I ignored them and have remained in my room. That was two days ago, and I have only gone downstairs to eat when they have insisted, refusing to speak to them and returning here to sit and stare out the window and sleep. It's only when I sleep that I escape the anguish.

His letter is tucked inside my pillowslip, but I no longer have to take it out to read. I have memorised it word for sorry word. He says he will think of me every minute, write as soon as he can, and has promised to return for me when the war is over. Until that day all I can do is hope and pray.

19 April 1943

It's been four months now since Samuel went off to war and there's been no word from him, or at least not as far as I can find out. When he left, Dad forbade me to mention his name again. He's such a bloody hypocrite – they both are. Many times at the dinner table he used to talk about what a hardworking, upright young man Samuel was, how he was more than ready to take on the manager's position, how he was so pleasant and amiable. That was all until he found out his daughter was in love with a black man. I can just imagine what he would have said to Samuel to persuade him to enlist. It sickens me to think about how patriotic he was – going off to fight for a country that barely recognises him as a human being and certainly doesn't consider him a citizen. Every day I pray to God to keep him safe and bring him home. Last week when Dad was away on business – again – I rode out to the camp on the outskirts of town. Samuel has an aunty there who raised him from a boy when his own mother died. He never knew his father – some white mongrel who got what he wanted and disappeared. I'd never been to the settlement before. To see the conditions the people live in brought tears to my eyes. The houses were nothing more than a stretch of broken-down humpies. Children played in the dirt beside dogs who greeted me with bared teeth and growls. At first I didn't think there were any adults there, until a voice yelled at the dogs to be quiet. Then a woman appeared from behind one of the huts.

'Whaddya want?'

'I'm looking for Aunty Beryl.' It was the only name Samuel had mentioned.

'Well, here I am.' The woman's stony face broke into a beaming smile. 'What can I do for ya?'

By this time I'd dismounted and tied Duke to a post. 'I'm Esther, a . . . friend . . . of Samuel Lailor. He used to work for my dad. I just wanted to see if there had been any news of him? If you'd had any letters?' My voice trembled. What if the news was the worst it could be? Did I really want to hear it?

Aunty Beryl dropped her hands from her hips and stared at me for what seemed like minutes but was in reality only a few seconds, then turned and vanished into the hut. Unsure whether or not to follow, I watched the children playing knucklebones. This is where Samuel would have played, grown up, I realised and the thought saddened me. I had only ever seen him on the farm, never with his own family, had never given a thought to what his life before I knew him must have been.

A sound broke my reverie and Aunty Beryl appeared, holding out an envelope. My hand shook as I took it and immediately recognised the writing.

'Came the other day,' she said.

It was dated 22nd March, four weeks ago. I slipped the pages out and unfolded them. As I began to read the letter silently, she interrupted. 'Can you read it out loud?' she asked. I realised then that she hadn't yet read the letter because she couldn't.

'*Dear Aunty,*' I began, trying to steady my voice. '*Sorry I haven't written but there isn't much time to sit around on our bums up here. It's stinking hot and the flies and mossies are monsters. I've been able to keep myself out of trouble so far but some of my mates haven't been so lucky. You need to keep your wits about you, but that's easy for a smart fella like me, eh?*' I could hear his voice in the words and I smiled through my tears.

'*Go on,*' Aunty Beryl urged.

'*I'm not sure how long we'll be stationed here before they move us on, but I wanted to let you know I'm doing okay and to tell you not to worry. I hope the small bit of money I left you from my wages has helped. Will write again when I can. Samuel.*'

I gazed at the curly S in his signature and ran my finger across the words. At the time the letter was written he was still safe, still alive.

'*He's a good boy,*' Aunty Beryl announced.

'*Yes,*' I whispered. When she took the letter back I had to resist the urge to snatch at it and push it into my coat pocket. This was the closest I had been to Samuel in months, and I wanted to hold his words close even though they hadn't been written to me.

'*You his girl?*' she asked matter-of-factly.

I nodded.

We both stood quietly, not knowing what else to say, watching the children, who had left their game and were now playing chasings at the back of the camp. Part of me wanted to stay there, where I felt closer to him somehow, because these were people who knew him and loved him as I did – but it was time to leave.

'*Thank you,*' I said, holding out my hand. She took it and pressed her fingers against mine.

'*You come back any time,*' she said.

As I rode away I turned back to wave but she had already gone. I knew in my heart that Samuel would have written to me and that my dad would undoubtedly have intercepted the letters. All I can do is continue to hope and pray for his safe return when this horrid war is over.

23 January 1944

Please God, do not let it happen. Please let it be nothing more than a dream this time.

It was as real to me as all the others, as if I were there with him in that jungle looking over his shoulder, his skin shiny with sweat, his dark eyes wide and watching for any movement, any sound. It was dark. Too dark to even see his hand as he held it up to his face, the knuckle of his thumb resting against his cheekbone, the rifle cradled by his fingers. He strained his eyes to see through the gloom. There was someone out there, but he didn't know where. He dared not even moisten his parched lips for fear of being heard. A mosquito whirred by his ear and landed on his cheek but he made no move to brush it away. Hunched forward, he peered harder into the night. A thick curtain of mist hung between the trees, and for a split second he thought he saw something move, but when he twisted his upper body towards the sound there was nothing. He had to get back to the others, somehow make his way back to base camp. The only noises now were the murmurings of the jungle: the rumble of croaking frogs, the hum of invisible insects, the intermittent hoot of a bird high up in the canopy. Usually his instincts were right, but this time the heat and the blackness of the night were disorienting him. He lowered his rifle and let it swing by his side as he lifted his left foot and then his right and began to make his way back in the direction he thought he had come from.

A stick snapped beneath his boot. Almost instantly his head jerked backwards, arms flailing, as the first shot hit and then a barrage of bullets shattered into him from behind, his body dancing a macabre jig before he crumbled to the ground, one hand still clutching his rifle. I watched from somewhere above or behind or around him, unable to move, unable to help him, as his soul left him and floated up into the ether. All that remained was the shell of him lying there alone in the pitch-black night.

I woke to the sound of my own scream, my sheets soaked with perspiration, my pillow wet with tears. All I could see in the grey shadows of my room was Samuel's face, the smile completely gone from his eyes. And I knew. Just as I had known about the boat.

Now I sit in my room and wait for the sun to rise, sick with misery, willing it not to be true but certain that it is. Death has paid another unwelcome visit.

31 January

I don't know how long my dad has known but at lunch today he deigned to break the news of Samuel's death. When I told him I already knew, that I had dreamt of it over a week ago, he refused to believe me and said I was never to mention such nonsense to anyone for fear they would think me insane. He said he was sorry that Samuel had died, that he hoped I had recovered from my girlish fantasies and then spouted some inanity about time healing all wounds. Mum, as usual, stood behind him blank faced, letting him do all the talking. When he had finished his sermon I asked to be excused, saddled up Duke and went for a ride along the beach. I think they wanted me to cry, to fall into some hysterical fit of grief so they could once again berate me for lowering myself. But I wouldn't give them the satisfaction. I waited until I reached

the cave, where Samuel and I had first loved each other, then lay
down against the wet sand and gave way to the sorrow that had
been welling inside me since my dad had begun to speak. It was
one thing to know in my soul, but to have the words spoken out
loud by the very man who had arranged Samuel's enlistment and
thereby condemned him to death was unbearable. Not until night
started to fall and Duke began to whinny did I rouse myself and
make my way home.

Miranda lifted her eyes from the page and tipped her head
back, rubbing at the crick in her neck. Tears welled as she
thought of Essie, forcibly separated from her lover, desperate
to hear news of him, alone in her bedroom dreaming of his
death. What a terrible gift to have been given, to be able to
foretell disaster and yet be powerless to stop it.

Night had fallen. She slipped her arms into the cardigan
and wrapped it tightly around her. Buster lay snoring at her
feet. The wick of the lamp flared as she wound it higher and
the smell of kerosene wafted through the cottage. She tucked
her feet up beneath her on the lounge. Samuel was dead. The
first chapter of Essie's life was over. The diary entries had
become more sporadic and there were only a few pages left
in this volume.

22 October
The days pass in monotony. My only solace has been in my music
and in riding. My parents have been busy with the farm and the
war effort. Leonard has visited often, supposedly as a guest but I
know for a fact that he has involved my dad in his black market
dealings – yet another act of hypocrisy from the upstanding Mr

Wilson, property owner and magistrate, who is selling meat illegally for profit. Leonard lavishes me with expensive gifts each time he visits and I suspect his interest in me is more than just friendship. I wonder if he would be shocked to know that the object of his attentions has lain with a coloured man.

16 August 1945
It's been some time since I've opened the pages of this diary. There seemed no point pouring my heart out onto the page when it has been irreparably broken. But the news that the war has come to an end does warrant recording. Japan has agreed to surrender now that the Yanks have bombed them. The papers are full of the news of course and the radio has nothing but reports about how soon the soldiers will return and what a wonderful victory Australia and our allies have won. But for those who have lost loved ones the victory is hollow.

The return of the men – even of my own brother – will only remind me of another who should have been returning. A man for whom I haven't even been allowed to grieve. Not publicly at least. Samuel's name has hung like a shroud over every conversation I have had with my parents since his death.

I have an offer to study at the Conservatorium, which would get me out of this house and away from my parents. Even though the thought of leaving the farm and Duke seems unbearable, perhaps it is the only way to shake off the weight of grief I have carried since Samuel's death. I know I will never love another man the way I loved him. Is it possible to ever be happy again?

Miranda closed the diary and ran her fingertips over the worn leather cover. When Buster startled at a thump on the verandah and ran to the door barking, she slowly unfolded her legs, staring nervously at the door, and moved to the edge of the lounge. Was somebody out there? What should she do? Her stomach twisted. Were the rumours that Esther had a gun true? And where would it be? She scanned the room but knew she wouldn't have a hope in hell of knowing how to fire it.

'Hello there, Miranda, it's me, Vincent.'

The tension in her body fell away as she stood and rushed to the door. Vincent? What was he doing here? 'Hang on.' She tried to smooth out her wrinkled shirt and fix her hair but gave up and opened the door.

And there he was, flashing her a beguiling grin. 'Thought I'd call by and make sure you were doing okay out here on your own.' He handed her a bottle of wine. 'Hope you like red?'

'Yes, I do,' she smiled back. 'Leave him alone, Buster,' she said, pushing the dog back into the house with her foot.

'So, can I come in then? If you feel like a visitor, that is.'

'Oh, I'm sorry, of course.' She tried to sound cool, calm and collected, as if she invited handsome strangers inside on a regular basis. 'Have a seat, I'll try and find some glasses.' From the corner of her eye she watched him take off his duffel coat and make himself comfortable on the lounge. Being outdoors with him today, with the horses as a distraction, had felt a whole lot easier than being at close quarters. Glancing down she noticed a stain on the cuff of her cardigan. Damn. If I take it off now he might think I'm up for it, she thought. She settled on turning it over so the stain wasn't visible. 'Not much to choose from, I'm afraid,' she said, holding up two glasses that were in fact recycled jam jars.

'I'm not fussy,' he said. 'A glass is a glass.'

As she handed him the first glass his fingers bumped hers and she felt a ridiculous tingle as he poured the wine. 'Thanks,' she said. The lounge was the only seat available, so she positioned herself on the other end of it, turned slightly towards him, grabbed a tattered cushion and placed it on her lap. 'It's good of you to come all the way out here to check on me.'

'Just wanted to make sure you were okay. It's a big call to be stuck out here in the middle of nowhere, especially for a city girl.'

She sipped at her wine. 'Actually I quite like it. Nice change from the chaos.'

'So what do you do up there in the big smoke?'

'I'm a lawyer. Corporate law.'

'Ohhh, a big shot, eh? Must be pretty exciting.'

'Not really. As a matter of fact, I'm pretty bored with the whole thing.' That was the first time she'd said it out loud, or even admitted it to herself. Maybe pursuing the partnership hadn't been such a good idea after all.

'So you just came here for a break?'

Should she tell him what had really brought her here? Maybe it would be better to wait until she was 100 per cent sure herself, and she really did owe it to Esther to tell her first. 'Yep, just got in the car and stopped where it looked good. How about you? I take it you don't come from around here yourself?'

'No, I certainly don't. I migrated out here from Wales when I was a kid. My parents bought a B & B in country Victoria. We had a few horses and I got into breaking and training. Dad sold the place a few years ago after Mum died and moved back to the UK. I've moved around a bit, doing odd jobs, some horse work. The boss saw me working with some horses down south, liked what he saw and offered me a job. I've been working at Garewangga for a couple of years now.'

'So you were headhunted?' she laughed.

'I guess you could say that.' He laid his head against the back of the sofa and sipped at his wine. Miranda found herself hypnotised by the stubble on his jawline and had to force herself to look away. 'This is the longest I've held down a job for quite some time. Usually I get itchy feet and move on around the one-year mark.'

'Well, after watching you with the horses today, you look like you're good at what you do.'

You look good. Full stop!

'Why thank you, ma'am.' He dipped his head in mock embarrassment. 'So you enjoyed your ride?'

'It was fantastic. I can't believe it's been so long since I've ridden. I'd forgotten what an amazing feeling it is.' She felt the thrill of the ride again now, like fireworks exploding in the pit of her stomach.

'Well, you'll have to come back and do it again.' He smiled and she felt herself swooning.

'I just might do that.' There was an instant when their eyes met and everything around her faded away. The sound of the waves in the distance, the snoring of the dog by her feet, the faint ticking of the clock above the stove, all of it dimmed and she was conscious only of the rising and falling of her chest and Vincent sitting dangerously nearby.

He refilled her glass, and then his own as he told her about Garewangga, the horses and life at Pelican Point. 'So how long are you planning on staying?'

'Well, I guess it depends on Esther.'

'You don't have to get back to work anytime soon? Or a boyfriend?'

'Why do you ask?'

'Just curious.'

She licked the red wine from her lips, hugging the cushion closer. 'I probably should be getting back. I'm supposed to be getting married in seven weeks.'

Vincent sat up and turned towards her. Had he shifted even closer at some stage or was she just imagining it? 'Supposed to be? You don't sound all that certain for someone who's about to tie the knot.'

'Oh, I am, it's just . . .' A slight tremble had started in her voice and she gulped a couple of mouthfuls of wine to wash it down. 'Everything's been pretty hectic. I just needed to get away for a few days.'

Who are you trying to convince?

'So what's he like?'

The question threw her off guard for a moment – she probably shouldn't be discussing her love-life with a man she hardly knew, but that same feeling of familiarity she'd felt on the ride had returned, now that her initial schoolgirl nerves had subsided. 'James? He's smart, good-looking, has a great job.' She stopped and thought for a moment – what else could she say about him? 'And he's funny, caring and considerate.'

'Sounds like a perfect match.'

'Yes, he is.' Perfectly boring, Belle would say, but Miranda felt a rush of guilt even thinking it.

He's safe. That's what he is.

'Is he your soul mate?'

Miranda frowned and took another swig from her glass. 'I'm not sure I want to answer that.'

'I think you just did.'

This was starting to feel a little like an interrogation, but two could play at that game. 'How about you? Attached?' The wine was giving her a bravado she didn't normally have, but what the hell, might as well go with it.

Vincent shook his head. 'Nope. Footloose and fancy free. The only females who've shown any interest in me lately have four legs, a mane and a tail.'

Miranda held her fingers over her mouth to stop the wine escaping as she laughed.

Vincent laughed too. 'Shit, that probably didn't sound too good, did it? I just meant, you know, I'm single.'

Single. The word hovered in the air in bold black type. Miranda shifted her eyes to her glass, finished off what was left.

'I thought I'd found the right girl a few years back. But it didn't work out that way.' He rose abruptly, rubbing his palms on the side of his jeans. 'Well, I'd better start my trek home, but how about coming out for a ride tomorrow?'

Miranda stood and folded her arms. Should she really be seeing any more of this man when she felt such an overwhelming attraction to him? Maybe not. Or then again, perhaps it was a good way of testing her true feelings for James, convincing herself once and for all that he was the man for her. Either way, it was probably best to play it cool. 'I'll see how I go, how things are with Esther.'

'I'm there all day – and the boss isn't – so I'll see you if I see you.' He shrugged himself into his coat and she followed him to the door.

He turned to say goodbye and she found herself standing within a breath of him. 'Thanks for the wine,' she said, avoiding his eyes, 'and the company.'

'My pleasure.' When he smiled she wanted a hole to open up in the floor so she could slide down into it and escape the almost painful yearning that had taken hold of her. Instead she stepped sidewards, opened the door and watched as he disappeared into the night, a single beam of torchlight bobbing along the ground in the darkness.

Esther

She struggled to open her eyes against the bright white glare of the lights. For a minute she thought she was somewhere else but the drip standing beside the bed and the hum of voices in the corridor reminded her she was in the hospital and the pain shooting through her leg reminded her why.

'Good morning, Mrs Wilson, and how are we this morning?'

'Well, I don't know about you, but I've certainly been better.'

The nurse raised her eyebrows as she placed her thumb and forefinger on either side of Esther's wrist, staring down at the floor in concentration. She stuck some kind of device in Esther's ear, removing it when it beeped.

'Lovely,' she said again in her oh-so-efficient voice, recording her findings on the chart. 'Your temp's come down quite a bit. Doctor will be in to see you soon, then we might be able to see about getting you something to eat.'

'I'm not hungry,' Esther replied. 'I want to go home.' She knew she sounds like a petulant child but she didn't give a damn.

The nurse's tone changed. 'You'll have to speak to the doctor about that.' And she clipped off across the linoleum floor and out the door before Esther had a chance to argue.

In the bed diagonally across from her a pale-faced old woman was curled into a foetal position, her head so small it barely made a dent in the pillow. There was an air of resignation about her, as if she was waiting to die, not just waiting for death but willing it. Esther thought of an orphaned baby bird left to starve in its nest that she once came across on the farm as a young girl. She'd wondered then how the parents could be so heartless as to just leave it to its fate, without a single soul in the world who cared whether it lived or died. Now she knew that life could be cruel and the only way to survive was to rage against it and not give in. The woman in the bed had given in.

But if they think I'm going to, they've got another thing coming.

Footsteps. A tall, balding doctor peered down at her over rimless spectacles. 'You seem to be doing much better today, Esther. Can you remember why you're in here?'

She frowned. 'Of course I remember. Fell and cut my leg and got some sort of infection from it. Can't see what all the fuss is about.'

He looked down at her chart. 'More than just an infection, I'm afraid. Blood poisoning. That's what made you so sick. You're lucky that young lady was there to help out or who knows what might have happened.'

Esther pictured Miranda, the look of concern on her pretty young face as she waved her goodbye at the cottage. He was right, she was lucky. Maybe there were still a few good eggs left in the world.

'The thing is, Esther, it's unusual for sepsis to set in so fast and be so severe – unless there are underlying complications.'

'Like what?'

'Things like diabetes, an autoimmune deficiency . . .' he hesitated. 'Or cancer.'

Esther scoffed. 'I haven't got cancer. Don't you think a person would know about it if they had cancer? I'm fit as a fiddle. Or I will be once this leg sorts itself out and I get out of this place.'

'I'm not saying you've got cancer, but there's evidence to suggest there's something not quite right going on. We need to get this infection under control, and then I'd like to do a few tests, just to rule anything else out.'

The tiny balloon of fear that had lodged itself in Esther's chest as they carried her out of the house began to expand, rapidly, and she had to focus hard to stop it from bursting.

The doctor rested his hand on her arm. 'It's just routine.'

Could she trust him? Could she trust any of them? Were they just telling her that to find a way to keep her here, looking for an excuse not to let her go home? If she had the energy to push herself up, she'd be out that door as quick as a flash, but her leg was anchoring her to the bed and the wooziness had returned, making her head spin. She'd have to go along with it for now, but as soon as she was capable of it she'd be out of here.

'Right, well, I'll see about getting those tests done. Try and eat something if you can, keep your energy up.' The doctor gave her another pat on the arm and a fatherly smile and was gone.

Cancer.

Could she really have cancer and not know it? Could her body be that much of a traitor? She glanced across at the old woman opposite, her eyes now closed inside her shrunken face. Probably what she's got. Well, I'll be blowed if it's going to get me. No use jumping to conclusions. Just take it one step at a time. Get the leg better, let them do their damned tests and then get out of here and back home to Buster.

Miranda

The corridor was blacker than a moonless night. It twisted in one direction and then turned in another, with doors on either side. Despite the lack of light she could tell some were wooden, painted in varying shades of the rainbow, others were metal, and some were covered in wrought-iron bars. Once or twice she stopped and tried the handles but none of them budged. A glow appeared under the doorway at the far end of the hall and she moved towards it, a strange sensation of weightlessness filling her body, as if her feet were no longer touching the floor. As she kept her eyes focused on the slender beam, the door opened and a voice called to her. She recognised the voice but she couldn't pin it down. Faster and faster she moved until she knew she was running, even though there was no sound echoing from her footsteps. Finally she pushed open the last door and just as her fingers touched the rough timber it slammed shut and she was left in absolute darkness.

Something wet and rough stroked her cheek and she woke to the sound of Buster slobbering in her face.

'Oh, morning, boy! I love you too, but really?' She threw off the blankets, rubbing her hands across the small of her back and circling her shoulders, twisting her head from side to side, hearing the knots crack. Buster ran to the door and she followed him outside. An army of clouds had gathered above the steel-blue field of ocean. More rain on the way, by the looks of it. Better get a move on. She had a sudden memory of a door banging shut in her dream as she padded back inside, but she shook it from her mind while she put on the kettle and organised some breakfast.

Today was Monday. Almost three full days since she'd last spoken to James. And in that entire time she'd barely thought of him. When Vincent had asked about him, she couldn't change the subject quickly enough. She'd assumed the dizziness and choking sensation she'd felt every time she thought about the wedding were just nerves. But what if they weren't? What if Belle – and the voice – were right? All her life she'd been ruled by her head, done what was 'right', what was expected. It was probably why she loved the escape of romantic movies so much – the characters made choices she only ever imagined and usually found their happy ever after. But what if she did throw caution to the wind and follow her heart and it all went horribly wrong?

That's a chance you have to be willing to take.

Esther had gone with her heart, followed her instincts, given herself completely to Samuel, and look where it had gotten her. Grief-stricken and alone. If she'd made a sensible choice in the first place, surely it would have been safer and worked out a whole lot better?

But she never would have known what it's like to love someone utterly and without fear.

She thought back to last night, to Vincent sitting beside her, the easy banter they had struck up, like old friends becoming reacquainted. Something stirred inside her at the memory of him, standing at the door, his hand on her arm, the way she had to force herself to keep her distance from him as they said goodnight. Of course she was going to be attracted to other people, but the thing was not to act on it, to control your impulses. Like she did last night. And like she would again today when she took him up on that offer of another ride. In a few days she'd be heading home, going back to sort things out with James, so she might as well get that horse ride in while she was here.

And then there was the mystery of Esther and Leonard. She was sure now that the two of them were her grandparents, but the riddle of Esther's supposed death and apparent resurrection was still to be solved. Miranda was pulled towards the diaries, and the answers they might hold, but the thought of riding across the hills one more time with Vincent tugged her in a completely different direction. She glanced out the window – those clouds weren't going to hold off for much longer, but the diaries would still be here when she returned.

Decision made.

On her way back through town she pulled over in a spot where she'd been able to get phone reception yesterday and made a call to the hospital. She spoke to the same nurse and got the same message: Esther was in a stable condition but there was no news yet as to when she would be discharged. Bugger. Before she could chicken out she dialled the office to say she was still too sick to come in. Judging by Jemima's frosty tone her absence wasn't going down too well. While she was on a roll she rang James who thankfully didn't answer so she left a voicemail to say she was fine and would call later. Relieved to have the calls out of the way she glanced at her watch – it was only 8.25, still early. Maybe a little too early to go visiting Vincent. Another shot of caffeine wouldn't go astray – and there was a café next to the grocery store, just across the road.

She ordered a double shot cappuccino and browsed through the local paper sitting on the counter. Above the shrieking of the milk-frothing machine a familiar voice boomed at her from behind. 'G'day, love, I hear old Esther's been carted off to hospital.'

She turned to see Norma swathed in a tropical print kaftan, a turquoise scarf wrapped around her yellow hair. News obviously travelled fast in small places.

'Yes, she's not too good.'

'And you're staying out at her place?'

Norma was fishing and Miranda decided she needed to be careful. 'Just looking after her dog for a few days.'

'Like dogs, do you?' Norma smiled and it was a relief to see her teeth were lipstick-free.

'Hmmm.'

'So how long will you be staying out there?'

'Until Friday,' Miranda said, which was probably true.

The young waitress emerged from behind the counter, a paper bag and takeaway cup in her hand, and approached a table in the far corner. 'Here's your order, Mr Wilson.' A man Miranda hadn't noticed until now stood and mumbled his thanks before leaving the shop without a word.

Richard Wilson. There was something about his pale eyes and the metallic tone of his voice that reminded her of a lizard. If her theory turned out to be correct, he was actually her second cousin. How could anyone be so cold and callous as to leave an old woman – his own aunt – living all alone in a tumbledown shack while he swanned it up in the family mansion? Surely Esther had more right than he did to be living in the place? That was something she'd definitely be looking into, something her legal training might actually come in useful for.

Norma's voice interrupted her thoughts. 'Well, watch out for yourself out there. Especially when the old girl gets back.' She snickered. 'If she gets back.'

It was a relief when the young girl handed Miranda her coffee. 'Oh, I'm sure she'll be fine,' Miranda told Norma.

Thanks for your concern.

Outside she held the cup to her nose, inhaled and took a good, long sip. Strong, hot and delicious. The perfect antidote to wash away Norma's irritating comments. Another mouthful and the reptilian image of Richard Wilson slithering from his lair in the corner of the café vanished too. Hopefully Vincent was right and he wouldn't be around today. Time to be getting along.

She slowed to a stop at the gates and pressed the buzzer, drove through and listened to them bang shut behind her. Whether it was the idyllic setting, the prospect of seeing Vincent again or the anticipation of riding one more time, she wasn't sure, but she was sitting just a little more upright in the seat than she had been and her palms were just a little bit moist against the steering wheel.

As she turned off the ignition she looked up at a second-floor window diagonally across from the old stone stable. Was this where Esther had stood at night and imagined what Samuel was doing? Miranda gave a melancholy sigh and looked around for signs of movement. Vincent was leaning cross-legged against the stable wall, hands shoved into the front pockets of his jeans, watching a horse pacing the fence at the far end of the grassed yard. He hadn't noticed her and she took the time to stop and have a really good look at what made him so enticing. The hair was certainly a drawcard, the way it fell in dark curls across his forehead, the way he pushed it back so nonchalantly. The body, of course, tall, broad-shouldered, just enough muscle. But his attractions weren't just physical, there was a relaxed self-assurance about the man that she found totally magnetic. It drew her towards him right now.

'Hi there.'

Vincent stood and smiled. 'This is a nice surprise. I wasn't sure I'd see you today.'

'Thought I'd take you up on that offer of a ride.'

He pointed at the horse. 'Got a new arrival on its way.'

'Seriously? A foal? She's about to have it?'

'Any time in the next hour or two, I'd say, by the way she's behaving.'

Miranda watched as the mare pawed the ground and tossed her head, then walked a few steps and did the same thing again. She was a gorgeous bay, with a thick black mane and tail. 'The poor thing. Is she in pain?'

Vincent laughed. 'I imagine so. I think you would be too if you were about to push a four-legged fifty kilo bundle of fur out of a very small orifice.'

She felt the rush of blood to her cheeks as Vincent put his hand to his mouth. 'God, I'm sorry, that wasn't the most tactful thing to say to a woman, was it?'

'Probably not.' She couldn't help but grin at his embarrassment and the two of them laughed together. 'Is there anything you can give her, or do for her? You don't need a vet or anything?'

'No, we'll just let nature take its course, unless things start to look complicated. I've got the vet on stand-by if I need her. Sorry about the ride, but I can't really leave at the moment. The foal's worth quite a bit – Dicko will hang, draw and quarter me if anything goes wrong.'

'That's fine, really.' She screwed up her face. 'You call him Dicko?'

'Only behind his back,' he said. 'I've heard other people call him a lot worse.'

'I bet. What is it with him, anyway? I just saw him at the café in town, he's positively creepy.'

Vince nodded. 'He's all about money. People, animals,

property – he only values them according to their capital worth. Or what he can get out of them.'

'Then wouldn't he be better off being nice to Esther?'

'Sucking up, you mean? He tried that – she got the shotgun out and told him to get off her property before she blew him off it. Read him like a book.'

Miranda smiled. 'I can just imagine. She strikes me as the sort who doesn't suffer fools.'

'That she doesn't. And he's the biggest fool around. Fancies himself as a hot shot racing man. He's going north for a week or two to visit some of his cronies.' Vincent watched as the mare circled and lay down on the ground with a thud. 'Looks like it's showtime. Want to stick around?'

'Sure.' Miranda followed Vincent to where the horse was lying. Her coat was soaked with perspiration and she was panting the way Miranda had seen women pant in those hideous films they'd watched in personal development classes at school.

Vincent crouched and stroked her face, speaking to her in soothing whispers. 'That's the girl, take it easy, you can do it.'

Miranda imagined him in a labour room holding her hand, reassuring her, talking her through the pain. For god's sake, get a grip of yourself. 'Is there anything I can do?' she asked.

Vincent kept his eyes on the mare but shook his head. It was probably best to give him and the horse some space and observe quietly. As a girl she'd always dreamt of having her own horse, raising it from a foal, training it, as Esther had done with Duke. And it hadn't been the only dream she'd given up. Living in Paris, working in New York, learning to paint, living by the beach – all of those crazy ideas that

had floated around in her brain at school and uni had
been squashed by reality – work, mortgage payments and
responsibility. The only thing she'd vaguely pursued had
been photography, but for the last few years even that had
fallen by the wayside. She remembered then that she had her
camera in the car.

'Would it be okay if I take some photos?' she said softly.

Vincent took a few seconds to answer, as if he'd forgotten
she was there. 'Sure,' he said without turning around, his
attention completely focused on the labouring mare, his hand
resting on her withers. 'But you'd better hurry.'

She raced to the car as fast as she could and grabbed her
camera bag. When she returned, the distinct shape of a hoof
shrouded inside an opaque white sac had emerged. Miranda
watched in awe as the mare struggled to her feet, walked a few
steps, bent forward on her knees and then settled herself back
down on the ground again. Just as a second hoof appeared,
she remembered the camera and snapped a few shots.

Vincent was crouching by the mare, who was now emitting
a low-pitched groan. 'Things should be moving a bit faster,'
he said, frowning. Before Miranda knew what was happening,
he knelt, grabbed the foal by the hooves and hauled it out.
'Phew, that's more like it.'

He pushed himself back up to stand beside Miranda, who
watched open-mouthed as the foal thrashed about, breaking
the seal to appear wet and dazed, long spindly legs stretched
out in front. It had the same white, lightning-shaped blaze
as its mother, who turned and stared at the smaller version
of herself.

Miranda felt tears spring to her eyes as the foal made tiny whimpers and inched its way closer to the mare who pushed herself up and gave the newborn a nudge. Legs splayed out in front, the baby responded by rocking itself forward until it was semi-upright, falling and then giving it another shot. With one almighty burst of effort it stood on teetering stilts, took two tentative steps and collapsed back on the ground in a heap.

Neither Miranda nor Vincent had spoken as they watched but now Vincent punched his fist in the air and gave a shriek. 'Yes, she did it, she did it, a colt!' He wrapped his arms around Miranda, lifted her off the ground and swung her through the air. She steadied herself against his chest as he put her back down.

'He's beautiful, just beautiful.' Then he leant in and pulled her close and kissed her, straight on the lips. Miranda kissed him back, and for a few moments the mare and the foal and the farm disappeared. His lips were on hers. She could smell the sweat on his skin and feel the strength of his shoulders beneath her hands. Something shifted deep down inside her.

'Woo hoo,' he whispered as they drew apart.

Yeah, woo hoo.

⌒

Miranda kept an eye on the foal while Vincent showered. He quickly returned with his wet hair tousled, wearing a fresh T-shirt and jeans. They spent the afternoon watching the foal stagger around on its gangly legs and talking easily together, Miranda helping out with the horse feeding and feeling more and more relaxed. When the clouds thickened and a brisk wind blew in from the sea, Vincent led mother and newborn into the shelter of the stable, where they both lay down and slept. Rain lashed against the windowpanes, turning the yard outside into a quagmire within minutes.

'Shocking weather we're having. Looks like you'll have to stay for a while.' Vincent smiled at her and she nodded. He took her hand and led her through a door adjoining the stable. They passed through a small, neat kitchen and a cosy living area, but kept on walking, climbing the stairs to an attic bedroom. It was neat and simply decorated but had the same smell of hay and earth she'd noticed in the stable. Or maybe that was Vincent? He turned to her, brushing the back of his knuckle beneath her chin and up her cheek, pressing his lips against the curve of her neck. She closed her eyes while his mouth lingered there, then arched away from him for a moment, pulling her shirt over her head, meeting the shine of his eyes as she ran her hands through his damp hair, letting her fingers catch in his curls. His hands were workman's hands but the power behind them was gentle as he ran them across her breasts and unfastened her bra. It dropped to the floor and she gasped. She unzipped his jeans and yanked his T-shirt up over his shoulders, pressing herself to him, warm flesh on flesh. In one languorous movement they fell together onto the bed. Kissing the inside of her thighs as he went, he slipped her pants off first and then her underwear, then slid out of his own so they were both completely naked. Lying beside her in the faint afternoon light, keeping his eyes on hers, he caressed her all over – her shoulders, her back, her belly, and finally, when she was so taut with longing she didn't think she could stand it for one more second, exactly where she wanted. She pulled him to her then, his body heavy against hers, and felt the flood of heat between her legs as they came together, the rush and shiver, and the completion of whatever had started that first day they met on the beach.

Later, nestled in his arms in the dark, feeling the rise and fall of his chest and listening to the constant beating of his heart, she thought about the day: the birth of the foal, how natural it had been when he'd kissed her, the smell of rain on the grass and the inexplicable joy as they made love. A door had opened and she had stepped through it. It had been her own voice calling to her from the other side.

Esther

They'd drawn the curtains around the bed so she couldn't see what was going on, but Esther knew by the hushed conversations between the nurses, the way they looked at her with forced smiles, that the woman in the corner had died. Better off that way than wasting away in a hospital. If the poor old thing had anyone who cared about her, they hadn't shown their faces over the last two days. But then Esther had no one either. That was how it had been for more years than she knew how to remember. And most times she was fine with that. Once there had been people who'd loved her, people she loved in return, but it didn't pay to dwell on the past. She'd built a wall around it and lived on the other side. Sometimes memories slipped through the cracks, like when she lost herself in the music, but they were usually the good memories, often of Samuel, and remembering him these days was a comfort rather than a torture. Not like the others. Thoughts of them were dangerously close now – being here brought them back. Soon the nurses would be coming to jab their needles in her veins and take more blood. She knew it had to be done, but the fear still lingered – were they trying to get her better or did they want to keep her here, stop her from going back to her . . . She almost said the word to herself then, but stopped just in time. Back to her house, and her dog and her garden, that's what she'd meant, her life out at the cottage.

Two orderlies appeared with a long metal trolley and vanished behind the curtains. There was some jostling around and then they appeared again, wheeling the woman away, her tiny body barely forming a hump beneath the starched white sheet. Esther turned her head to look out the window, watched a train of thick grey clouds roll across the sky. All these years she'd fought to stay alive, to keep waking up every morning and making the most of every day. For what? For who? Was it really worth it?

Maybe the woman was better off.

Maybe death would be a release.

Miranda

'Shit!'

Vincent stirred in the bed beside her as she dived out and scrambled around for her clothes. 'What is it? What's wrong?' His voice was still groggy with sleep.

'I forgot about Buster. I've left him on his own all night.' She pulled on her jeans and stretched her arms into her shirt. Gathering her hair into a ponytail at the back of her head, she wrapped it into a knot.

'He's a dog, he'll survive. Might be a bit hungry, that's all.'

He climbed out of bed and pulled on his jeans but was still bare-chested. She had to force her eyes away and make herself concentrate. Where the hell were her boots?

'If you're looking for your shoes, they're not here. Come on.' He led her back down the stairs and out into the stable, where she remembered now she'd taken her muddy boots off at the door. She pulled them on while Vincent went to check on the foal.

Right. Just chill. The dog will be fine.

She found him standing at the stable door watching the foal, who was standing gawkily, his head tucked beneath his mother's belly, drinking. 'I could watch them all day,' he said.

'I know what you mean. He's adorable.' She tucked some loose strands of hair back behind her ears. 'Look, I have to go. Thanks for . . .'

He looked at her, waiting for her to finish the sentence.

What exactly was she thanking him for? she wondered. What was the etiquette here?

'No need for thanks,' he said. 'The pleasure was all mine, believe me.'

Not sure what else to say, or whether or not she should kiss him goodbye, she smiled. 'Well, see ya.'

She went to leave but he held her back and kissed her. 'Bye.'

Part of her wanted to stay, wanted to lie down with him in the stable right there and then, but she knew she had to go. And not just because of Buster. At the door she stopped and turned. 'Vincent, I just want you to know, I don't usually do this sort of thing.'

'What sort of thing?' he teased.

'You know, sleep with strange men.'

He folded his arms. 'So I'm strange, am I?'

'That's not . . . I'm just not a casual-sex type of girl. I just wanted you to know.'

'I know.'

'Thanks.'

As she walked to the car, her boots squelching in the grass,

she felt as light as air, like a leaf drifting on the breeze, like
something inside her had been set free.

⁓

Buster greeted her at the door with a chorus of barks before
spinning around like a dervish chasing his tail and racing
outside.

'I know, I know, boy, I'm so sorry.' She went straight inside
to the fridge where she found a couple of sausages, chopped
them up and put them in his bowl with some dry food she'd
left in a container on the bench. She took it outside to the
verandah and he launched into his food like he'd never eaten
before. Slumping into the seat by the door she stared up at
a sea eagle circling just beyond the headland, its white body
stark against the black arc of its wings, as it rose and fell
on currents of air. As Buster gulped at his breakfast beside
her she was overcome with guilt, initially at her neglect of
the dog and then, as she thought of last night, about her
betrayal of James. Everything that she'd worked for over the
last few years was slipping through her fingers – her job, her
hopes for the future, her life with her fiancé. If she didn't
have any of those things, what would she really have? Who
would she be?

Yourself. You'd still be yourself.

And who would that be? It had all been so easy when she'd
had a plan and followed it. What was it that had steered her
so off course, sent her life spinning out of control? Since she'd
turned thirty last year, things had slowly started to go awry,
not on the outside, but somewhere deep inside in a place that
she'd refused to acknowledge. When she thought back now,

the first time it had really bubbled to the surface had been when she was looking at herself in that wedding dress. She'd assured herself it had just been pre-wedding jitters. Just as she'd told herself that it was nerves that made her baulk at the partnership and that she was searching for Esther out of curiosity. She'd pretended this whole trip south had been about her mother, finding the missing pieces to *her* puzzle, but it had really been about herself. She'd run away, pure and simple. And in the process she'd discovered a whole lot of things she *didn't* want: she didn't want to work in the city in a job that bored her, she didn't want to pander to her mother's moods any more or make choices that pleased her parents. And she didn't want to marry James. There, she'd admitted it, if only to herself.

Exactly what she did want, she wasn't quite as sure about – the thought of not having her life sorted into boxes that fit neatly on a shelf, colour coordinated, side by side, made her stomach spin. But not as much as the thought of locking herself into a marriage – and a life – that she knew now she didn't want.

Was that what Esther had done when she'd married Leonard? Was that why she'd left and come here to live out the rest of her days alone? Miranda went back inside, picked up the basket of diaries and returned to the verandah to find the answer. There was only one diary left, and as Miranda flicked through it, scanning the dates at the top of the pages, she saw that the entries were brief. She settled in to read, tucking all thoughts about James – and Vincent – into a quiet little pocket in the back of her mind.

27 January 1946

The last few weeks have been a whirlwind of packing, goodbyes and new sights and sounds. The hardest goodbye was to Duke. I swear he knew. When I went out to his paddock he stood at the far end and refused to come to me. Even when I held an apple out to tempt him, he just turned his head away. Before I even reached him the tears started to flow and it was impossible for me to hold them back. I threw my arms around his neck and buried my face in his soft, warm coat. For the last eight years we have been virtually inseparable. I have ridden him almost every day, groomed him, tended to him when he was sick, even slept in the stable with him that time he went down with colic and the vet told me he doubted he would survive. Saying goodbye to him was like saying goodbye to part of myself. And not only to myself but to Samuel and to his memory. Duke and I have made frequent visits to the beach since his death. I would leave Duke there on the sand while I went into the cool shadows of the cave, touching my fingers to our initials and the heart Samuel had carved around them, remembering. Each time I would emerge, Duke would come to me and nuzzle his head against my shoulder. It was as if he shared my grief, or at least acknowledged it, something no one else has ever done. I sobbed as I stood there in the early-morning chill, feeling like a traitor for leaving him behind, unable to turn back as I returned to the house, where my parents were waiting to accompany me on the drive to Sydney.

We talked very little on the journey north, me wrapped in my own thoughts and them battling to adjust to the idea of me leaving the farm and moving so far away from home. It had been my choice in the end to study at the Con, an excuse to get away and live my own life without them constantly watching me, worried no doubt that their wayward daughter might take up with another unsuitable man. They have tried everything in their power to marry me off, first to Clarence Pratt, god help me, and then to a string of other eligible local boys. Dad has even made overtures about Leonard, but I have refused all their suggestions. My life from now on will be lived on my own terms and nobody else's. I will study, learn, improve my playing and one day travel the world. But my heart will always be there on the farm, and I know that one day I will return there for good.

So Esther had moved to Sydney and studied at the Conservatorium. Miranda thought back to that first day when she had watched Esther playing the violin through the door, remembering the beautiful melancholy of the music. She felt a curious sense of pride at the young woman's decision to leave her family and follow her dream. The next section of the diary talked about her lessons, the routine of her days, friendships made with fellow students and the excitement of life in the city.

12 May 1946
My life has changed so drastically since moving to Sydney that it is hard to imagine what it was before. I am boarding with an old family friend of my dad's, Mrs Beatson, who has a house in Glebe, so it is not too far for me to travel to the Conservatorium each day. My schedule is gruelling, with lectures and tutorials and rehearsals crammed into each day so that by the time I get home in the evening I am completely exhausted. It's so wonderful to be immersed in my music again. My tutor is a German fellow, Mr Schmidt, who was interned during the war. Fortunately, because of his talent, his application to stay on here in Australia was accepted. He is

almost impossible to understand – his accent is so thick – but he
explains things so precisely and is so encouraging that my playing
has improved enormously. He says it is so expressive that I must
have experienced great pain to be able to make the instrument sing in
such a mournful way. I just nod and thank him for the compliment.
Losing myself in my music again has helped revive the part of me
that was dead. I am actually finding myself enjoying life here in
the city, making new friends and even joining them at dances and
socials when our schedule allows. Leonard has called on me on
a few occasions and has brought me stockings and even leg tan,
which he says he obtained from his 'connections'. He really is quite
debonair. At dinner last week we talked about the boat sinking and
the rescue. It seems so long ago, as if that was another version of
myself, one I hardly remember. Tomorrow night he is taking me to
a ball at the Sydney Town Hall. I have a lilac silk dress that my
horseshoe necklace will go perfectly with, so I think I will wear
it. I'm sure he will be impressed.

14 May 1946
What a spectacular night we had, Leonard and I. It was the most
amazing party I have ever been to – waiters dressed like penguins
in their white shirts and black tuxedos, one hand behind their backs
as they filled champagne glasses, bowed and then waddled away;
women in all shades of chiffon giggling and flirting; men in dinner
suits smoking cigars as they chatted around tables, the band in the
background playing all the latest songs from people like Sinatra,
Perry Como and Frankie Lane. I wore the necklace – Leonard
was very pleased. He was watching me across the dance floor as
he chatted with some of his friends and I couldn't help but smile
back. I have known him for so long and feel comfortable in his

company, but since coming to Sydney I am starting to think of him as more than just a friend. I know nothing of his business dealings other than that he works in 'the import trade', but he seems to have plenty of money to splash around. He is very interested in my music and has been to recitals at the Conservatorium a few times now, but last night something changed. When the band played the final song, 'Some Enchanted Evening', he came and took my hand and led me onto the dance floor. He placed his arm around my waist and pulled me close and I rested my head against his shoulder. I could smell the fragrance of his aftershave and the scent of tobacco on his skin. As we moved and swayed in time to the music, something awoke deep inside me, a longing I had locked away and forgotten. I pressed my body against his and our hips moved in perfect rhythm. When the song was over we stood there until the movement of those around us brought me back to myself and I reluctantly pulled away. I looked up into his eyes and I smiled and he knew what that smile meant. We both did. We sat side by side in the cab as he dropped me home, hardly speaking. He walked me to the door, and when he said goodnight, I lifted my lips to his and we kissed. When he ran his hands down my arms, brushing his fingers against my breasts, I thought I would burst with desire.

'I'll see you tomorrow night,' he murmured in my ear before turning to leave.

Can it be possible that I could really love another?

13 November 1946

Today was the final fitting for my dress. My wedding dress. I can hardly believe it. Everything has happened so swiftly it hardly seems real. It is only six months since my relationship with Leonard changed from one of friendship to something else. If I hadn't known

*him for such a long time I am sure I wouldn't have allowed things
to develop as they did. There had always been that bond between
us, ever since that night, the bond of two people who have faced
death and survived, and of course he has been trying to win my
affections for a very long time. Finally he did. Perhaps it was wrong
of me to spend the night with him so soon, but being that close to a
man again, a man who professed his love and wanted me so badly,
brought out a part of me that I had only ever known before with
Samuel. Of course it has been different with Leonard – he is a man
of the world. I am sure that he has had plenty of practice! But he
assures me I am his one and only and will always be and I believe
him. Since he assumed I was a virgin, I said nothing to persuade
him otherwise. He says he is happy about the baby, although when
I first told him I thought I saw a tremor of panic wash across his
face. It was a shock I suppose, as it has been for me. We thought
we had that side of things taken care of, but apparently Mother
Nature had other ideas. It has been an effort getting up to early
classes, trying desperately to swallow back the nausea. The hardest
part has been breaking the news to my parents. Mum has taken
it particularly hard but is of course relieved that we are to be
married so quickly. Dad is over the moon about having Leonard as
a son-in-law. We have arranged to have the wedding here in Sydney,
using Leonard's business dealings as an excuse, and I know it is a
relief for my parents not to have to explain my condition to their
friends, although I suppose they will all find out soon enough.
The wedding is to be held at Paddington with a small reception
afterwards. Fortunately there are only four more weeks left at the
Con, which means I just have to muddle through and make the best
of it. My clothes are getting tight but I should be able to make do
if I have some waistbands let out and wear looser fitting shirts.*

The wedding will be the day after my final classes for the year. I haven't yet told them that I won't be returning to complete my studies. It is the one aspect of this situation that I cannot stand to think about. My dreams of pursuing a career in music have come to an end. Fate – and of course my own impulses – have seen to that. Each time I lift the violin and feel the cool smoothness of it against my chin I choke back a morsel of regret. Life has other things in store for me now and there is no use pining over what might have been. I have done enough of that already in my time.

It feels so strange to know I have another being growing inside of me. That soon I will be a mother. I feel guilty for writing this, but I hope that I will be a better mother than my own has been, that my daughter – for I'm sure that it is a girl – will feel at ease with me, happy to be in my company when she is older, unafraid to confide in me. I can picture us now, Leonard, myself and our children, sitting on the verandah of our home, a property not too far out of the city so Leonard can still continue with his business, watching the horses and cows graze in the paddocks. Once the baby has arrived and we've found just the right place, I'll organise for Duke to be sent up. It's been months since I have seen him and I long to ride again although that won't be for a good while now. As much as I have loved the chaos of the city, it will be good to get a place of our own and be able to soak up the smells and colours of the land again.

My dress is exquisite: rose-patterned French lace with an underlay of silk. When I tried it on today and looked at myself in the mirror I couldn't stop staring. Not because I thought I looked beautiful, although in this dress any girl would feel like a movie star, but because I didn't recognise myself. It was as if I had stepped out of my body and was standing a short distance away trying to

PAMELA COOK

work out where the real Essie, the girl who had ridden so freely and loved so defiantly, had disappeared to. Was this really her or was it some brazen impostor who had stepped into her skin and taken her place? Growing up on the farm seems so distant now even though it has been such a short time since I left. The girl I was then is so different to the woman I have become in such a short space of time, but there is no going back. Life presents us with choices and it is up to us to make the best of them.

Miranda recalled the photo secreted away in her mother's closet, the dress with rose-patterned lace, just like her own wedding dress. She re-read the last two pages of the diary: Esther had fallen pregnant with Leonard's child, had married him to avoid scandal, convinced herself that she could love him as much as she'd loved Samuel. She too had felt like a stranger to herself as she looked in the mirror that day, but she had dreams for a happy future with Leonard. Did they come true? The next few pages were blank and the following entry was dated some time later.

5 July 1947

The baby never stops crying. Night and day, day and night, no matter how often I hold her to my breast, how tightly I swaddle her or how long I rock her, she sleeps for only an hour or two at a time and then the crying begins again. The clinic nurse I visit each week has given me various remedies – gripe water, peppermint tea, even a drop of whisky – and I have become so desperate that I confess I have tried them all. I am a walking corpse, my skin sallow, grey circles and bags bulging beneath my eyes, my hair always pulled back into a bun as I have no time to wash it or to worry about my own appearance. Mum came last week for a visit, and as much as she tried to help, I found having her here only made things worse – another dinner guest to worry about on top of the men that Leonard insists on bringing home to wine and dine, their cigarette smoke clogging the room, forcing me to keep Kathleen closeted in the bedroom until they leave. Leonard tries to help in his own way, picking her up and nursing her, and it irritates me to admit that she does seem calmer when he holds her. But his fatherly attentions are few and far between, he is so busy with his clients, out entertaining them at gambling houses and restaurants, that for the last two weeks I have hardly seen him. When he comes home at night I hear him stumble into the room, humming away drunkenly to himself, not even caring if he wakes the baby, oblivious to the fact that it has taken me hours to feed and settle her, and anger rises like bile in my throat. He crawls under the sheets and I feel his whisky breath in my face, the hot skin of his palm pressing against my ribs as he wraps his arm around me. I shut my eyes that little bit tighter and feign sleep, ignoring the words he whispers in my ear until he sighs and rolls away onto his own side of the bed. It has been a month now since Kathleen's birth but I have neither the energy nor the inclination to be amorous. The nurse assures me that it will take some time for the baby and I to settle into a routine and that I need to be patient. If only I could sleep for longer than a few hours at a stretch I'm sure I would feel more like myself again.

There it was – Kathleen. Esther and Leonard's daughter was named Kathleen. Buster stirred as Miranda bounced from her seat, squealing. 'This is it,' she said, tapping at the page in the diary. 'This is the proof – Esther really is my grandmother.'

She bent down and hugged him and he jumped up, smiling, as if he knew exactly what she was talking about. But there were still so many unanswered questions. From the tone of the diary, it seemed the romance soured between the couple shortly after the birth. Miranda sat back down, filled with an even mixture of elation and apprehension as she read on.

11 February 1949

There has been no time for me to write down my thoughts here and not much to record. The days pass in a fog of nappy washing, house cleaning and cooking. My life on the farm and even at the Conservatorium are such distant memories now that I try not to let myself think about them. Leonard and I have become ships in the night. He is rarely home, preferring to spend his evenings at the pub or out at restaurants with his workmates but the smell of perfume on his shirt collars and the way he refuses to look at me when I ask him where he has been tell me otherwise. I knew within months – even before Kathleen was born – that I had made a huge mistake. Once we were married, I became no more than a possession to him, a trophy, and an increasingly plump one at that! He would brag to his friends about my bravery, telling them about the rescue and making it sound as if fate had destined us to be together. When we were out, he would fawn on me, making out he was the gentleman, but once we were behind closed doors he virtually ignored me, locking himself in his office, supposedly working on business. I know now what I only surmised before, that many of his dealings are suspect, if not completely illegal. Of course he worked in the black market during the war – I heard enough of his conversations with my dad to be sure of that. Since then he has said only that he works in the 'import/export business' but I know he spends a good deal of his time in gambling houses with reprobates and I wouldn't be at all surprised if he is buying and selling stolen goods. Or worse. Talk of moving onto a property has ceased and every time I bring it up he snaps at me and tells me he's not made of money and we will just have to wait. I try not to think about the farm or my happy days as a young girl riding across the hillsides – or Samuel. I find that I am pregnant again, the result of too much Christmas cheer and a notion of wifely obligation. Although my life with Leonard is not what I imagined it would be, I love Kathleen with all my heart and look forward to giving her a brother or sister. Leonard too loves her in his own way but he is not really father material and only spends time with her when it's convenient. She watches him with those wide blue eyes of hers and waits for him to pay her some attention. My children will never want for material things but it is up to me to give them the love and support they need – I will have to be both father and mother in one. When the baby is born in a few months' time I will pack up our things and head south to the Point for a few weeks. I want the children to know about more than just life in the grey shadows of the city. Who knows? I may even be able to convince Leonard that a life on the land would be better for all of us.

Once again the next few pages were blank and then what looked like a hurried note:

18 September 1949, Douglas born 3.49 pm

Douglas – that would be Uncle Doug, her mother's brother who lived in Queensland. There were only two years between them. The remainder of the diary was blank. For some reason Esther hadn't written much leading up to her son's birth and nothing at all afterwards. From the sound of the last few pages, Kathleen had been the only ray of light in her otherwise difficult life. Miranda thought back to the earlier entries: the vibrant young Essie who had loved life so much had certainly vanished.

Closing the diary she stood and looked out over the trees to the wide expanse of sea and sky. Now she had the proof she'd come here to find. Esther was undoubtedly her grandmother. The remaining mystery was why Kathleen thought that she was dead. Had she walked out on the family? It was easy to see how she might leave her husband, but hard to believe that she would walk away from her children. All Miranda had ever been told was that her grandmother had died when Kathleen was eleven. If there were no more clues in the diary, there was only one person who was going to be able to give her the answers, and that was Esther. For some reason Esther had chosen to stay away from her family for all these years and Miranda knew it wasn't going to be easy finding out why. She looked down at Buster, who had wandered over to sit beside her, gazing up at her adoringly. There was no way she could leave him here alone, again.

'You up for a road trip, boy?'

He thumped his tail on the verandah in reply.

⌒

The hospital was just over an hour's drive south. Buster sat beside her in the passenger seat peering through the window and taking in the scenery. Miranda tried to concentrate on the road and block out the carnival that was going on in her head. How was she going to prove to Esther that she was in fact her granddaughter? And how would the news be taken? There was no way of telling what Esther would say or even if she was in any condition to have a conversation. All she could do was wait and see.

She followed the TomTom's directions and drove into the car park. It was the largest regional hospital on this part of the coast and looked like it had recently had a face lift, the outside walls painted in strips of fuschia, khaki and tangerine, with a curved corrugated roof spanning the entranceway. She pulled up in the shade of a huge old banksia, and leaving the windows down a little, gave Buster a pat on the head.

'I won't be long.'

He hung his head as she closed the door and when she turned around he had his paws up on the dashboard, nose pressed against the windscreen. So much for my nice clean car, she thought, smiling to herself. She stepped up to the entrance and the automatic doors hushed open.

The girl at the main reception counter directed her along the corridor and to the right. Esther had been moved out of intensive care, which meant she could have visitors. In the ward, Miranda fluttered her brightest smile at the nurse behind the desk.

'Hello, I'm here to see Esther Wilson.'

'A visitor for Esther?' the nurse asked, one eyebrow raised. 'She told us she didn't have anyone who would be visiting. Are you a friend of hers?'

There was no point trying to explain the whole story. 'Yes. Yes, I am.'

'Down the hall, second on the left,' the nurse pointed. 'Good luck.'

'Thank you.'

It sounded like Esther was being her usual cheery self. As Miranda's shoes squeaked along the floor she thought of that Mary Poppins grandmother she'd conjured up in her imagination as a child, the way she would throw her arms around Miranda and shower her in kisses smelling of butterscotch and tell her stories about the olden days. That make-believe grandmother was a far cry from the woman she was about to visit.

At first she thought the nurse had made a mistake and sent her to the wrong place. Both the beds by the door and the one in the far corner were empty. A screen was drawn across the only other bed in the room and Miranda tiptoed across to it.

'Hello, Esther, are you there? It's me, Miranda,' she called quietly.

When there was no reply she poked her head around the curtain. The woman in the bed bore little resemblance to the one she had found in the cave on the beach. Even though she'd been hurt then, there had been colour in her cheeks and a feistiness about her despite her injury. The face that lay against the starched white pillow gazing out the window into the garden was pallid and defeated.

Miranda walked around to the other side of the bed and stood directly in Esther's line of sight.

'Hi, Esther – do you remember me?'

The old woman's eyes moved to Miranda's face and

hovered there for a minute before they widened slightly in recognition. 'Buster. Where's Buster?'

'He's out in the car. I'm pretty sure they won't let me bring him in. He's fine. But he misses you, of course.'

A smile drifted across Esther's lips. Miranda leant in closer as she started to speak again. 'They won't let me out of here. Doing tests.'

'They'll soon have you back on your feet again. Once you're feeling better.'

Esther shook her head. 'They're giving me the drugs again – to keep me quiet.'

'That would just be painkillers. To help you sleep, take the edge off.' Maybe they were making her a little delirious too?

Miranda pulled up a chair. She wasn't really sure what she'd expected but she hadn't counted on Esther being so listless, so forlorn. Maybe finding out she wasn't all alone in the world was just what she needed to hear. Miranda took a deep breath and began.

'Esther, I have something to tell you, but I'm not really sure how to go about it, so I'm just going to say it. You remember I told you I was getting married?' She paused to wait for a response, but none came, so she pushed on. 'Well, I was looking for something old to wear to my wedding and I remembered this necklace that my mother had – a horseshoe pendant set between two amethysts on a double string of pearls.'

A slight flicker behind Esther's eyes gave Miranda the courage to continue, despite the tumbleweed of anxiety rolling around in her stomach.

'When I found it there was also a newspaper clipping inside the box about a girl rescuing someone from the sea on a horse just off Pelican Point. The girl's name was Esther Wilson and the man she saved was Leonard Clarke.' Was she explaining it properly? Did any of it make sense?

'Why are you telling me this?' Esther's voice shook.

'I did some research into my family tree, and, well, Esther and Leonard were my grandparents. My mother's name is Kathleen, and she has a brother called Douglas.'

Again, a glimmer of recognition.

'I don't know what you're talking about.'

Miranda wasn't sure where to go next. If she told Esther she'd read her diaries, she would lose the woman's trust completely. An idea came to her. She pulled out her phone and scrolled through the photos until she found the image of the young woman in her wedding dress and held it out for Esther to see.

'Is this you?' she asked softly. She watched Esther's eyes fall on the picture and saw the way her mouth drew itself into a line just before she shook her head. 'And this is the necklace,' Miranda said as she flicked to the next image on her phone.

Tears brimmed in the old woman's eyes as she stared at the screen. Miranda's chest ached as she watched them spill over and trickle down the wrinkled cheeks. She bent her head to hide her own sorrow.

She placed her hand on Esther's. 'I'm your granddaughter,' she whispered. 'Kathleen's daughter.'

'Is she alive? And Douglas?'

Miranda nodded. Esther turned her head away, a torrent of sobs wracking her body. Whatever had isolated this woman from her family was something so deep and traumatic it had kept her separated from them for the best part of her life. It was the pain of that separation that Miranda was now witnessing. She sat quietly by the bed and waited for Esther's anguish to subside.

'And what might be happening here?' The nurse's voice shocked Miranda back to her surroundings, but Esther seemed unaware of what was going on around her. 'Is everything all right, Mrs Wilson?' the nurse asked.

Miranda willed Esther to speak, to tell the nurse this was her granddaughter, who had found her after all these years, but Esther's eyes were closed as she wept quietly now.

'I'll let you get some rest,' Miranda whispered and patted Esther's hand again. 'I'll be back.'

She picked up her bag and followed the nurse to the desk.

'I believe Esther was having some tests done. I'd like to speak to the doctor about her condition.'

The nurse organised some papers, refusing to look at Miranda. 'I'm afraid the doctor will only speak to family members.'

Miranda sweetened her tone. 'That's good. Because I'm actually her granddaughter.'

The woman looked at her in disbelief.

'You can confirm it with her if you like.' This was a bluff and Miranda wasn't exactly sure that Esther would answer in the affirmative.

'We were led to believe – by Mrs Wilson – that she didn't have any family.'

'She doesn't have any family *here*,' Miranda said. 'I've come down from Sydney.'

The bluff worked. 'Right, well, if you wait I'm sure the doctor would be keen to speak with you.' The nurse tossed her head and scurried up the corridor.

It took all Miranda's willpower not to rush back into the room and continue her conversation with Esther, but she'd probably had enough of a shock for one day and right now it was more important to find out exactly what was wrong with her.

A middle-aged man with auburn hair approached, wearing a white coat over his blue-striped shirt and tan corduroys. 'So I hear you're Esther's granddaughter,' he said. 'I'm Dr Sommerville.'

Miranda shook the hand he offered and smiled.

'Were you the same woman who found her on the beach and called the paramedics?'

'Yes, I was.'

'But when she was admitted, the records said there was no family?'

She couldn't blame him for questioning her, the whole situation must seem extremely bizarre. Because it was. 'There've been some family issues,' she said.

'Right. I see.' He raised his eyebrows and folded his arms. 'We were concerned about the intensity of Esther's infection – it's unusual for sepsis to take hold so quickly unless there's an underlying issue. So we decided to run some tests.'

Miranda could tell he was choosing his words carefully. Couldn't he just get to the point?

'I'm afraid the results aren't good news.' He rubbed his index finger across his bottom lip. 'Esther has lymphoma – it's a cancer of the blood. It affects the immune system, which is why the infection set in so quickly after her fall.'

Cancer. Cancer. The word ricocheted around inside Miranda's brain. 'Is it treatable?'

'We can treat it with chemo and possibly some radiation therapy. Unfortunately, the treatment itself can be as aggressive as the disease, especially for elderly patients like Esther.'

'Does she know?'

'Yes, she does. And she doesn't want any treatment.'

'But that's ridiculous.' She looked up at the doctor through blurry eyes. This wasn't just any old woman, this was her grandmother, the grandmother she'd only just found, and there was no way she was going to let her just curl up and die.

'She's eighty-nine years old. It's not uncommon for patients her age to prefer to go in peace rather than suffer through the chemo. She does have the right to refuse it.'

Miranda slouched against the wall, holding her head in her hands. This was not supposed to happen. The doctor's voice cut through the haze of her thoughts.

'We'll keep her in here for a few more days, until she's completely over the infection, and then she's free to go home. Of course in her condition, you may want to think about some care arrangements. It probably isn't wise for her to be on her own.'

'I will. Thank you.'

She wasn't exactly sure what she was thanking him for, but it seemed the right thing to say. He nodded and started to walk away. 'Oh, I meant to ask, Esther seems to have an almost morbid fear of doctors, of medical staff in general. She's been quite hysterical at times. It's been what you might call an effort getting her to cooperate. Do you know of any reason why?'

'No, no, I don't.'

'Natural at her age, I suppose, but I was just curious.'

She watched him disappear through the plastic swinging doors. It probably wasn't a good idea to discuss all this with Esther now – not after the shock she'd already had. But there was one person she needed desperately to talk to, somebody who had at least some of the answers.

And this time Miranda wouldn't be backing down.

Esther

She could see her face as clearly now as the day she was born, the tiny veins on her eyelids as they closed against the glare of the hospital lights, those fine wisps of fair hair and the perfect crescent shape of her fingernails. Kathleen, they'd called her, after Leonard's mother. And later Douglas, her own father's middle name. Beautiful children, the both of them, like a pair of angels sent down from God for her to cherish. And she did. She loved them so much, clung to them as her marriage disintegrated, as he spent night after night away from home. But something happened – something terrible, something she dreamt about and tried to stop but couldn't.

From then on the voices kept echoing in her head, her parents' voices, night after night, over and over again, pleading for her to help them, before it was too late. And no matter how much she tried to block them out, the only thing that worked were the pills. Just a few at first, to ease

the grief and blur the pain, but soon she'd needed more just
to get through the day. Then that one day came – the day
she couldn't remember.

Miranda

It was dark as she turned into the driveway of her parents' house in Oatley. She turned off the motor, and talked herself through what would happen next. She'd knock on the door, smile pleasantly, tell her mother she needed to talk to her about something and then get straight to the point. If she thought about it too much she might get cold feet.

No you won't.

'No. I won't,' she said out loud. Buster stuck his head over the back of her seat and gave her a lick.

'You must be desperate to get out, buddy, come on. Let's see what sort of reception we get.' She clipped the dog's lead to his collar and hopped out of the car, letting him have a pit stop before she walked resolutely up to the front door. Her finger floated above the doorbell for a few seconds. How do you tell your mother that the woman who had given birth to her, the woman who she thought had died when she was a child, was alive and living only five hours away? It wasn't as if Miranda was even able to explain what had happened but surely her mother had to be told the truth?

You can do this. You can.

She pressed the buzzer and listened as footsteps thumped towards her along the hallway.

'Hello, sweetheart – we weren't expecting you tonight.'

'Hi, Dad – just popped over for a chat.'

Her father pushed open the security door and Buster bounced at him. 'And who do we have here?'

'This is Buster, I'm looking after him for a friend of mine. Is it okay if I stick him out in the yard for a bit?'

'Suppose it's okay. I'll take him out if you like. I hope he likes cats.' He lowered his voice conspiratorially and gave Miranda a wink. 'No need to mention it to your mother. She's in the lounge room watching one of her silly shows.'

'Thanks, Dad.' She gave Buster a pat and headed through the dining room and stuck her head around the door.

'Hi, Mum,' she said in her breeziest voice.

'Miranda, what are you doing here? I called you the other night but there was no answer, I've been worried about you.'

'I've just been away – down the coast – had a few things to sort out.'

'What's going on? Are you and James having problems?'

This was not going exactly as she'd hoped. Her mother was already on edge and Miranda could feel her resolve fading.

Remember the drill – straight to the point.

'Look, there's something I need to talk to you about.' She sat in the armchair opposite her mother and picked up the remote. 'Do you mind if I turn this off for a minute?'

Her mother nodded vaguely.

'Mum, do you remember after the dress fitting when we had that conversation about the necklace, and you got upset?'

Her mother's eyes darted towards the door. 'Why are you still going on about that, Miranda? I told you I know nothing about a necklace.'

There was no way Miranda could avoid it, she was going to have to confess to snooping. 'Well, I couldn't stop thinking about it. When you and Dad were away a couple of weeks ago, I had a look in your room . . .'

Her mother moved forward in the chair, eyes like saucers. 'You came over here and poked around in my bedroom? How dare you!'

Her mother's shrill tone brought her father in to see what the fuss was about. 'What's going on?' he asked.

'Miranda has been nosing around in my belongings, that's what's going on.' There was already a frantic edge to her mother's voice, but Miranda pushed on. 'Dad, Mum, please just hear me out. This is really important. Yes, I did go stickybeaking in your room and I'm sorry about that, but when I found the necklace I also found the newspaper excerpt and photo you'd stored away in the case. Like I said, I couldn't stop thinking about it, so I did some research on the internet to find the names that were mentioned in the clipping.'

As she spoke, Miranda watched the blood drain from her mother's cheeks, and noticed the stern look on her father's face, but there was no turning back now. 'I found out the names of your parents, Mum – Leonard and Esther – and when they were born, and when your father died. But there was no record of your mother's death.' Kathleen shrank back into her chair. It was almost as if she was becoming physically smaller.

'She died when I was eleven years old. I've told you that,' she said in a voice Miranda didn't recognise.

It was an effort to keep her voice steady as she tried to find the right words. 'I know. I know, Mum. But . . . with the wedding and everything, I've been a bit stressed. I needed to get away for a bit, so I drove south, to the place mentioned in the newspaper report.'

'Pelican Point.'

'Yes, that's right. Well, I asked around and . . .'

Just say it.

'And I found her. Your mother. Esther. She's still alive.'

Nobody spoke. Miranda felt like a kid playing statues, afraid to move in case she was caught, her body frozen. She kept her eyes on her mother's face, watched it collapse in confusion, saw her father's bewilderment as he sat on the side of the wing-back chair and put his arm around his wife's shoulder.

It was him who broke the silence. 'If this is some kind of sick joke, Miranda, you can just leave. You've no right coming over here and upsetting your mother like this.'

She hadn't been prepared for her father's anger, had never in fact experienced it. 'Dad, do you think I'd joke about something like this? I've met her. She lives on her own in a shack by the beach. I've been staying there for the last five days. You have to believe me. I don't know why or how she happens to still be alive but I'm telling you she is.' She was pacing, unsure what else she could say to convince them she was telling the truth. Kneeling on the floor by her mother's chair, she took her hand.

'Mum, I know you've never wanted to talk about this, but how were you told about your mother's death? Can you remember anything?'

Her father stood and glowered at her. 'That's enough.'

'No, Brian, it's all right.' Kathleen still spoke softly, her voice wavering, but she gestured to her husband, who sat down again beside her. 'I found her. Lying on her bed. Her hair falling around her face. She looked like an angel. Douglas had gone to a friend's house to play. I was the only one home. I remember I ran into the room and saw her there. At first I thought she was asleep, but when I called to her she didn't stir. I knew something was wrong then. I held onto the doorframe and called her again, over and over. Then I walked towards the bed and I saw the bottle of tablets. She told me once that she took them to settle her stomach. The lid was off the bottle and it was lying on its side, empty. I put my hand on her arm and shook her. "Mum, Mum," I said, but she didn't move, she just rolled backwards and forwards on the bed. I don't remember going next door to the neighbours' house, but I must have because they called an ambulance. The siren was like someone screaming. There were all these people out on the footpath watching as they carried her out. She was so still, not moving at all. I just stood there and watched while they pushed her inside the ambulance and shut the door. They wouldn't let me go with her. That was the last time I saw her.' Kathleen looked up at Miranda, tears filming her cheeks. 'My father collected Douglas and me from the neighbour's house that night.

It was dark. The house was cold. He sat us down in the kitchen side by side. I could smell the liquor but he wasn't drunk like he often was. "Your mother's not coming back," he said, "she's dead. It's just the three of us now." He left us there, me and Dougie, and went to bed. Just like that. We sat there crying, hugging each other. We didn't know what to do. After a while we went to bed, both of us in my bed, and we cried ourselves to sleep.'

Miranda wanted to say something comforting but there were no words. She squeezed her mother's fingers gently.

Kathleen continued. It was as if the seal on her grief had been broken and she had to pour it out. 'I tried to ask my father the next day about what had happened but he went into a rage. "You're never to speak of her again, do you hear me? She's gone and that's that." There was no one else I could ask. My mother's parents had died a few months before in an accident and we had very few friends. I kept thinking of her lying there on that bed and wondering what I could have done to save her. It wasn't until I was older that I realised she'd taken her own life.'

'I don't get it.' Her father rested his hands on his knees and looked at Miranda. 'If Kathleen saw her there on the bed and then taken away in the ambulance and then her father told her she was dead, how can she possibly still be alive?'

Miranda shook her head. 'I don't know, Dad. The only person who can answer that is Esther.' She looked back at her mother, trying to gauge how much further she should push. *Only one way to find out.* 'So your father didn't ever speak of her again?'

'No, he forbade us to mention her name, said she'd done a bad thing and we were to forget about her. He started coming home earlier for a while, trying to be a real father, but it didn't last. Before long he started calling by the pub on his way home, staying out later and later, and I was left to look after Dougie.'

'But you were only a child yourself.'

'I had to grow up fast. After a year or so, Dad told us it was too hard for him to look after us on his own any more and he sent us to a children's home. I'd turned twelve by that time. And I'd never gotten over losing Mum. Dougie and I were separated and after a while a family came and took him into foster care. I didn't see him for years afterwards.' Kathleen dropped her head and wept, the sound of her sorrow filling the room.

'It's all right, love, you don't have to say any more.'

Miranda watched as her father put his arms around her mother and held her close. The two of them rarely showed any physical affection for each other, but there'd always been a tenderness between them that Miranda knew was love.

'I'm so sorry, Mum,' she whispered.

Her mother shivered. 'I still remember the smell in that place, a mixture of urine and bleach. The beds were set out in rows and some of the girls would wet the bed, they were so afraid of the nuns. The older girls, like me, would have to scrub the floors and wash the linen, look after the younger ones. We were like slaves. If you complained or didn't do exactly as you were told, they'd hit you on the hand or on the behind with a wooden stick. Sometimes I'd lie in bed at night with my eyes closed, imagining my mother would knock on the door one day and gather me up in her arms and take me home. But when I crawled out of bed and knelt down on the cold floor for morning prayers, I knew that was never going to happen.'

'Didn't your father ever come and visit you?' The idea of a father abandoning his children like that was more than Miranda could fathom.

'At first, once a month on a Sunday, but then the visits grew less frequent, once every few months or so, and when Dougie was fostered out he hardly came at all. After a while I just accepted that this was the way it was. I kept my head down, did what I was told, learnt to shut myself off when other girls were being beaten or verbally abused.'

'How long were you there, Mum?'

'Four years, and seven months. The day I turned seventeen they gave me a slip of paper with the address of a boarding house on it and the phone number of an office where I could get a job. I packed up my few belongings and left. I had no idea if my father was still living, but when I went back one day to our old house, he'd gone. Dougie wrote to me a few years later to say he'd been notified that he'd died. Sclerosis of the liver. Drank himself to death.' Kathleen's mouth twisted into a sneer. 'A shame it took him so long.'

The ticking of the clock on the mantelpiece marked the seconds as Miranda thought about what to say next. She'd had no idea where this whole conversation was headed when she started and the revelations about the difficulties of her mother's life had completely floored her. Her father looked just as baffled. He rubbed his palm across his forehead and stood.

'Are you sure that this woman is really your grandmother, Miranda?'

She unfolded her legs and pushed herself up. 'I'm positive, Dad. She had a fall – that's how I first met her, on the beach – and she ended up quite sick and had to be taken to hospital. I stayed at her place and minded her dog . . .'

'That would be Buster, the dog in our backyard,' said her father.

'That's him.' She ignored the quizzical look on her mother's face. 'Anyway, while I was there I found some diaries, and I couldn't help myself, I had to find out, so I read them.'

'You're getting to be quite the detective, young lady.' He smiled at her and she lifted an eyebrow in reply. 'So how did you raise the subject with her?'

'I went to visit her in the hospital and told her I'd been researching the family tree. I told her about the newspaper clipping and just sort of fudged over the rest.'

'I see.' While Miranda and her father talked, Kathleen sat straight as a post, braced against the back of the chair, staring at the floor.

'Well, I'm completely confused about where this leaves us,' said her father. 'How did she – Esther – how did she take the news that you were her granddaughter?'

'She didn't believe me to start with, not until I told her about Mum, and Uncle Doug. When I mentioned their names, she broke down.'

'You're one hundred per cent certain it's her?' Kathleen's voice drifted up from the chair.

'I am, Mum.'

'So she deserted us then.'

'What?'

'She tried to kill herself, and when that didn't work, she refused to come back. She left Dougie and me, knowing what our father was like, left us to be neglected and end up in a home.' The poison in her voice made the hairs on the back of Miranda's neck stand on end.

'We don't know that, Mum. I thought maybe you could come back with me and we could talk to her together, find out what actually happened.'

Her mother sprang from the chair. 'No. That will not be happening. If this woman is my mother, as you say she is, then she clearly hasn't made any effort to find me or my brother in all these years. She abandoned us, and as far as I'm concerned she died fifty-five years ago and that's the end of it.' Before Miranda could say anything, Kathleen stormed from the room and down the hallway, the slamming of the bedroom door signalling the conversation was over.

Her father sighed and collapsed onto the lounge.

'Should I go talk to her?' Miranda asked.

'I think it's better if we just leave her, love. Give her some time to come to terms with the news. She might come around.'

'Or she might not. Dad, there's one more thing I haven't told you about Esther.' She sat down beside her father. 'When they took her to hospital she had blood poisoning. They did some tests to find out why it was so severe and found out she has cancer.'

'Shit.' Her father ran a hand across his eyes. 'Does she know?'

'Yes. And she's refusing to have any treatment.'

'Do you know how long she's got?'

Miranda shrugged. 'No, I don't.'

'Right. Well leave that one with me. I don't think your mother needs any more surprises tonight.' He shook his head again. 'I can't believe it. All these years and I never knew what she'd gone through. She told me her parents were both dead when we met but never wanted to talk about it. I respected that. We were happy. It wasn't until after you kids were born that I knew there was something wrong. She'd be miserable for weeks on end for no apparent reason, then just snap herself out of it. I didn't know what to do to help her.' Her father's voice cracked.

Miranda moved closer and hooked her arm through his. 'I know, Dad. There wasn't anything you could do. Any of us.'

'It was just easier to wait it out, go along with her moods. You know what she was like – she always came good in the end.'

Miranda thought back over her childhood to the days and weeks where her mother had hardly spoken, the times she would hear her crying behind a locked door in the bedroom, and the better times where she would laugh and they would all feel like a family again. 'We all did the best we could, Dad, just like she did, I guess. Do you think she'll come around? Agree to see Esther?'

'I don't know, love. It's been a huge shock for her. Let's just see how she goes.' The look of despair on her father's face told Miranda he wasn't hopeful. She threw her arms around his neck and gave him a good long hug. 'Have you eaten?' he asked. 'There's some leftover casserole in the fridge if you're hungry.'

'Nah, I stopped on the drive up and had a snack.' She

glanced at the clock. It was nearly half past nine. Time she was getting home. 'I have to get going.'

'Of course you do. James will be keen to see you.'

She stood quickly, hoping her father wouldn't see the look of panic on her face. 'Dad, there's something else.'

'Really?'

She heard the fatigue in her father's voice and saw his face, heavy with worry. He'd had enough for one night. 'Yeah, would you mind if I leave Buster here for a day or two? Until I sort something out?'

'I suppose so. I'll just keep him out of your mother's way.'

He saw her to the door and kissed her on the cheek.

Back in the car she heaved a sigh of relief. Or was it exhaustion? Had Esther really abandoned her children as Kathleen presumed? And if not, why had Leonard told the children she was dead? There were still questions left unanswered, but for now they would have to remain that way. It was time to face the music with James.

She gripped the wheel and reversed out of the driveway, trying to ignore the stabbing pain in her chest every time she thought about what she had to do next.

Esther

There was a voice trying to pierce through the fog. A high-pitched, frantic voice. The voice of a child. Calling to her. 'Mummy, Mummy, please answer me. Can you hear me? Mummy, please say something.'

Kathleen. It was Kathleen. But she was so far away.

She tried to open her mouth, to tell her daughter that everything was all right, that she was just having a rest, but as hard as she tried, nothing came out. If she kept her eyes closed for a bit longer then she'd be able to speak. She'd taken some extra pills, just to help her escape for a while, but they'd wear off soon.

The voice was still there but now it was distorted, like a record on her father's old gramophone player when it hadn't been wound enough, the words twisted and garbled. Not her little girl's voice any more but a man's voice. One of *them*. The ones that wouldn't let her out of the room, who made her sit in the chair by the window all day, looking out at the jacarandas and the wide green stretch of grass that reminded her of home, taunting her every time they turned the key in the lock.

She pinched her eyes shut, trying to stop the memories churning around in her head, praying that when she woke up she would be back in her home, her real home, Garewangga, with Kathleen and Douglas and her parents by her side.

Miranda

iranda arrived at the apartment just after ten o'clock. She sat in the car looking through the dust-streaked window at the plain white facade of the building with its sleek lines and louvered shutters, the steel door covered by a security gate – a far cry from the never-locked tumbledown shack she'd been living in for the last week. Somehow Esther's cottage had felt more like a home, despite the drafts that snuck in beneath the crooked door and the lack of modern comforts. Or maybe because of it. But it was the thought of what lay in store for her inside the apartment that was of more concern to her right now.

Since she'd made up her mind to break off the engagement her resolve hadn't faltered. Until now. Now, when James was only a few steps away from her, when what she had to say would change the course of both their lives. She played with the diamond ring on her finger. James had got down on one knee while they were at Noosa for her thirtieth birthday and she hadn't even hesitated. But there'd always been something missing: real passion. The toe-curling, heart-stopping kind of passion that meant you couldn't stop thinking about the person, that meant you couldn't wait to see them again. Like she felt for Vincent. No matter how much she tried to dismiss what had happened between the two of them as a crazy fling, a wild moment of abandon, she hoped in her heart that it was more.

But this wasn't about Vincent, it was about James. Five years. He was her best friend. Even so, she'd kept him at a distance, kept a small piece of herself tucked away, had never been totally open with him. Their relationship had become a habit, one that she knew deep down wasn't good for her, but one that she was too afraid to break. Recently that fear had been replaced by a greater one – the fear of marrying a man she didn't truly, madly love. There was no question about it – she was making the right decision, for herself and for James.

You deserve better. And so does he.

She gave a slight nod, picked up her handbag and locked the car door behind her. The key clicked in the security door and she walked in, stood and listened for a moment. Nothing. Perhaps he'd gone out to grab a late bite. The kitchen light was on and there was music playing on the sound system. The heels of her boots tapped loudly on the tiled floor. A few takeaway containers sat on the table along with a couple of empty beer bottles. A noise in the bedroom upstairs made her start. He was home after all. Her stomach lurched. Can I really go through with this?

Before she had a chance to think any further, James was on the stairs.

'Hi,' she said when he was almost at the bottom.

He tripped at the sound of her voice, gripping the railing to balance. 'Mindy, shit, I didn't know you were here.'

'Sorry, I just got in.' She was trying not to sound formal and awkward, but it wasn't working.

James came straight over and threw his arms around her, kissing her hair. 'God, I've missed you. You smell so good. I was just about to have a nightcap, feel like one?'

'No thanks. You go ahead.' Alcohol might bolster her courage but she wanted to say what she had to say with a clear head.

'So, how was it? Have a good break?'

He stood at the fridge filling a glass with ice from the dispenser. He was wearing the retro Hawaiian boxers she'd given him last Christmas and a loose navy blue T-shirt. She watched as he poured himself a bourbon, the dark amber liquid glugging into the glass, crackling over the chunks of ice.

'Mindy?'

'What was that? Oh, the break, yes, it was fine.'

He took a sip of his drink and put the glass on the bench, then scratched the tip of his nose.

'Is something wrong?'

Where would she start? Probably with Esther and work her way up. 'I need to talk to you about something. Do you remember that argument I had with Mum, about the necklace?'

'The one where she went all hysterical and smashed the glass?'

'Well, yes, sort of.' She was feeling more protective of her mother now she knew the truth about her past. Not that that was the issue here. Continuing with her story, Miranda told James all about what she'd found at her parents' house, coming across Esther on the beach, reading the diaries, and the final confirmation in the hospital, ending with her mother's reaction and revelations at the house just hours before.

She finished her story as James poured himself a second drink. 'You really have been busy, while you've been away. Why didn't you tell me any of this before?' There was an injured tone to his voice that once again stirred Miranda's guilt.

'I wanted to be sure before I told anyone.'

'Even me?'

She looked at him and knew it was now or never. 'I wasn't lying last week when I said I needed to get away for a while. It wasn't all about my grandmother. The last few weeks, probably months, I've been feeling really nervous about the wedding.'

James nodded. 'Pretty normal, I'd say.'

She held up a hand, tried to keep her voice steady. 'Please, just let me finish. It's more than nerves. I've made a mistake. I can't marry you.' The last sentence sent her over the edge, tears streaming down her cheeks. There was an awful silence as James lowered his glass but didn't say a word. Resting his hands on the benchtop, he hung his head, so that Miranda couldn't see the expression on his face or in his eyes, but she could tell from the heaving of his chest that he was fighting to contain his emotions. She sat wordlessly and waited, willing him to speak, to say anything rather than prolong the sudden tension that had thickened the air between them.

When he finally raised his eyes and looked at her, the hurt that filled them almost brought her undone. 'Is there someone else?'

'No. Maybe. I don't know.'

He slammed his fist down beside the glass, sending it skittling sideways, but Miranda caught it before it fell to the floor. 'Jesus, Miranda, what the hell do you mean, you don't know? How can you not know, either there is or there isn't. It's not that fucking hard.'

'I met someone, while I was away.' Her voice was so muted she wondered if he'd actually heard what she said.

'While you were away? This week? So you're going to throw five years together down the toilet for someone you just met. I don't believe this.'

'This isn't about him, James. It's about me. I've been having doubts for a while now, but I've pushed them aside, tried to ignore them. Being away just gave me the space to be honest with myself.'

'What's his name?'

'It doesn't matter.'

'Did you sleep with him?'

It was the question she'd been dreading, the one she had prayed he wouldn't ask. 'I told you it's not about him!' She was yelling back now, spurred on by James' anger, angry at herself.

'You did, didn't you?' His voice was quieter again now, breaking. 'You screwed some guy you just met, even though you're supposed to be marrying me.'

'James, please, it wasn't like that,' she sobbed, hardly able to see him through her tears. This whole scenario had played out so differently to how she'd hoped. But what could she expect? That he was going to be happy about it? Hug her and send her on her way? What could she say to make him understand?

Somehow she made her way towards him, stood in front of him and took his hands in hers, and he didn't resist. They'd shared so much of their lives together. Surely he deserved to know why she was doing this, to hear the truth. As she started to speak, he looked directly at her, but she didn't flinch or break her gaze. 'I'm so sorry. I've hurt you and I can never make up for that. But I can't marry you when I know in my heart that you love me more than I love you. It's not fair, to either of us.'

Sliding the ring from her finger, she placed it in his palm, folded her fingers around his and rested her head against his shoulder one last time, remembering how much she had once loved him.

⤙⤚

Lights quivered on the black water of the river. A man in a hoodie walked by with his dog. She pressed the button and heard the car doors lock as the pair wandered away, and she thought of Buster, wondered what he was making of his city sojourn. When she'd left the apartment she had no idea where she was going, all she knew was that she had to get away. Her first thought had been to continue driving, pick up Buster and make a beeline for Pelican Point, but after driving all that way earlier in the day and her two confessions tonight, she really didn't have it in her. A ravenous hunger had consumed her and she'd stopped in for a burger at an all-night diner, then parked here by the river to devour it.

She screwed up the wrapper and threw it onto the floor of the car. The food had physically filled her stomach but a gnawing sense of emptiness still gripped her. Images of James flickered in her brain like a broken neon light. In one way it was a relief to have finally told the truth, been honest with him, and with herself. But now that sense of release had been replaced by an overwhelming loneliness. Tears stung her eyes. She made a weak effort to blink them away before she dropped her head against the steering wheel and let them fall. Her relationship with James was over, and her mother was so traumatised by the news she'd delivered that she'd locked herself in her room, where Miranda had no doubt she still remained. Everyone she knew and loved would think her mad, hate her for ruining the wedding, for breaking James' heart. Her closest friend was the one person who would understand, who wouldn't judge her, and she needed to see her right now.

⁓

'Who the hell is it?'

'It's me, Miranda.'

Belle unlocked and opened the door, wrapped in her purple velour dressing-gown, squinting in the glare of the porch light. 'My god, woman, do you know what time it is?' She looked closer. 'What's happened? Come in, come in.'

Miranda followed her friend down the narrow hallway to her lounge room. She could feel herself shaking but wasn't sure whether it was from the cold or the events of the last few hours. Either way, there was nothing she could do to stop herself trembling.

'You're fucking freezing, Mirry, here, put this around you.' Belle grabbed a crocheted blanket and wrapped it around Miranda's shoulders before guiding her to the lounge and helping her sit. 'I'll get us a coffee.'

She returned with two steaming mugs and placed them on the table in front of Miranda. 'Now tell me what's happened.'

'I've called off the wedding. You were right – James isn't the man for me.'

Belle, who had just picked up her coffee, put it straight back down. 'Shit. Really?'

Miranda sipped at the dark, sweet brew and nodded. 'And there's a good chance I won't be practising law for much longer, either. I've probably been sacked and if I haven't there's a good chance I'll resign.' That was another admission she hadn't put into words until now.

'So what are you going to do?'

'Short term, I'm going back to Pelican Point to look after my grandmother. Long term, I have no particular plans.'

'Well, good for you.' Belle gave her a hug, and despite the throbbing in her head, Miranda mustered a weak smile in return.

'Is it okay if I bunk down here for the night?'

'Absolutely. On one condition.'

'What?'

'I get the whole story, start to finish, over breakfast in the morning.'

'Deal.'

Esther

'I met your granddaughter yesterday. Lovely young woman. She's very concerned about you.'

Esther barely listened as the doctor's gravelly voice rambled on. There was nothing more he could tell her that she wanted to hear – only that she was allowed to go home.

'She asked me about possible treatments and I told her you didn't want any.'

She shifted her head on the pillow. 'You told her about the cancer?'

The doctor nodded his head, hands stuck in his pockets.

'You had no right.' How dare he tell the girl her business? If she wanted her to know, she'd tell her herself. If she ever saw her again.

'As your next of kin, I thought she had the right to know. When you were admitted we didn't have any relatives recorded.'

There he was, at it again, prying. She'd learnt not to trust any of them. Turned your words around and tried to make out you were saying something you didn't mean. Used it against you. Better not to say too much even now.

'What about her parents – are they alive? I presume one of them is your son or daughter.'

Her son Douglas.

Her daughter Kathleen.

The children she hadn't allowed herself to think about for all these years. She couldn't even remember how long it was since she'd seen them. Dougie hadn't been there that day. Only Kathleen.

The doctor gave a slight shake of his head and picked up Esther's chart. 'Looks like we've finally got this infection under control, anyway, so we should be able to discharge you in another day or two. Let's just see how you go over the next twenty-four hours, shall we? And if you do change your mind and want to discuss further treatment, get one of the nurses to let me know.'

She angled her head and gazed back out the window. White roses, her favourites, were in bloom. A magpie flew down and landed on the edge of the cement birdbath in the centre of the garden, dipped his head in and splashed about before flapping away again.

'It would buy you more time, Esther. But that's up to you.'

More time? Time for what? Remembering? Regretting?

A tiny voice whispered inside her head.

Hoping.

Miranda

The drive back was longer than she remembered. It didn't help that she was stiff and sore from sleeping on Belle's couch. She'd kept her end of the bargain, filling Belle in on all the gory details of the scene with James and then what she didn't know already about Esther. Belle had insisted that she would break the news about the wedding to all their friends and cancel the flowers, gift registry, music and photographer, while Miranda herself would handle the church, the reception house and her parents. And that's where she'd headed – to her parents' house – straight after yet another enormous bear hug from Belle.

Despite her trepidation, her father had listened sympathetically while she told him about James, omitting the details about Vincent. If her mother had been up and about, Miranda was sure she wouldn't have been so understanding, but there was nothing to worry about on that score: Kathleen was still in bed and that's where she was likely to stay for the rest of the day. They decided not to make things worse by telling her the additional news just yet. After a long, tear-filled morning, Miranda grabbed Buster and kissed her father goodbye.

It was a long stretch in the car to Pelican Point, so she'd decided against visiting Esther today. It was another hour's drive and she needed to get Buster home. In that in-between time of day where activity has stopped and night hasn't yet fallen, she drove through town. The only movement on the inlet was a lone pelican floating across the velvety surface of the water. There wouldn't be a scrap of fresh food at the house, so she pulled over at the grocery store, thankful there was a young boy manning the till instead of Norma.

When she got back to the car, Buster was barking raucously, his paws on the rim of the passenger seat window, nose streaking the glass. The pelican had waddled onto the sand and was only a few metres away from the car – she could see the black centre of his beady eye and the fleshy sack of his beak. So could Buster. 'Righty-o, that's enough, leave the poor thing alone.' He whimpered as he sat down, turning his head towards the bird, which spread its enormous wings and lifted into the sky when Miranda started up the engine. 'You're a funny old thing,' she said, reaching over and giving Buster a rub on the neck. She'd grown so fond of the dog in such a short space of time, she could imagine how much Esther must be missing him.

As she approached the end of the access road she saw a car parked at the barrier – Vincent's black ute. What was he doing here? She hadn't planned on seeing him yet, but just the thought of him made her legs go weak. Bags in hand, she started off at a brisk pace, keeping her eyes on the track now that dusk had fallen. Waves rumbled out past the headland, a sound that she never tired of, so welcoming after the traffic and noise of the city. But not very much further along, a strange scent made her stop and sniff the air. What was it? Not the usual perfume of bush mint that she so loved out here, or the salty smell of the sea she'd grown accustomed to. No, it was something else. Buster had noticed it too and lifted his head.

Smoke.

But where was it coming from? The wind was blowing from the north-east, the direction she was heading in. It was impossible to see in the shadowy light, but the closer she got to the cottage the stronger the smell became. If it was a bushfire, it must be awfully close. She walked faster, stumbling over a tree root and almost falling flat on her face. What would she do if there was a fire? Grab what she could of Esther's belongings – definitely her diaries – and get out as fast as possible? Vincent would be there; he would know what to do.

As she made her way out of the shelter of the trees and into the clearing at the bottom of the property she saw that it wasn't the bush that was on fire. It was the house, or at least the back part of it. The shed and laundry were alight with bright orange flames, growing larger with each burst of wind.

'Shit!' Dropping the bags, she ran past the chicken coop, where the hens were clucking madly, Buster at her heels, the heat from the fire becoming more intense as she got closer.

There was another smell, too, not just smoke, but something more acrid. Petrol.

When she reached the out-buildings the fumes were even stronger. The fire was spreading quickly. Her head was spinning. The only hose she'd seen on the property was attached to the tap at the back of the laundry. Right where the fire was burning. There was nothing else for it, she had to act. Stripping off her jacket, she pulled it over her head to shield her face. Even so, the heat from the blaze was overpowering, forcing her to the ground, where she crawled along towards the tap. Just a little further and she'd make it. There. She pushed herself up, kneeling and reaching for the tap. The hot metal stung her palm but she forced herself to keep going, turning the handle as far as it would go. The hose was coiled around a reel. She grabbed the end and yanked, moving away as fast as she could until she could tolerate the heat, then turned and aimed the nozzle towards the fire. Flames sizzled beneath the force of the water. Steam billowed into the air. Buster ran in circles behind Miranda, rushing forward every few seconds, growling at the commotion.

'Get out of it,' Miranda yelled at him, 'do you want to get yourself burnt?'

Vincent. Where the hell was he? Why would he park his car there and just disappear? Surely if he was in the house the disturbance would have brought him outside, if not the smell.

It was almost dark now, but in the glow of the fire as it died down Miranda could make out the outline of the house, which looked to have escaped without any damage. As she peered through the smoke-filled gloom, a movement in her peripheral vision made her turn. A tall figure was loping away through the bush. Her scalp bristled. Her heartbeat pounded in her ears. Someone had been here the whole time, someone who was wearing a black duffle coat and was now fleeing.

'Vincent?' She heard her voice call his name as she watched whoever it was disappear. 'Vincent,' she repeated to herself.

The fire was just about out. Drifts of smoke curled above the smouldering framework of the laundry and shed. But still the petrol odour stung Miranda's nostrils. The thought that someone else had been here – that *Vincent* had been here – and that he had fled rather than help her put out the fire, made her feel physically sick. Had he *lit* the fire? Had he doused the place with petrol first? She dropped the hose and fell to her knees on the sodden grass, retching over and over until she sank to the ground, giving in to the sobs that came from somewhere so deep inside that her body shook violently. When the tremors finally subsided she reached out to Buster, who sat quietly by her side.

Struggling to her feet she grabbed the hose again and wet down the outside of the house, making sure to cover every inch, washing away the petrol stains she imagined must be there. When the walls were well and truly soaked she stumbled back and turned off the tap. Somehow she retraced her steps and found the bags she had dropped beside the chook yard and made her way into the house.

Fumbling her way to the table she found the matches and lit the lamp. She stood and stared at the puddle forming around her boots. The realisation that she was drenched from head to foot sent a new series of shudders through her limbs. She curled her arms around her middle in an effort to stem the shaking but seemed unable to will herself to move any further. It wasn't until Buster jumped up at her that she was able to snap herself out of the trance.

Take off the wet clothes. Get warm. Feed the dog. Eat.

She went through the motions, concentrating so hard on each task that her mind didn't have time to wander. When all of that was done, she huddled up on the lounge, pulling the blankets over her, and allowed herself to think.

It was definitely Vincent's car she'd seen parked on the track – an R.M. Williams sticker emblazoned across the back window. And the figure who had run off through the bush looked around his height and was wearing a black jacket, like the one he'd been wearing that first night he came to visit. But why would Vincent try to burn down Esther's house? He'd been the one person around here who actually seemed to like her. And he'd put himself out to help when she'd been so ill, called the ambulance, made sure Miranda was okay. He'd seemed so genuine, so honest. The only motivation he could possibly have was money. And Richard Wilson had plenty of that, enough to be able to pay someone to do his dirty work for him. Could she really have been so stupid, falling for a man who was such a scoundrel, who would put an old woman out of her home, who could lie straight to her face?

The anguish that washed through her as she'd watched him vanish into the night was morphing into something else: a dark anger that was beginning to burn. There was no way he was going to get away with this. He might have blinded her with his charm but he was going to have to answer for this – first to her and then to the police. There was a good chance he'd be gone when she got there but in the morning she'd be going out to Garewangga to see what he had to say for himself, before she made sure both he and his criminal of a boss paid.

She lifted her head and flipped the pillow over, pounding it into submission with her fist, over and over until the hollow in the centre was as hollow as her heart.

Esther

Sometimes they still came to her in her sleep, just as they had that night in her dream, all those years ago.

Her father at the wheel of the car, straining to see, her mother clutching her handkerchief in the passenger seat, her face pale with worry, rain pelting onto the windscreen, the wipers sweeping backwards and forwards like the pendulum of a metronome, clearing the glass for only a second before it was again covered in water. It was early morning and the fog that had thickened the sky at daybreak still cloaked the mountain. In the opposite direction a truck hurtled along the highway. From where she looked down on the scene Esther could see it gathering speed as the driver took the bend way too fast. The back of the trailer wobbled as he hit the brakes, the screech of the tyres choked by the wet asphalt, the whole thing skidding sidewards over the centre line and then the sickly sound of crunching metal as truck and car collided.

There was no scream.

No sound.

Only perhaps a slight intake of breath as her mother looked up and saw the huge beast bearing down. And after a few desperate seconds of silence, the deafening bellow as the truck exploded into flames, the car crushed beneath. Fat black clouds of smoke poisoned the mist and the smell of burning flesh scorched the air, until Esther thought she herself would suffocate.

That night she'd woken gagging, coughed until her throat was raw and her eyes bulging, her body seized by an uncontrollable shaking. The house was in darkness. From the next room she could hear Leonard's drunken snore. Throwing back the blankets she tore from her bed and ran to the hallway, picking up the receiver of the phone. One ring, two, three, four . . . each of them like a siren sounding in her brain. *Come on, answer, pick up.* But it rang out. She dialled again, and again, each time more urgently until she fell to the floor in despair. This was all her fault. She had blamed her father for years for Samuel's death, until time rubbed away her grief, but since her own children had been born she'd learnt that a parent will do anything to protect their child, no matter how misguided. She'd come to value her parents for all they had done for her and adored the way they doted on Kathleen and Dougie. They were coming to collect her, to take her home to Garewangga, and although she hadn't told them yet, she wouldn't be returning to Sydney. Or to Leonard. And they were coming tomorrow.

She had to do something, try to stop them from getting in that car. The only way was to drive there herself. There was no telling exactly when the accident might be – it could be days or weeks, but it could be sooner. Could she risk leaving the children here with Leonard or should she wake them now and take them with her? No, it would be too frightening to drag them from their beds out into the cold, wet night. They wouldn't understand. Leonard was their father, he could take care of them. It would only be for a day or two, just long enough for her to warn them.

Rushing to his bedroom, she switched on the lamp. 'Leonard, Leonard, wake up. Please.'

She placed her hand on his shoulder and shook him, gently at first but then harder, his head rocking from side to side on the pillow, until he peered at her through half-closed lids.

'For Christ's sake, what is it?' he croaked. The sour smell of whisky stained the air.

She moved back slightly from the bed now that he was awake. 'I need to go to Garewangga. Tonight.'

'What the hell are you talking about?'

Unsure of how to explain herself and afraid of arousing his anger, she calmed herself and began again. 'Do you remember when I rescued you from the sea that night and I told you I'd dreamt the whole thing, that was how I knew about the boat sinking?'

He looked at her blankly.

'Well, I've had other dreams that have been the same, that have come true. And I . . . I've just had a horrible one about my parents being in a road accident. I've tried calling them but they won't answer. I need to go down there and stop them getting in the car. I need you to mind the children.'

Leonard pushed himself upright in the bed. His hair, usually combed back from his face, hung in greasy strands across his forehead. It had been some time since Esther had bothered to look at him this closely and she could see now how haggard the years of drinking had made him. When he spoke, the venom in his voice forced her to take a step back. 'Are you mad? Did you think I ever believed that ridiculous story you concocted about dreaming of my boat sinking?' His laugh echoed in the dark corners of the room. 'And if you think I'd let you take my car off in the middle of the night on some wild goose chase, leaving your duties here at home, you can think again.'

'But, Leonard, it wasn't a story and this isn't . . .'

He was on his feet in an instant, the back of his hand striking her temple, forcing her off balance. She toppled backwards, heard the crack of her skull as it connected with the corner of the table. And that was that.

It was a night she'd pushed right to the furthest recesses of her mind, but as she thought of it again now, lying here in the hospital bed, it seemed to have happened to someone else. Another Esther. Not the spirited country girl Essie, who had lost the man she truly loved, but another woman, who had made the wrong choices, and who'd become an imitation of herself rather than staying true to who she was and who she might have been. That night had been the beginning of the end: the end of her parents' lives, the end of her plans to escape Leonard and the miserable existence they led together, the end of any hope she might have had of living a normal life with her children. Pain and grief and guilt had engulfed her and the pills became her only relief. Her only escape.

Miranda

S he woke groggy and shattered, the smell of stale smoke
stinging her nostrils. Buster lay beside her, refusing to
move until she extricated herself from the tangle of
blankets. When she ventured outside to inspect the damage
in the daylight, the sight of Esther's ruined laundry and shed
made her throat ache. The fire had been dangerously close to
the house, had in fact singed the timber boards flanking the
back door. If Miranda hadn't arrived when she did, scared
off the intruder, the whole place would have been burnt to
the ground.

The intruder.

Vincent.

Let's see what he has to say for himself.

The farm was quiet, the only horses nearby being the mother
and foal. Ordinarily Miranda would have smiled at the

perfect picture they made against the pristine backdrop of the rolling hills and the wide, blue ocean. But this morning she was on a mission. And she wouldn't be fobbed off with excuses or lies. She lifted her fist to the door and bashed again. 'Vincent, open up. Now.'

Just as she was about to bang once more, the door opened and there he was, in nothing but a pair of jocks, rubbing sleep from his eyes. Obviously recovering from last night's antics. 'Well, this is an unexpected visit.' Was he serious? She stepped back, raised her palm and slapped him across the face. Hard.

'What was that for?' he asked, incredulous, rubbing his cheek where a red welt was already beginning to appear.

'You know damn well what that was for. I was there last night, remember? Or are you going to pretend you didn't see me, just ran off because you got cold feet?' The nerve of this guy was unbelievable.

Hands on his hips, he narrowed his eyes at her and frowned. 'I haven't got a bloody clue what you're talking about. I was up half the night dealing with the mare with the new foal – she's got mastitis. I was squeezing milk from her teats if you must know, trying to avoid being kicked in the head for most of it.'

'So that wasn't your car I saw parked on the track, and that wasn't you racing away from Esther's in your duffle coat.' He could bullshit as much as he liked – she wasn't buying it.

'Running away from Esther's? I have no idea what you're talking about, Miranda.'

He was good, she had to give him that. 'Don't bother trying to explain yourself to me. Save it for the police. Oh, and for Esther. She might like to know why the only friend she has around here wants to burn her house down. Or at least find out how much you were getting paid for your dirty work.'

'Burn her house down?'

'You're doing a very good job of looking surprised, I must say. I'm sorry to disappoint you, but I put the fire out before it damaged the house. So if you and your fuckwit boss planned on stopping her from coming back, you can think again. Your arson attempt didn't work.'

'Whoa, there. Hold on a minute.' He held his hands palms up in front of him in defence. 'Like I said, I've been here all night, and Richard's away, so you're barking up the wrong tree. I'm not saying he definitely wasn't involved in this – I wouldn't put it past him – but if he was behind it he was paying somebody else, not me.'

'Someone who drove your car and wore your clothes.'

'Ah, okay.' He nodded his head slowly. 'I dropped my car at the mechanic in Mullawa yesterday, but I got caught up here with the mare and didn't have time to collect it. The guy said he'd drop it back today. As far as I know, that's where it was last night.'

'So you're saying some random person stole it and went out to Esther's on a whim to burn her house down? I don't think so. I'm going to the police on my way to the hospital, so you'd better come up with something more believable before they arrive.' She could feel her voice cracking. 'I honestly thought you were a decent person.' Dropping her head to hide the tears, she turned to walk to her car. She felt his fingers around her arm, his voice low and pleading.

'Miranda, please. I don't know what happened or who did this, but please, let me do some investigating before you go to the police. If I haven't come up with anything concrete by tomorrow, go then – just give me a chance to prove to you that it wasn't me.'

She didn't want to look at him, knew that if she did her determination could waver. All the evidence pointed to Vincent, and after all, he had no real reason to be loyal to Esther, or to her for that matter. If Richard was prepared to pay him handsomely for his services, why wouldn't he have done it?

Give him a chance.

For a second she didn't quite believe what she was hearing. Was that the voice, suggesting she give in, back down, when it had always instructed her to be more forthright, more assertive?

She turned her head slightly, saw the look of desperation in his eyes. Was it desperation not to be caught or desperation for her to believe him? She wasn't quite sure. For all she knew he could be lyng through his teeth, but that look – and the voice – persuaded her to give him the benefit of the doubt.

'I know what I saw,' she said, conscious of how close he was and the strength of his grip. 'But I'll give you until tomorrow. Then I go to the police.' She tugged her arm away and strode towards the car, climbing in and slamming the door without bothering to look back.

Esther

All she wanted to do now was go home, fill her days with books and music and memories. The good ones, the memories that always came when she closed her eyes and drew the bow across the strings, memories of Samuel, of course, and Duke, and maybe even Kathleen and Dougie when they were small and she took them to the farm for visits, sat them on the back of a horse, walked along the beach collecting those tiny shells, filling jars and jars with the pearly pink and brown cones. What were they called? For the life of her she couldn't remember.

It was only at night that the more ominous images crowded in. The cold, white walls. Wailing that shattered the quiet from somewhere down the corridor. The sound of a key turning in the lock and the slide of the bolt on the outside of the door. It was only since she'd been in here, in the hospital, that they'd broken into her thoughts again, fractured her dreams. Once she was home she would be fine.

There was no point digging up the past. Nothing could be said or done now to give her back all the years she'd missed with her children, all the years they'd gone without a mother's love. Better to leave things as they were and see the rest of her days out in peace. Better for everyone. She'd tell the girl that when she came back. If she came back.

Miranda.

Could she really be my granddaughter?

Miranda

Miranda stood just outside the door of the hospital room, nerves nailing her feet to the floor. Hopefully Esther would still agree to see her, talk to her. It wouldn't be a good idea to mention anything about the fire – that poor woman had had enough shocks for the time being – but she needed to find out why Esther had hidden herself away for all this time, decided to leave the children with Leonard. She needed to find out for her mother.

Perfume from the wildflowers she was holding wafted up to her nose, a bouquet of pale pink and sulfur-yellow proteas mixed with sweet-smelling boronia and a few creamy white flannel flowers. She licked her lips, pulled back her shoulders and walked through the door wearing her sunniest smile.

'I'm back,' she announced, stepping up to the bed.

Esther moved her eyes from the window to the flowers in Miranda's hand. There was a dullness about her, as if the fight had gone out of her.

'I thought you might like these.'

A nod.

Miranda placed the flowers on the table and pulled up a chair. 'Feeling any better?'

'You didn't have to come back. A young girl like you must have better things to do. Like get back to that fiancé of yours.'

'He's actually not my fiancé any more. I've broken off the engagement.' She looked down at her bare ring finger. 'Long story. And I didn't come back because I felt obliged. I came back because I wanted to. But you didn't answer my question – how are you feeling?'

'Better. They say I can go home in a day or two.'

Miranda chose her next words carefully, aware that she and Esther were still really only acquaintances, despite their blood connection. 'So the doctor told me . . . that there's complications.'

Esther snorted. 'It's cancer – would you call that a complication?'

There it was, out in the open. 'He did say the treatment is often effective.'

'Well, I won't be bothering with it. No point at my age. Going through all that chemo and whatever else they want to do to me. Dragging myself in here god knows how many times every week. For what? To get a few more months and to be sick as a dog while it's all going on?'

'I'd be happy to stay on and help. In fact I'd like to. We could get to know each other better.'

Esther rubbed her fingers across the fold of the sheet. Her knuckles were bony and lined, brown blotches tarnishing the back of her hands. In the corridor outside, trolleys clattered past. A burst of laughter erupted from somewhere down the hall, snippets of conversation drifted by, but still Esther didn't speak. Miranda opened her wallet, pulling out the laminated family portrait she kept tucked inside one of the pockets. She stood and moved closer to the bed, holding the photo out in front of her for Esther to see.

'This is my family.' Miranda pointed. 'Me and my brother, Simon, and that's my dad, Brian. And there's Mum.'

Esther took the offering, holding it between trembling fingers. 'Kathleen,' she said softly.

Miranda looked away at the flowers, biting her bottom lip. She had to stay calm, in control, for Esther's sake.

'Does she know about me?' Esther asked, without moving her eyes from the image.

Miranda nodded. 'Yes, she does. I think she's in a bit of shock, finding out you're alive after all this time.' That was an understatement, but there was no point upsetting Esther any further with the details. 'She just needs some time to get her head around it all.'

'She thought I was dead?' Esther stared up at Miranda.

'Yes. That's what her father told her when – well, after you were taken off in the ambulance and didn't come back. He told Mum and Uncle Doug that you had been very unhappy and that you took too many pills and that you'd died in the hospital. Doug couldn't remember any of it, apparently, but I'm pretty sure Mum did.' Miranda thought of the heartache on her mother's face when she'd told her about that day. 'I don't think she ever really got over it.'

'That rotten bastard. What kind of man would do that to his own children? Did he take care of them?' The old woman's eyes were pleading, begging Miranda to say yes, but after all this time didn't she deserve to know the truth? Hadn't there been too many lies already?

Miranda took Esther's hand, felt the papery fragility of the skin beneath her palm. 'I wish I could tell you he did, but after a while he told them he couldn't take care of them on his own and they were put in a children's home. Dougie was fostered out to a lovely family and moved to Queensland. He still lives there.'

'And Kathleen?' Esther asked, her voice cracking.

'She was twelve when they went into the home. She stayed until she turned seventeen and then moved out into a boarding house. I didn't know any of this until I told her about you. She never spoke about her life before she married Dad.'

Esther's eyes closed. A single tear rolled silently down each weathered cheek. Miranda stood and dabbed at them with a tissue, laid her forehead against Esther's and held her close. So much pain, so much suffering. She felt her grandmother's body break as the sorrow of all those lost years sank in. Finally, when the trembling eased, Miranda lifted her face and brushed a strand of silver hair from Esther's brow. The hardest question of all still remained unasked: Why had Esther never come home? Should she push any further? Would it be too much?

Esther coughed and began to speak before Miranda voiced the words. 'He had me locked away. Told the doctors I had a history of mental illness, that I was a danger . . .' Her voice faltered but she composed herself and continued. 'A danger to the children. He told them I had hallucinations, that it was for my own good. And they believed him. It was called a sanitorium in those days. Eighteen years I spent in that prison. Drugged to the eyeballs half the time because I dared to argue with them and tried to run away. The more I told them I wasn't mad, the more they refused to listen. Treated us like animals. Or worse.'

Miranda covered her mouth with her hand, shaking her head, trying to comprehend Esther's words. When she heard her own voice it sounded faint, distant. 'How did you get out?'

'They closed the place down and dumped us all in halfway houses. To help us readjust to the outside world. But the world I knew was gone. My children had grown up. I had no idea where to find them. Since they'd never been to see me, I presumed they didn't want to know me any more. That they were ashamed of me. Leonard wrote a letter telling me as much. I'd become ashamed of myself. I stayed in the house until we were forced to move on and then caught a bus back home.'

'To Garewangga?'

Esther nodded. 'I didn't know what else to do. Martin was the only one left. Nearly fell over when he saw me. He was dying and thought I was a ghost come to collect him. He promised me I'd have a home at the farm for as long as I wanted, much to his son's disgust. But I was happy to have the shack. I'd spent all those years locked away. Didn't know how to deal with people any more. So he left me the cottage and the land it sits on to live in until I die.'

The last word echoed in Miranda's head.

'I tried my best to put it all behind me. Even went by my maiden name so I could start fresh. But you never forget.'

'Oh, Esther, I'm so sorry.' She didn't know what or who she was apologising for, but there was so little else she could say. She thought back to Esther's diaries, to the young woman who had galloped across the hills with her lover, full of life, dreaming of their future together, and her heart split in two. So much had been taken away from Esther and yet she had survived. Now it was time for her to be looked after and comforted, to live what remained of her life surrounded by love.

Esther

She packed the last of her things into the small overnight bag. It all still felt like a dream. Not one of *those* dreams – which was a blessing. This whole business with Miranda coming and finding her after all these years. If the girl hadn't been so persistent she never would have known, would have died believing that her children had disowned her. But what now? From the way Miranda had spoken, there was a good chance that Kathleen would never come to see her. And what about Dougie? They'd grown up thinking that she'd killed herself, abandoned them. Which was exactly what their mongrel of a father had wanted them to think. Her blood boiled when she thought about the lies he'd concocted, the life he'd deprived them all of for all those years.

I hope he's rotting in hell.

A rapping on the window caught her attention and there was Miranda, waving, and standing next to her at the end of his lead was Buster. Esther knocked on the glass and the dog looked up, saw her, and barked, his tail slicing the air.

'Hello, my boy.'

She stood and looked at them: the girl with her beautiful thick blonde hair, so much like her own had been when she was younger, waving and laughing; the dog with what could only be described as a smile on his face, so pleased he was to see her. Something that had been dead inside for a very long time began to stir.

She was going home.

Miranda

It was a long, slow walk back to the cottage, but they were in no hurry. On the way Esther told Miranda what it had been like to grow up on the farm – days spent on horseback, her love of music and books, all the good things – back in the days when she was called Essie. Miranda listened as if hearing the stories for the first time – now that she had gained her grandmother's trust, she didn't want to risk losing it by confessing to delving into her diaries.

Before they rounded the final bend in the track, she paused and turned to Esther. 'There's something I have to tell you. Someone vandalised the house, tried to burn it down. I came back late the other night and caught them in the act. I put out the fire but I'm afraid the laundry and shed are gone.'

Esther staggered a little but Miranda grabbed hold of her and helped her regain her balance. 'Did you see who it was? What he looked like?'

'I'm not sure. It was dark. Whoever it was ran off when they realised I was there.' She tried not to look directly at

Esther, afraid she might see the lie in her eyes. She'd find out it was Vincent soon enough, but for the time being Miranda decided to keep the details vague. Esther had suffered enough betrayal for one lifetime. 'I thought I'd get you home first, then go and make a report to the police.'

'Tell them to start with my nephew. He's been trying to get me out of here for years. Thinks as soon as I'm off the place it will go to him. He's always been a coward but I never thought he'd stoop this low. His father would be ashamed of him.'

'Well, he might have picked a fight with the wrong person. I studied property law as part of my degree.'

Esther broke out laughing, a long, hearty laugh that was so infectious Miranda joined in. It was a good minute before they pulled themselves together enough to finish the walk. There was a crispness to the air that reminded Miranda it was well and truly autumn. Whipbirds called from somewhere far behind them in the bush. The sea pulsed onto the shore in the distance. In Esther's garden white moths flitted between the rows of cabbages and beans, and bees hummed among yellow nasturtiums.

They stopped to look at the damage done by the fire. 'Bloody mongrel,' Esther growled.

Miranda bent her head but didn't speak, recalling the heat of the flames as if they were still blazing, and felt once again the pain of Vincent's deception. She urged Esther on, rounding the corner of the house to the front verandah, as Buster ran around in circles in his usual crazy fashion, pleased to see his mistress home.

'Ahhh, that's more like it.' Esther sighed into the armchair on the porch.

'Would you like a cup of tea?'

'Thought you'd never ask.'

When Miranda pulled open the flyscreen door, an envelope tucked between the wire and the frame fell to the ground. She picked it up and held it in her hands. Her name was printed across the front.

'What's that?' Esther asked.

'It's addressed to me,' she said in surprise. She slid her index finger below the seal, and sat down on the step as she ripped the envelope open.

> Miranda,
>
> A mate of mine spotted the apprentice mechanic driving through Mullawa in my ute and assumed he was taking it for a test drive. When I put some pressure on the kid about the fire at Esther's, he told me Richard had put him up to it – Richard knew my car was booked in there that day. I called Dicko and had it out with him. He denied knowing anything about it to begin with, of course, told me to come up with the proof, but when I threatened to go to the police about some of his other, shall we say, shady business dealings, he came clean, admitted he'd paid the kid to do his dirty work. My coat just happened to be on the back seat. He threatened to sack me if I went to the police, but I resigned before he had the chance. We had a chat and let's just say I think I've persuaded him to see a solicitor about Esther having

more permanent ownership of the property. As for me,
I'm in need of a job, so if you're looking for someone
to repair the house, I'm your man. For the time being
I'm at the caravan park.

Vincent

Miranda folded the letter and slid it back into the envelope.
She looked out across the grey sea to where it blurred with
the sky. He'd told her the truth and she'd doubted him – more
than doubted – accused him of lying, and was all set to have
him arrested. He was a good, honest man, so why hadn't she
just believed him? The same reason she'd gone so far down
the road to marrying James and the same reason she'd stayed
so long in a job for which she had no passion. Because she'd
always played it safe, listened to her head instead of her heart.

'That letter from anyone I know?' Esther's voice reminded
her she wasn't alone.

'It is, as a matter of fact. Vincent Kennedy. He says he's
convinced his boss to back off and leave you alone, or he'll be
going to the police with some evidence about the fire – and
some of your nephew's other pastimes.'

'Good for him,' Esther laughed. 'He's one in a million,
that Vincent.'

I think you might be right.

Miranda jumped to her feet, not even attempting to
disguise her smile. 'How about that cuppa?'

Esther

It was good to be back, sitting here on the verandah looking out across the sky, back to her own bed, back to her garden and back with her dog. Buster looked up at her as if he knew what she was thinking and she gave him a pat. Even though she'd always loved the isolation of the cottage, she had to admit, at least to herself, that having Miranda here was a blessing. Luckily the girl had been able to take some more time off work, although the way she was talking it didn't sound like she'd be going back. They shared their stories over cups of tea as the days became shorter, laughed and cried together, got to know each other. She could see the Kathleen she remembered in her granddaughter's eyes and mannerisms – the same wrinkling of the forehead when she asked a question, the way she touched her tongue to her upper lip when she was concentrating. Both of them were cautious not to dig too deep, to just scratch away carefully and gradually, learning a little more about each other every day.

Vincent had called by a few times now, brought some timber and paint to rebuild the outhouses. There was definitely a spring in Miranda's step whenever he was around and Esther couldn't help but notice their familiarity. Maybe more had gone on while she was away than the girl had let on? And what if it had? They were young, had their whole lives ahead of them as she'd once done. It was right here in this shack that she and Samuel had dreamt about a life together.

If I'd been braver, stood up to my parents and run away with him, things would have been different.

But it was too late now. She'd played the hand life had dealt and now the game was just about over.

She picked up her violin for the first time since she'd come home, breathing in the musty smell of the timber. Martin had kept it for all those years, along with a few of her other belongings, even though he'd thought her dead. Almost as if he'd known that one day she'd come back. The tune vibrated through her body, along her arm and out through her fingertips, a heavenly symphony of notes riding on the air. They were there with her, all the people she'd loved, deep within her heart: Samuel, her mother and father, Martin, her children. Never forgotten. And she sensed her granddaughter standing somewhere close by, listening. How lucky she was that the girl had taken the time to find her, that they had found each other. She let the notes form themselves, soar, mingle with the melodies of the birds and the sighing of the sea.

The creak of the wire door broke her reverie, and as she opened her eyes the music stopped. Miranda stepped onto the verandah, looking towards the track at the bottom of the hill. When Esther followed her gaze she saw a woman in a cream coat walking towards them, blonde wisps of hair bobbing in the breeze. Miranda stood still a moment, then rushed down the steps and threw her arms around the woman, who collapsed onto her shoulder. As Esther looked on her throat thickened and her stomach clenched.

Could it really be? After all this time?

Slowly she placed the violin back in its case, closed the lid, and held onto the arm of the chair while she stood. Her legs were scraps of straw beneath her and her heart knocked so fiercely against her ribs she thought they might crack. The two women were getting closer now, leaning on each other, and the resemblance between them was undeniable.

One step, the second step, the tread of feet on the crooked boards. Miranda paused as the woman came forward, took Esther's hand and held it to her cheek.

'Mum,' she whispered, and they fell into each other's arms, the years and distance between them slipping quietly away.

Author's note

Essie's early life was inspired by the true story of sixteen-year-old Grace Bussell who, along with Sam Isaacs – an Aboriginal stockman who worked for her family – rescued survivors from the wreck of the *Georgette* off the coast of Western Australia on 1 December 1876. The story was reported by H. C. Barrett on 31 January 1877. Some versions I read suggested Grace had dreamt of the event before it occurred. While I have used this incident as part of Essie's story, the rest of her tale, including her relationship with Samuel is entirely fictional and any similarity to any real person or event is totally coincidental.

Acknowledgements

To everyone who has helped me in the writing of this book, I offer my heartfelt thanks and gratitude . . .

My writing partners and friends in The Writers' Dozen, for your constant support – Jen Tomasetti, Yvonne Louis, Angella Whitton and especially Monique McDonell and Terri Green for reading the early drafts and providing much needed feedback. And to the late Pauline Reynolds for her enthusiasm and encouragement over many years. You are greatly missed, Pauline.

Krystina Hill and Wanda Wiltshire for reading and giving constructive criticism – you really helped me improve those early pages. Alison Manning from Mindspan, for coaching me through a difficult patch. My mother Gwen, who told me tales about life during the war and the years following. And to Clare for sharing part of your own story.

All my family and friends who have been so supportive since the publication of my first novel. You have helped make this whole experience truly special.

The wonderful team at Hachette: Vanessa Radnidge for your encouragement and continual faith in me, Kate Stevens for your keen eye and honest suggestions, Elizabeth Cowell for your detailed editing and Sarah Fletcher for meticulous proofreading. Thanks also to Anna Hayward and everyone who has helped behind the scenes.

To my husband, John, for your unwavering belief, and to my daughters, Freya, Georgia and Amelia, for putting up with me while I ignored everything else to write. Thank you for making this all possible.

. . . once again you have all helped make my dream come true.